BRISTLECONE

Books by Richard S. Platz

Novels

OF MAGIC AND DELUSION

PROJECT DIVINE WIND

APPOINTMENT AT ANGAHUAN
(Co-Authored with James A. Kline)

Short Stories

MEMORIES & OTHER FICTIONS

DREAMTIME

VANISHING POINT

BRISTLECONE
A Novel

By Richard S. Platz

Blue Lake Press

Cover photo by author taken at Great Basin National Park, Nevada

BLUE LAKE PRESS
A Western Division Subsidiary of the
Chicago, Whitewater & Mad River Company
P O Box 797, Blue Lake, CA 95525

ISBN: 978-0692078754

Contents

PART ONE

Cedarville, California

June

A SOLITARY FIGURE knelt before the raw headstone. Balancing on one knee, Shadrack Smithers tried as he might to avoid focusing on the letters freshly chiseled into the granite face, but his eyes betrayed him and read them anyhow: *MATHILDE SMITHERS, Wife and Mother.* As if that summed it all up, which it most certainly did not.

The position was painful for the old man, but he had something to get off his chest. He plucked a dandelion and twirled it between gnarled fingers, then cleared his throat. "Well . . . this here jus' might be m' las' visit." His eyes were moist, but he was in a sore perplexity to be understood. "Or one a'em anyhow."

His speech faded into the otherwise empty cemetery. The afternoon sun had passed behind the spreading canopy of honey locust trees, whose yellow blossoms swirled down with each puff of breeze. Shadrack twirled the dandelion as he worked up the gumption to go on. He heard himself mumble a few words about local doings and how the bookstore might be closing, but quickly fell silent again. It was taking him a heap of time to get his mind just right for the meat of this conversation. But it had to be said.

"I made up m' mind, I have," he declared at last. "An' I'm a'bound and determined t' go on an' take me one final trip. Try an' make it back t' the Ozarks where we growed up. Missouri was a'where we met an' was a'married. An' whar Donny was first born. You knowd all o' that. But there's where I'll be bound." He paused and hung his head. "I got the cain't-he'p-its all the time now, seems. Got 'em bad and cain't seem t' get nothin' a'tall done no more." He waited for more words to come, but they were slow in coming.

He took a long breath and blotted an unwelcome tear from the corner of his eye before plunging on. "Anyhow . . . I know what you' be a'thinkin' 'bout me tryin' t' travel nowadays, particular with me a'sayin' t'hell with standin' in line tryin' t' get one o' them damn' travel permits. They warn't never gonna gimme one o' them anyways. I ain't got no chance for no travel clearance, tha's fer sure. I ain't got no long haul trucker license. An' I ain't got no 'critical skills,' as 'ey call 'em. No ma'am. An' there ain't no qualifyin' reason for 'em t' justify the burnin' up o' nash'nal resources jus' t'get me back there t' Missouri. But I don't give a damn an' that's the truth! An' I don't want you a'askin' 'Why for?' like ya always used t'do. 'Cause I don't have a notion why for. I simply do not. I jus' knows it's somethin' I jus' gotta do. An' that's the open an' shut of it."

Shadrack rose stiffly and bent backwards until his spine crackled. He gazed up at the open sky and recalled the days when the wild blue was criss-crossed with drifting white plumes of vapor trails from everybody and his uncle flying somewhere or other for no damned purpose at all. He'd done so himself, maybe a half-dozen times, long ago, way back when anybody could just lay down some cash on the barrel-head and jump aboard any old plane and fly. But those days were long gone. Now the national policy was for you to stay put, just where you was and as you was. Nowadays you couldn't ever borrow a car and drive across county lines without holdin' a permit of some kind. And they sure as shooting weren't gonna issue him no permit. What for would they? He wasn't nothing to them.

Stiffly he knelt back down on the other knee to finish this business. "I'm gonna have t' think this 'ere through mighty careful, I grant y' that. There's that civil insurrection still a'ragin' over by Denver, so I plans t' scoot aways south o' all that. An' things is still a little warm with the cattle ranchers an' seper'tists over there in Nevada, though they mostly been kilt or else rounded up and stuck behind bob wire. An' a'course there's terrorists ever'where a'blowin' 'emselves up, but I figure I can work m'way 'round them techy spots perty easy. I been a'rock houndin' all o'er this here territory fer years. As you well know. Anyhow, all it'll take is jus' t' hook up with some local fella here what still got an operatin' pickup hid away somewheres. An' some gasoline. There mus' be plenty a' fellas 'round here, I reckon. I'll jus' buy the sucker offa 'im fer cash money, paint it up black, an' ride out by moonlight." He thought about it for a while, then added, "Four wheel drive'd be highly pr'ferred."

He thought some more while his back and knee throbbed, but couldn't think of anything else to say, except, "I al'as loved ya. But you knowed that anyways. An' I don' wanna have t' leave ya har all alone. But it ain't like I'm a'leavin' without ya, 'cause . . . I'll be a'carrin' ya with me ri'chere." He pounded a bony fist against his breast. "Al'a's have been . . . but you knowed that." Shadrack rose painfully and turned, paused in thought, then turned back. "But ya gotta remember one thing . . . you's *dead*. So g'bye now." He shuffled away without looking back.

ELAN GROVES was rocking in his front porch swing, rereading an old Faulkner novel, when he glanced up to see a scarecrow approaching. A loose worn work shirt flapped emptily in the breeze above faded overalls cinched up tight about the specter's bean-pole waist. Elan blinked, and the vision resolved itself into a human figure with a full snaggle of beard, a head of sparse shaggy gray-white hair, worn work boots, and a limp in his right leg. The fellow was no stranger. Few who lived in and about Cedarville were. But it took Elan a couple of heartbeats to place him. He was the husband of Tildie Smithers, who had worked with Elan's wife Bess at the Nuevo Niños Reading Project a few years back. The Smithers owned a small farm a few miles down the road toward Eagleville. Tildie had passed away recently, he had heard, and Elan had seen the fellow around town more since she passed. But he couldn't recall his first name. Something odd, but he couldn't recollect what. "Howdy," he called out, rising to his feet. "Something I can do for you this fine morning, Mr. Smithers?"

"Shadrack," the visitor corrected, waving a bony hand. But he spoke no more until he got right up close. Then low and confidential he said, "P'raps there might be."

"And what's that?"

Shadrack squinted about uneasily. Up close his bones seemed strapped with wiry farm-labor muscles, and he exuded that tangy old-man aroma of stale sweat. He muttered, as if to himself, "Your wife make it back home?"

"No. Bess is still caught up in Portland with our oldest girl, Ginger. She's started college up there last fall, and Bess went up to help her settle in a month ago. She's still up there waiting for her travel permit to come back home."

"Them permits!" Shadrack spat.

"I've been aggrieved about them myself," Elan agreed. "Ever since those clowns in Washington went crazy and declared a state of emergency and diced up the whole country into sectors. Isolated everybody. And for what? It might make some kind of sense in combating terrorists some places, but not out here in the Warners."

"No, sir," agreed Shadrack. "Ya got that right."

"I was teaching Business Accounting at the Community College over in Alturas when the new regulations came down. Now I'm on suspended leave, because I can't get through the roadblock at the old agriculture inspection station. It's now a sector checkpoint."

Shadrack grunted accord and sympathy. "So you's outta a job?"

"For now anyway."

"Got no paycheck a'comin' in?"

"Unfortunately not."

Shadrack grunted again and looked down at the old flop hat he gripped in his hands.

"You look like you might've lost a little weight since I last saw you, Mr. Smithers."

"Shadrack. An' ya'd be right 'bout that. Don't eat reg'lar much since Tildie passed, no sir. Got me no appetite. Don't do much a'tall anymore. Ain't even got the late potatoes outta the ground yet."

"I was sorry to learn of your wife's passing," Elan said. "She worked with my wife, Bess, you know. You have my deepest condolences."

Shadrack fidgeted, figuring that enough chit-chat had flowed between them to grease the skids, so he came to the point. "I un'erstan' ya might have somethin' I'd like t' offer t'buy offen ya. Cash money it'd be. New gov'ment issue. Good as gold."

"Oh?" Elan closed his book. "And just what might that be, my friend?"

"They say y'got a ol' four-by-four truck still runs good. 'Zat a fac'?"

Elan considered him carefully. "Now who might be telling you such a thing?"

"Oh, 's'jus' the word 'bout town. Nobody in particular, I guess."

"And just what do you want a truck for, if I might ask. You can't go much anywhere anymore. Not without a permit. But I'm sure you know that."

Smithers nodded. "Ever'body know'd that, right 'nough, I guess." He paused for a moment, then pressed on, "But 'chew got a four-by-four, I hear tell. Ain't 'at so?"

"You haven't told me what you might want to use a truck for."

So Shadrack Smithers drew in a deep breath and hunkered down on his haunches. He let it out in a long sigh, then told Elan what he had just told his dead wife, using mostly the same words he had used with her.

"The Ozarks. My goodness. Missouri or Arkansas?"

"Missouri, but it might's well be t'other."

"That's a long way to try and go in a pickup truck nowadays."

"That might be's it is, I guess. But it's whar Tildie and me was married. An' whar'r first born was begot. An' tha's where I'm hankerin' t'get back to."

Elan nodded. "The permitting is going to be a nightmare. And I'm assuming you haven't got a permit to travel that far yet?"

Shadrack shook his head. "Don't wanna make that no business o' yourn. I'll take on the 'sponsibility of havin' a permit 'r not. Don't worry yerself none about it."

Elan smiled. "I appreciate your consideration in keeping me out of trouble, should there be any unlawful travel contemplated. But . . ." He fell silent again.

"But whut?"

"But . . . well . . ." Two competing trains of thought were vying for his attention. He chose the simpler one. "Well . . . for one thing, why don't you just hitch a ride along with some trucker? One of the long-haul ones that come through town now and again. They all carry commercial permits."

"None o' 'em I talked to'll take me on. Scared t'death, they are. Might get their license 'spended. 'R get 'emselves locked up someplace behind the bob wire. 'R even worse."

"That bad, is it?"

"These's troubled times, son. They might jus' get shot down like dogs, from what I hear. And it's not a'knowin' jus' *what* might happen t'em's got 'em so spooked."

Elan was quiet for a long while. At last he nodded. "Come with me, Mr. Smithers—"

"Shadrack."

"Sorry . . . Shadrack . . . let's go take a look see at what's available out in the old barn." He stepped down onto the grass. "I've collected some vintage vehicles out there over the years. At least I used to collect them. Now I restore them up, when I can find the time. Kind of a hobby with me. But I never get to take any out on the road anymore."

"Whyn't?"

Elan grinned. "Haven't got a travel permit."

The barn's red paint was faded and flaking, and the foundation blocks were separating in places. Elan fished a key out of his pocket, unsnapped the padlock, and ground the big red door back on its squealing track. He flipped a wall switch and an overhead fluorescent flickered on. The large, low space inside was sifted with bits of hay and dust and pigeon droppings. An abandoned concrete feed trough ran down the far side with rusting car and tractor parts leaning against it. Farm implements hung from the walls. "Watch your head," Elan cautioned as he led them through a second low opening into a larger section. That space was brightly lit by work lights beneath a canopy of surplus parachutes strung overhead to kept the workspace clean. It had the feel and smell of an old auto repair garage. Surrounding them were auto relics, stripped down for painting or major overhaul.

"Great Lordy!" gasped Shadrack. "A feel like a chile in a can'y shop!" He was admiring the three vehicles in the center beneath the lights. They had been cleaned up and polished and looked ready for the road. One was a three-decade-old black Toyota pickup, the one Shadrack had inquired about. Its coat of dull primer black paint seemed to absorb the bright light. Beside it was a stubby GMC school bus with the passenger seats removed and the original yellow paint sanded down and partially primered gray in spots, giving it the character of an old piebald workhorse. And beyond that sat a humvee in desert camouflage livery, a restored relic of the Persian Gulf War.

Elan grinned at him. "As you see, I suffer from a bit of wanderlust myself. Like you, I've been considering getting away on a road trip of my own."

"You?" Shadrack wondered.

"Yes, sir."

"How y' gonna get a permit t' travel?"

"Well," explained Elan, "when I began restoring these vehicles, you didn't need any such thing. And now that you do . . . well, it's all become a kind of compelling fantasy. You might call it an obsession. I kept putting it off, what with work and a wife and two daughters and all that. And now that I've got the time, it grieves me that it may be too late. Anyway . . . what you were saying about *your* travel permit being *your* problem is correct . . . but I guess it would become *my* problem too, don't you think, if I decide to come along with you for the ride."

"Come along? You?"

"Yes, sir. That's what I'm thinking. With Bess and Ginger away, I've got a whole lot of spare time on my hands. But I'd have to figure out how to make arrangements for Katie. She's my youngest, and she's just a junior at Cedarville High. She lives at home with me. Just the two of us, until Bess gets back. If she ever does. Anyway, I'd have to think this through very carefully and talk to my wife. And to Katie, of course. But it's a possibility. That's what I'm saying. A real possibility. A road trip. What do you think of my crazy idea?"

Shadrack turned away, grumbling mostly to himself. "This ain't what I come o'er here fer a'tall. I jus' come t' see if'n ya might have yerself a pickup I could buy off'n ya. This here seems t' be gettin' a way more complicated than I'druther. An' I'm not sure I like where she's a'driftin'." He turned to confront Elan. "I was a'plannin' t' go this'n by m'self, y' un'erstand. No offense intended, mind ya."

"No offense taken, Mr. . . . ah, Shadrack. But you think it over, will you? And I'll do the same. We can talk again in a couple of days."

"But ya might sell me one o' these here?"

"I might."

Shadrack scowled. "Coupla day's too long. How 'bout tomorrow? Same time."

Elan nodded. "Tomorrow afternoon it is."

KATIE GROVES could sense that something was up. She felt it the moment she walked through the kitchen door. Something was not quite right. She stacked her books carefully on the corner of the sideboard and turned to sniff for a clue.

Her father was sitting at the table just staring at her. No *Hi ya Kiddo.* No *What did you pick up in school today, honey?* He sat there with a piercing gaze and a grimly down-turned mouth.

"What?" she demanded. Katie was a tall slip of a girl on the threshold of becoming a fetching young woman. Pale green eyes. Pony tail of chestnut hair. Athletic body. She ran cross-country in the spring. Played soccer in the fall. And she was just about to turn sixteen. "*What?*"

Elan glanced away.

"What's wrong? Oh my god, did something happen to Mom?"

"No, nothing happened to your mother."

"*What is it then?*" She demanded.

"Oh, nothing. I was just thinking of something is all."

"What?"

"Oh . . . of maybe . . . taking a little trip."

"A trip? Like how can you take a trip? Where to?"

He raised a puckish hand to pacify her. "We can talk about it at supper," he smiled. "How did things go at the bookstore today, Kiddo?"

She turned fierce bright eyes on him. "What are you up to now, Dad?"

"Nothing at all. I just . . . sort of ran into . . . well . . . you remember Tildie Smithers, don't you? Your Mom's friend"

"Sure. She came in and taught us some Spanish back in, you know, sixth grade. But she just died, didn't she?"

"Yes, she did. But her husband, Shadrack, came by this after-noon—"

"Isn't he that scary old farmer from down the road? With the wild beard?"

"Well, I wouldn't say 'scary' exactly. But you know who I'm talking about. Anyway . . . Mr. Smithers . . . Shadrack . . . he's thinking of leaving the area here and I was thinking of offering him a lift."

"A *lift?*" The concept baffled her. "Why would you do *that?*"

"Well . . . it's just that I never get to take my trucks out anymore . . . and I wouldn't mind a bit of a road trip myself."

"A *road* trip? How far were you planning on driving him."

"I wasn't *planning* on anything just yet. Just mulling it over. And I kind of wanted to talk to you about it first. Make sure you would be alright here by yourself for a few days. You know—"

" A few *days*? How far are you planning on going?"

"We haven't really worked that out exactly . . . but—"

"Dad! Come on. Tell me. How far?"

"Well . . . maybe as far as Missouri, but—"

"*Missouri?*"

"Just the southwest corner. Barely out of Oklahoma. Anyway, that's his plan. Not really a plan. This is all very tentative, as far as I'm concerned."

Katie stared at him. "Why are *you* involved?"

"I wouldn't say I was *involved*. 'Involved' is too . . . well . . . it's not the right word."

"Dad, there's something here you're not telling me. And this is about *me* too, you know. I need to know, like, how *I* fit in. Just let me *think* a minute."

The clock ticked on the wall until he couldn't stand it anymore. "Katie, I know—"

"Shush! I'm thinking."

Mutely they both listened to the clock ticking. He sitting. She standing. Finally her face broke into a radiant smile, a beam of sunshine bright in her eyes. "I want to go too," she announced.

"Wait," Elan coughed, "I'm sorry, but I don't think that's possible."

"Why not?" she wanted to know. "You're like always going on about the splendors of this wonderful country. You know, the purple mountains. The wide open deserts. The wildlands and the forests. The waves of grain from shore to shore and all that. And I've never been off to see any of that. *Any* of it. I've spent my whole life right here in Cedarville—"

"Katie, you know that's not true. We've taken you to Reno and San Francisco—"

"That's not the same thing, for sure, and you know it. And the way things are going, I'll probably never get another chance."

"I . . . ah . . . don't think I could get a permit for you, honey."

She stared him in the eye. "I bet you and Mr. Smithers haven't got any permits for yourselves either."

He glanced away. "I couldn't take you, honey. There might be some . . . well . . . some danger involved, you see. And I can't put you in any danger. Your mother would skin me alive."

"I'll talk to Mom," she enthused. "I can make her see my side. You don't mind if I do that, do you?"

"Well . . ."

"*I want to go along!*"

SHADRACK SHOWED UP the following afternoon, right on time, aboard his ancient gray Farmall as it rumbled noisily into the driveway. He shut the tractor off and climbed down, a dirty brown paper grocery bag pinched under his scrawny arm. Elan had the doors open to the back half of the barn and was gunning the Toyota pickup's engine while he adjusted something under the hood. When he saw Shadrack, he pulled out and straightened up and leaned into the cab to shut off the engine.

"Looks like ya got 'er a'runnin' perty nice 'ere," Shadrack told him. "Sounds real solid."

"I tuned her up just this Spring. I like to run them all at least once a week. Worst thing you can do to a motor vehicle is to let it just sit. What have you got there in the bag?"

"Well sir, I brung along some money. We ain't talked about price yet, 'an I's a'hopin' it's 'nough. But I brung the deed t' m' farm, too, jus' in case the cash money don't cover it. How much 're you a'askin', anyhow?"

"Now hold on, Shadrack. We still have something else to discuss, don't you remember?"

Shadrack pulled off his slouch hat and scratched his head. "Nothin' all that much 's I recall."

"Remember me telling you that I might want to go along on the trip?"

Shadrack shook his head. "I recall you a'spoutin' somethin' 'bout that, but I reckon I told y' 'no' on that there partic'lar notion."

"I didn't hear you if you did. As far as I'm concerned, it's still up for discussion. And it would certainly affect the purchase price of the truck, if I decide to sell at all." Elan paused to let that sink in. "And now I know someone else who might just want to tag along, too."

Shadrack blanched. "An' who might 'at be?"

"My daughter Katie."

"Your *daughter*! I'n't she a one still in high school?"

"That she is."

"Well . . . but . . . I declare . . ." Shadrack sputtered, drawing back, "ain't *that* a crazy notion. This jus' ain't a'gonna do." His eyes narrowed. "An' y' figure ya can come up with all 'em permits, do ya?"

"Now hold on," Elan laughed. "Why should *we* worry about a permit, if *you* don't?"

"Don' seem a'tall right fer either one a ya t' think a'coming along without no permits. No sir. 'S just not right. An' again' the law. It be a mighty dangerous thing. An' she bein' jus' a girl! I'd never take my girls 'long on somethin' 's chancy 's this here might be. An' besides . . . an' besides, they jus' ain't 'nough *room* fer three a' us in that little ol' truck a' yours."

That was the opening Elan had been waiting for, and he pounced. "Now *that's* where you'd be wrong. I figured we'd do better if we took *two* vehicles. You in the truck, maybe. Katie and me in the bus. Mostly you would be by yourself and wouldn't even have to talk to us. But we could switch drivers from time to time. Spell each other maybe. Make the long drive easier. And we would find safety in numbers, just in case one of the vehicles breaks down. Besides, Katie and me might not want to go the whole way. Probably would not. A couple of days out and back ought to be enough for us. Then you'd be on your own."

Shadrack was shaking his head gloomily. "This ain't . . . this jus' ain't a'tall—"

"Well, give it some thought anyway. We can go over the logistics if you're on for it. In the meantime I'd like to know what route you were planning to take. Why don't you come on into the kitchen for a cup of coffee. I've got some maps spread out on the table in there. And I'd like you to meet Katie."

"Don't know 'bout that," Shadrack grumbled as he followed across the wide lawn. "Ain't much good with the young'ns. 'Specially the girls. Jus' don't cotton t' me a'tall. M'own all moved out years ago, soon's they finished high school. Never bother t' gimme a call anymore."

"Didn't they come out for the funeral?" Elan asked as he led the way up to the house.

"They did. But t'warn't fer t'see *me*, I reckon."

KATIE WAS ADJUSTING the flame under the coffee pot when the kitchen door banged open. With a wan smile she turned to face Shadrack Smithers as he stepped grudgingly through the doorway. "Hello there, Mr. Smithers—"

"Shadrack," the old man growled, taking Katie aback.

"Katie," her father intervened, "I'd like you to meet Shadrack Smithers. Shadrack, this is my daughter Katie."

"Would you care for a cup of coffee?" Katie tried again.

"Don't drink no coffee," Shadrack grumped. "Not no more. Angrifies m'bowels, it does."

Katie stood clutching the pot. She turned to her father for help.

"Have a seat here, Shadrack," Elan said. "Is there something else I can get you to drink?"

"Water'll be fine." Sullenly he drew out a chair and eased himself down. "These the maps you'us a'talkin' 'bout?"

"Yes, sir. Some of them, anyway. See, here we are in Cedarville."

Shadrack followed the finger, then pushed it aside with his own yellowing nail, almost a claw. "Ri'cher?" He leaned closer and squinted. He tapped his nail on the spot.

"That's where we are alright." Elan caught a glance from his daughter.

"Dad, can I talk with you for a second?" She made eyes urgently toward the doorway.

"Oh . . . sure . . . okay. Would you excuse us for a moment, Shadrack?" He followed her into the hallway.

Katie whispered in exasperation. "This isn't, like, going to work out, is it?"

"That's what I was trying to tell you, Katie."

"How about you and me just, you know, going off on our own?"

"That sounds just wonderful, sweetheart."

His daughter stared at him. "But . . . what?"

"I didn't say 'but' anything."

"I heard it in your tone, Dad."

"Well, yours is a good idea. A great idea. Just you and me out camping. And I think your mother might even go along with it. But . . . here's the thing . . . maybe we could just follow him along in our own vehicle for the first day or so. He seems to know the country pretty well. Better than either of us. Better than a tour guide, and we might learn something new."

"But he smells so . . . so *bad*."

"I'll see if I can talk him into taking a bath."

She thought about it. "Make it part of the deal. For sure."

Elan sighed. "I guess I could do that. Maybe offer him a soak over at the hot springs."

Katie considered, then shrugged. "Whatever." She smiled and gave her father a big hug. "This is going to be *fun*."

By the time they stepped back into the kitchen, Shadrack had familiarized himself with the map. "Now this's how I see 'er," he announced. "They a'gonna stick up roadblocks on the big highways and the choke points. Th'ain't got the manpower t' patrol all them highways an' dirt roads a'runnin' through here." He swiped his hand over a broad swath south and east of Cedarville. He scratched his head. "Now, do ya suspect we need a permit jus' ta travel there anyhow?"

"I don't know," Elan replied. "The state line runs down the east side of the Surprise Valley. But the sector checkpoint is over west of the Warners. That leaves us in a kind of no man's land between the two. It's like they sliced off the northeast sliver of California."

"Arrr. But did 'ey stick 'er onto Nevada, I wonder?"

"I don't know. Maybe for sector and travel purposes they ceded us to Nevada."

"Might be. But might not. An' anyways, might not make no diff'rence, bein's ya got California plates on all the veh'cles."

"Good point, Shadrack. When they see those plates, they're going to stop us and start asking a lot of questions either way."

"*If'n* they see 'em. Now I knows all them Nevada dirt roads perty good m'self from years a' rockhoundin', an' I think I can a'slip us on past all 'em checkpoints."

Elan nodded. "So you're alright with Katie and me coming along then?"

"I guess it ain't none o' my never-mind, 's'long 's yous be a'drivin' that other rig a' yourn." Shadrack glanced up. "But why you'd be a'takin' that ol' school bus, rather'n the big jeep, confounds me, it surely does."

"Well, for one thing, the bus gets better mileage. I put a 4-cylinder diesel into it, and it just sips the fuel now. And its got a built-in stove and a sink and storage cabinets and a lot more room inside for sleeping mattresses and our gear and supplies."

"But no 4-wheel drive?"

"No, but it's got duals on the back with aggressive treads for sand and gravel and a new transmission with plenty of torque."

"She got a winch?"

"Not yet. There's one on the pickup, of course. And I think I've got another one I can mount on the bus, if that would ease your mind."

"We ain't got no time fer a whole lotta shop work."

"Won't take long. And we'll have to put the shell back on the pickup. Give us another place to sleep if it rains."

Shadrack grunted. "Y' prob'bly right 'bout the bus. Hummer'd be too wide fer some 'a the shortcuts I was a'plannin' on."

"Shortcuts?"

"Yeah. Like ri'chere." Shadrack tapped the map with a fingernail. "Ain't no sense in a'tryin' t' run through Gerlach an' Reno, when we'd do better a'cuttin' down through the High Rock Canyon, then a'swingin' north'a the Black Rock Desert an' a'stayin' north a'the highways, then droppin' down t'cross under the Interstate at a cattle pass I know this side'a Winnemucca, an' catchin' Highway 50 eas'boun' t' Utah."

"Utah?" Katie asked. "We're going into Utah?"

"Might be," said Shadrack. "Er me'be we'll cut straight on down t' Arizona. Have t'see the lay a'things."

"But U. S. 50 is a major east-west route," observed Elan. "There would probably be checkpoints on it, wouldn't you think?"

"Nobody uses 'er much. Jus' a few truckers, mostly screamin' 'long in the night, high on meth. An' tha's why they calls it 'the Loneliest Road In America.' They ain't gonna be so stupid as t' deploy no troops out thar. They'd jus' plum die a' boredom. Anyways, we' be a'drivin' 'er in th' dark a' night."

"But . . . they'll see our headlights."

"Me'be. But how'll they know we's not jus' 'nother truck? Them commercial trucks all got stickers t'travel."

IT TOOK THEM the better part of a week to get things ready. Together they bolted a winch onto the front bumper of the bus and wired it up, secured the canopy shell over the bed of the truck, welded on brackets for jerry cans of gasoline and diesel, bolted a propane tank to the rear bumper of the bus, changed the oil and filters, checked the brakes and belts and hoses, and drove both vehicles out for a test run on the alkali flats of the valley and dirt roads in the foothills across in Nevada. Elan found and installed mattresses in each vehicle. Water jugs were filled and groceries and a porta-potty stowed away inside. Elan gave Shadrack free use of the truck to ease the commute back and forth from his farm, and they pulled the Farmall under a shed roof at the end of the barn.

At Katie's request, Shadrack brought over two heaping baskets of his dirty laundry, which she washed and hung out to dry. After she took them down and folded them, Elan handed Shadrack a stack of clean clothes, a bar of soap, and a towel and sent him over to the Surprise Valley Hot Springs with a coupon for a bath and a good soak.

When he returned, Katie whispered, "He looks like a new man."

"Smells like one, too," her father agreed.

While Shadrack continued to bemoan the time they were "a'wastin'," his protests grew milder as he settled into a comfortable working relationship with Elan and Katie. Shadrack showed up each morning with the dawn and performed the tasks and chores assigned to him with competence and growing enthusiasm until the dark set in. When he ran out of things to do, he wired a cut-off switch into the brake lights in the pickup, then found a hoe in the shed and attacked the weeds in the flower bed, neglected in Mrs. Groves' absence. Katie prepared three square meals a day, and they ate mostly together in the kitchen, planning their route, arguing the details, and marking things off their checklists.

Shadrack confronted Elan one morning as they were walking up the dewy lawn from the barn for breakfast. He was holding out his grocery bag in one hand. "Now y'still ain't tol' me how much y'want fer that ol' truck a'yourn," he said. "You ain't gonna be a'goin' all th' way t' the Ozarks, that's fer sure. So I'd like t'settle up with y'right now, y'hear?" He opened the bag and peered inside. "How much d'y'be a'wantin' fer the truck?"

"Well," said Elan, stopping in the grass and stretching his back, "that's something I've been giving a lot of thought to."

"Ya have, have ya?" Shadrack waited.

"How much money have you got in that poke of yours?"

Shadrack gave him a suspicious look. "Wha's'at got t'do with 'er? You set a price, an' I'll consider it, fair an' square, I will. I got m'deed in here too."

"Just tell how much cash you've got. Okay?"

"Um," Shadrack grumbled. "'Bout . . . me'be . . . two thousand dollars."

"That's it? That's all you've *got*?"

"Me'be twenty-five hun'ert. Any more'n 'at I need fer food an' gas, I reckon."

"Total amount in the bag, Shadrack. Come on, how much?"

"Twenty-eight hun'ert. Little bit more, me'be."

Elan clasped a hand over his mouth in thought. "Alright. Here's the deal. I'll sell you that old truck for twenty-four hundred—"

"Twenty-four hun'ert!"

"That's a fair price. It's worth more than that. But I only want three hundred cash down right now. You can sign an IOU for the rest, and I'll sign the pink slip over to you. You can pay me the rest when you get back."

"But I ain't a'comin' back!"

"Well then, you can send me the rest in installments after you get your feet on the ground there in Missouri. Alright? We got a deal?"

Shadrack hung his head. "I'm a'willin' t'pay ya the whole dang price right'chere'n now 'n' be done with it."

"No," said Elan. "You're going to need every penny of your cash to live on for a while. And maybe more. My mind's made up."

"But, I got—"

"I said my mind's made up. Now, what're you going to do about that farm of yours? Someone's going to have to look after it while your gone?"

"I ain't plannin' t' come back."

The kitchen door opened and Katie waved. "Breakfast is ready!" she sang out. "Come and get it!"

Elan waved back. "We'll be right in!" He turned back to Shadrack. "But you *might* be coming back. You've got to keep an open mind about it. In the meantime, someone's got to look after the place. If later you do decide to sell it . . . and not come back here . . . well, then someone will have to be here to sell it for you and pay the bills and send you the net proceeds."

"You?"

"That's not what I had in mind. But . . . well . . . I might be willing to help you find someone to farm it and keep it up and pay the bills and taxes while you're away."

Shadrack thought about it. "Tollitson might do it."

"Teddy Tollitson?"

Shadrack nodded. "Yeah. 'S'got that big ranch next t'mine. An' lots a' other prop'ty. Runs cattle mostly. Y' know 'im?"

"Sure. He used to teach an Ag class at the college. We used to drive over to Alturas and back together when our classes lined up. Have you talked to him yet?"

Shadrack groaned. "I never figured t'take th'time fer all 'at. *We gotta get a'move on.*"

"Hold on. Now just hold on. This won't take all that long. But you're going to have to sign a power of attorney naming someone here as your agent and giving them the legal right to look after things while you're gone."

"I should'a jus' sold th' dang place," Shadrack grumbled.

"Now *that* would have taken a lot of time. Months, probably, to get a good price. Do you know Wiley Baxter? He's the attorney in town."

"Heard a'im."

"Ever met him?"

Shadrack shook his head.

"Too bad. Nice fellow. He did our wills. Mostly retired now. But

I bet he could draw up a power of attorney for you real quick. Advise you on it. Get it signed and notarized. Why don't you call Tollitson to see if he'll serve as your agent for you?"

Shadrack gazed down at his boots and shook his head slowly. "No, sir . . . Tollitson'n me've never seen eye to eye on much. Had us some . . . problems, I might say . . . o'er th'years." He looked up. "But how's 'bout chew? You could do it fer me?"

"Now wait a minute," Elan held up his hand. He glanced up and saw Katie was watching them from the porch. "Okay. I *might* do it. You've got that deed of yours in there?"

Shadrack held up the paper bag. "Yes, sir."

"I would have to . . . find a renter for the house." He ticked it off on a finger.

Shadrack nodded.

"Find someone to farm the land." Another finger.

Shadrack nodded. "Tollitson, me'be. Might run 'is cows."

"Open your mail and pay the bills. Keep an accounting." He ticked two more.

Shadrack nodded.

"And I would pay myself an administration fee . . . and expenses . . . out of the income, I guess." He held up his thumb.

Shadrack shrugged. "Ain't never been much a'that."

"You sure you want *me* doing all that?"

"Yes'r. If'n yer a'willin'."

"Alright . . . I'll think about it," Elan sighed. "And we can give Wiley a call and see if he can see us right away." He glanced up to the house. "But let's not keep the cook waiting any longer."

The power of attorney paperwork cost them another two days. But the delay allowed the moon to wax gibbous for better night driving, which comforted Shadrack. In the meantime, on several occasions Elan and Katie spoke by phone with Bess, still awaiting her travel permit from Portland, in a tag-team effort to secure her approval for the unfolding adventure. Neither mentioned Shadrack Smithers or his quest to return home to the Missouri Ozarks. Nor anything about the likelihood of crossing security sector boundaries without a travel permit. Nor of the detention camps in Nevada or the unknown perils lying beyond. Bess was thrilled to hear of a little father-daughter bonding on a short camping trip in the old school bus. Enthusiastically she bestowed her unenlightened blessing.

DEPARTURE DAY ARRIVED at last. Shadrack appeared with the pickup in the early gray gloaming. He had conceded that the first day's route through narrow canyons and rocky mining roads would best be undertaken by daylight. Nobody would be driving those back roads anyway. But after that, he insisted, by god, on driving at night.

Elan and Katie had already finished loading the school bus. Their slickers gleamed in the porch lights from a steady, light drizzle. Down on the playa a pack of coyotes howled. Elan walked over and handed Shadrack a two-way radio through the open window.

Shadrack held it by the antennae like a vermin. "Wha's'is fer?"

"So we can keep in touch while we're driving. You know how to use it?"

"Course I do. But they kin hear them things, y'know. Trace'em right back t'ya."

"So I've heard. But we'll have them just for emergencies. Keep yours turned on while we're driving, okay?"

Shadrack grunted and dropped it on the already crowded passenger seat beside a long burnished metal barrel.

Elan leaned in. "Is that a rifle?"

"Shotgun," Shadrack corrected. "Double barrel. Breach loader. Twelve gauge. Med'yum choke. Got'er loaded with double-aught buckshot."

"Do you think we're going to need it?"

"Jus' might. Ya never know. A'huntin' rabbits an' squirr'ls mos'ly, I reckon."

"I . . . ah . . . I think I read in the paper that the emergency regulations prohibit carrying firearms in motor vehicles."

"Well sir, I had this'un fer most a' my life, an' I ain't a'gonna leave 'er behin'." Shadrack turned and lifted the gun and stuffed it down behind the seat. He covered it with a red plaid flannel jacket. "Now . . . y'ready t'get a'goin'?"

Elan sighed. "Katie? You ready?"

"Just have to use the bathroom and lock up the house," she enthused.

"Guess we're good as we'll ever be," Elan said. "We'll follow you."

Behind the wheel of the pickup Shadrack led them the short way east on Highway 299 into Nevada, where the paved two-lane degraded into a graveled road. The rain had stopped and the rising sun lit a few scattered thunderheads looming a dazzling white against cerulean sky on the horizon. At the abandoned town site of Via, he turned south on gravel route 34 behind the Hays Range. No one else was on the road. After an hour of dusty washboard road, Shadrack slowed, looking for something in the sagebrush to his left. In a half mile he came to an intersection with primitive Duck Flat Road and wheeled the truck around heading back northward. When the bus pulled alongside, he rolled down the window and told them, "Musta missed th' turnoff."

"For what?" Elan asked.

"Li'l High Rock Canyon."

Elan had to cut and back to turn the larger bus, and by the time he caught up with Shadrack, the pickup had turned off onto a rough, unmarked dirt track descending into the sagebrush toward a cleft in the mountain rim. There was no road sign. They crawled down the narrow, bumpy path, gunning across a few muddy ruts, hoping they would not have to turn around. At a fork, Shadrack chose the one to the right, which curved toward the canyon. The track circled above a dammed reservoir a quarter full of water, then dropped to a muddy stream crossing in the middle of a broad wet meadow. For 30 feet the road was a bog where the stream flowed through deep, sloppy ruts.

Shadrack climbed out to look it over. Elan and Katie joined him. An amazing abundance of cow pies adorned the green sward, and cattle watched them from the surrounding tall sage. Bits of black obsidian peppered the rocky, alkali dirt.

"Can we get through?" Elan asked.

"Truck can. Don' know 'bout th'bus. Prob'bly. She's got good high clearance."

"Well, we always have the winches."

One after the other the vehicles waded in, wheels spinning to their hubs, but both crawled up out of the slop. On the far side the road climbed a hill, then forked. The right-hand fork wound down toward the cleft in the mountain. Lichen stained the interior walls yellow. Sage frosted the slopes like mint icing. As they approached, it began to look like a chocolate-lemon layer cake that had been sliced open and a single piece removed. The road dropped for a half-mile until they came to a gate at the canyon's narrow entrance. A barbed-wire fence stretched high enough up into the rim rock on each side to keep the cows out. The wire gate lay wide open in neglect or defiance. In Nevada, you never knew which. They all climbed out.

The walls were stunningly high rock cliffs, the bottom beautifully green and inviting. A definite trail followed the creek along the canyon floor, but Elan could not see past the first bend, so could not tell how far. No signs were posted, but he surmised that they stood on the threshold of the wilderness.

"It's beautiful," Katie whispered, stepping backwards up the road to get a panoramic picture with her smartphone.

The two men passed through the gate and followed the trail. "You've been here before?" Elan asked. "Driven through?"

"Been 'ere. Walked 'er. Number a'times. But ain't never druv through."

"Can we make it?"

"I reckon so. Stream's shallow. Bed's rocky. But 'er's only one way t'find out fer sure."

"What if we get stuck?"

"We brung th' winches."

"What if we . . . break an axle?"

Shadrack stared at him, shook his head, and turned back. "You ain't gotta follow me. But I'm a'goin' ahead."

Meanwhile Katie had climbed to a ten-foot high strata of white alkali deposits exposed in the cliff above the road. There, before a shallow cave, lay the skeleton of a complete dead cow, ribs sticking into the air and a bit of hide still clinging to the hoofs and snout. She wondered if it had died naturally in that unlikely place, or if someone (or some *thing*) had dragged it there to eat, or as a warning to wolves, or rustlers, or to keep the herd in line, or for some mysterious dark ceremonial purpose only the Nevadan mind could grasp. She shivered, snapped a quick photo of the canyon, and scrambled back down to the bus.

Elan followed Shadrack into the canyon, the wider bus squealing against one of the fenceposts, and immediately crossed the shallow creek on smooth wet rocks, following the cattle trail onto the narrow valley floor. The canyon curved sharply right, then slalomed back and forth beneath ever rising rimrock painted yellow with lichen. As they descended, the canyon opened. The trail cut through tall sagebrush, eight-feet high in places, and crossed and re-crossed the creek as it meandered from wall to wall. Wildflowers brightened the slopes and meadows. A bright sun played peek-a-boo with the lingering low clouds.

"It's *so* beautiful," Katie murmured again and again, oblivious to her father's bare-knuckle battle with the wheel, around rocks big enough to bend an axle, up and down cut banks and point bars, smashing down stream-side willow saplings and serviceberry which had sprung back up after the pickup passed, and plowing blindly through sagebrush and meadow grass and wild rose and chokeberry. A massive quantity of horse and cow manure marked the well-used corridor, which was probably a thoroughfare for working buckaroos, but was unmarked by tire tracks in this roadless area.

After a while the floor of the canyon broadened into a 300-feet wide pastureland. Sagebrush grew short and sparse, replaced by lush green rye and bunch grass. The creek curled in a wide arc to the left, still and deep and muddy with alkali runoff which turned the water milky. There in the grassland they stopped for a rest. Swallows and magpies darted among the cliffs. Chukar scolded from the rimrock. A red-tailed hawk soared high overhead.

"I *love* this place," Katie exclaimed.

Shadrack heard her and admitted, "Kinda partial t'it m'self."

"Why don't we, like, stay here tonight!" she enthused.

Shadrack shook his head. "Cain't. Gotta get through these canyons a'fore nightfall." But his eyes sympathized with her disappointment.

"Well," Elan chimed in, "then how about a little lunch? I'm hungry."

Katie took her time making tuna fish sandwiches while gazing around the cliffs and meadow. The men inspected the vehicles for damage. They found no oil drips. No soft tires. Nothing bent under-neath. Except for an ugly scrape on the bus's right side, everything looked sound.

After lunch they resumed their pilgrimage. The canyon narrowed and seemed to drop more steeply. Rock slides intruded from one side after the other as they zig-zagged their way slowly down. Katie tried closing her eyes and leaning against the headrest for a nap, but it was like trying to snooze aboard a bucking bronco. In two places boulders stopped them. Elan was sure they would have to turn around. But each time Shadrack managed to set a choke around a big rock to winch it out of their pathway. In a third place the pickup managed barely to scrape over a rock slide, but the bus high-centered and had to be winched, scraping and squealing, onward to level ground. Their progress was glacial, but as Shadrack had expected, they encountered no other souls, Homeland Security or otherwise.

The afternoon was almost gone by the time they emerged from the canyon onto the Smokey Canyon Road, a rugged favorite with 4-wheelers and off-roaders. It was a rough and rocky track, but a relief after the roadless canyon. Shadrack headed north, where the road skirted around the west side of High Rock Lake, a waterless dry playa ringed by rough black lava walls. Soon the track merged with the graded Soldier Meadow Road, where Shadrack picked up speed and Elan fell back to avoid eating his dust.

Katie followed their progress on the map through the Summit Lake Indian Reservation, where they turned east. But as the sun prepared to set, she dozed and soon lost track of where they were. "Circling north of the Black Rock Desert," her father explained when she awoke, although in truth he too was lost. It had grown fully dark, but the gibbous moon offered some light. Just not enough to see the big water bars and potholes coming.

"Hand me the radio, honey," he said. Elan thumbed the button. "Shadrack, come in."

No reply.

"Shadrack, we've got to stop for the night. I can't see the potholes coming anymore."

No reply.

"Shadrack?"

No reply, but ahead the brake lights of the pickup flashed through the dark and the dust. After a half mile they pulled up alongside. "Didn't you hear me?" Elan asked.

"I heared ya."

"But you didn't reply. Don't you know how to—"

"I knows how. Jus' don' like them things."

"Well, we need to stop for the night. Before I break an axle."

Shadrack nodded. "There's a good spot up at the pass, as I recollect. Be a li'l cooler thar. An' high 'nough fer timber cover."

"How far?"

Shadrack considered. "'Nother . . . twen'y minutes. Me'be half'n hour."

Elan glanced over at his daughter. She nodded. "Okay. Lead the way."

ONCE SHADRACK CRESTED the ridge, he turned left up a narrow dirt track that led a short way to a hunter's camp at a clearing in the forest. Here there was flat ground, a fire ring filled with burned-out tin cans and fallen branches, two sturdy sitting logs, and even an old wood-sided pit toilet with half the roof blown off.

They shuffled the vehicles into level positions. Then Elan popped up a small dome tent and tossed in a futon and his sleeping bag. Katie would sleep by herself in the bus. Shadrack had cleared a space in the back of the truck and was spreading out a blanket on top of an old foam pad. Evan flashed a light inside. Shadrack's shotgun lay beside his bed, barrel pointed out across the open tailgate.

"Planning on doing some hunting tonight, are you?"

Shadrack glanced up at him. "Well . . . there's critters ya hunt . . . and' there's critters 'at hunt you. An' this here's a wild country."

"Okay. But just make sure you don't shoot me or Katie if we get up to pee in the dark."

"Hardly likely."

Katie had prepared freeze-dried dinners, which they devoured hungrily before a kindling fire. Even Shadrack seemed to have an appetite. Afterwards, her father went out with the headlamp to gather chunks of juniper and pinyon for firewood.

This was Katie's first time alone with Shadrack. She eased herself down into the blue bucket of the folding camp chair next to the log where Shadrack perched upwind of the campfire. "I was so sorry to hear about your wife's passing, Mr. Smithers," she said.

"Shadrack."

"Right . . . okay . . . I mean, I'm sorry . . . *Shadrack*." She adjusted her hips in the uncomfortable fabric sling. "How have you been getting along?"

Shadrack stared into the crackling fire without looking at her. After a while he sighed. "Oh . . . she's been kinda rough, I reckon. Days're long. Cain't seem t'do ma' chores. Chores's been m' life. It's what I done. All these years. Now . . . they don't give me no more sat'sfaction. Don't wanna bother with 'em no more. What fer would I? 'S'all fer nothin' no more. Ya see?" He searched for the right words. "Nights're longer still, they are. All b'myself . . . in that ol' empty house. Empty bed." He scratched at his neck whiskers. "Got t'do ever'thing fer myself now. Aw, I don' min' th'work . . . no ma'am . . . but . . . somehow . . . it mos'ly jus' don't seem worth th' trouble."

"Well, I'm sorry. Tildie must have been a wonderful companion."

"That she war." They sat in silence, watching the flame lick the wood and the smoke curl away into the night. After a while Shadrack spoke quietly. "We *had* us somethin', we did. Tildie 'n' me. An' now . . . now it's all plumb slipped through m'fingers, it has. An' the only place I know whar ta look fer it ag'in . . . well . . . is whar it all started out."

"Is that why, you know, you're going back to the Ozarks? If you don't mind my asking."

Shadrack pondered on it for a while, then said, "'S'a funny thing . . . an' hard t'splain in words . . . never was much good with 'em nohow . . . but . . . well . . . I got me a debt t'pay." With that preamble spoken, his eyes brightened. "An' them Ozarks . . . oh my! . . . the smell a' the pines after a rain me'be. The way it all feels *right*. Inside 'n' out. Feelin' things's be all jus' a'gettin' better an' better . . . an' a'goin' someplace." He paused in his recollections, then turned his face to her. "It don't make a lick a' sense. None a' it. Ya think I don't know that? Well, I do. But what else've I got t'do? Cain't go on like this, I reckon. Might as well jus' put m'self outta m'mis'ry an' be done with it all." He turned back to the fire.

"I . . . I feel that way too sometimes," Katie said. She drew a deep breath and let it out. "Oh . . . I've never had that feeling you're talking about, I guess . . . but I *want* to have it. Someday. For sure. I want to feel like . . . like I belong somewhere. With someone. But everything just seems to be . . . you know . . . so laid out in front of me. Like by my parents. By my teachers. By my friends. And it's all in one long, straight, dreary line. Like a . . . railroad track. And I'm not sure I want to *go* that way." She paused to find the right words.

Shadrack looked over at her and nodded.

"I have no clue, like, where it's all going," she continued, gazing at the firelight flickering in his eyes. "But I'm . . . searching for something that . . . you know . . . that gives my life . . . *something*. A purpose, maybe. Something that gives all this, like, *meaning*, I guess." She fell silent.

"I un'erstan'," he said.

"You do?"

"Arrr. But you's jus' a young'n still. Me, I's nearly spent. Fer me, it's all 'bout gone past a'ready. Seems like two shakes o' a lamb's tail." Slowly he smiled. It was the first time she had seen his gap-toothed smile, and it brought a kind of gentle beatitude to that gnarly, bewhiskered face. "Oh, thar's a mighty lot I could tell ya 'bout . . . but I ain't never been much good with words. An' besides, it warn't do no good. *My* path ain't *yourn*. Like the song says . . . ya gotta walk that ol' lonesome valley . . . an' ya gotta walk it by yerself."

Something snapped in the woods and Katie jumped. "What was *that*?"

"Jus' yer pa, I reckon. A'bustin' up sticks t'fit the fire."

She laid her small hand across his larger one. "Thank you, Shadrack."

Awkwardly he pulled back his hand. "Fer whut?"

"For . . . like . . . listening to me . . . for understanding, I guess. Dad never has time to really listen."

"Uh. Whole world's got in such a rush nowadays. He's a'bound t' mellow as he gets older. An' it ain't no easy thing being no parent, neither. No, sir. I can tell ya that. You's near growed up now, but yer pa, he cain't see it yet. No, sir. He still sees y' as that little girl he's gotta pertect an' keep safe from the big bad wolf outside 'cher door." He dropped his eyes. "But 'ere's one thing I ken guarantee y' for certain. Some day sure he'll come t' regret not getting t' know 'is own chil'en better when he had 'is chances."

She waited for more, but when nothing came, she asked, "Are you . . . talking about my father, Shadrack . . . or . . . or about yourself?"

He barked out a laugh. "Same difference, I reckon." Slowly he creaked to his feet and arched his back. "Sometimes it seems like the same ol' sorr'ful thing . . . over'n over ag'in . . . don't it?"

MORNING LIGHT CAME too soon for Katie. But long before the sun rose she was up and dressed and cooking oatmeal on the propane stove in the bus, while the men broke camp. When her father hauled in his tent to stow beneath the cabinet, she asked him, "Do you think it would be alright if I, like, rode along with Shadrack for a while?"

"Ow." The question so startled Elan that he banged his head on the cabinet door. "Ride along with *Shadrack?*"

"I was just thinking . . ."

"I thought you didn't like the way he smells."

"Oh, that's not so bad anymore. Or maybe I'm just getting used to it. Anyway, I guess it would be better than breathing his dust all day long. He seems kinda lonely . . . and I know how you cherish your morning time to yourself."

Elan rubbed his head. "Have you asked him?"

"Not yet."

He thought about it. "Go ahead. See what he says."

When she brought up the subject with Shadrack, he grumbled, "I'd haf'ta move all this stuff outta the front seat."

"I can help," she offered.

"Now hol' on. Hol' on. I . . . uh . . . don' rightly know. Lemme think on't." But when she returned, the passenger seat had already been emptied. "You ask yer pa 'bout this?"

"He's okay with it if you are. He likes to spend some time by himself in the mornings. And we can switch back whenever anybody wants."

The sun rose hot and dazzling through the pickup's windshield as they descended into the next basin of pale dry desert. The thick alkali dust kept the bus at bay far behind. Shadrack appeared uncomfortable at first with a companion aboard, and they didn't have much to say to each other. So they rode along in a bumpy, rattling silence. After a while Katie asked him, "So, how did you and Tildie meet?"

It took Shadrack a long time to put the words together in his head. So long that Katie thought he hadn't heard, or worse, that she should mind her own business. But finally he spoke. "First laid eyes on 'er 'n . . . St. Louie . . . 's'I recall. She was . . . jus' . . . a'walkin' down the sidewalk thar . . . an' . . . an' I jus' thought . . . why, ain't she the pertiest senorita I ever see'd?" He smiled as the memory absorbed him.

"But . . . how did you actually get to *meet* her?"

Shadrack glanced over. "Shucks, I jus' stepped right up an' tol'er howdy an' how perty she looked." He broke into his gap-toothed grin. "An' she cottoned t'me right off, she did. I believe I cut me a perty manly figure m'self, back in 'em days."

Katie laughed. "What were you doing in Saint Louis?"

"A'workin'. Got me a job as a survey'r's helper fer the Corps of Engineers. Diggin' ditches an' holdin' flags an' poundin' iron stakes an' such. Right'char on the bank a' that ol' man river. Y'ever seed 'er?"

"The Mississippi?"

"Thass right."

"No, I haven't."

"Well . . . y'outta."

"So you weren't . . . like . . . dressed up in your finest."

"Lordy, no! Jus' my dirt boots an' work clothes." He shook his head in wonder. "But she took a shine t'me anyhow. Right away, she did." He pondered a bit more, then added, "An' ta this day I still cain't reckon why. But I knew right'en. I'uz th' luckiest man on this earth. An' I still b'lieve it."

"Was she . . . if you don't mind my asking . . . a US citizen?"

"Was after I marry't her." He thought about it. "Her pa, y'see, he come over as a bracero. Down in Texas somewheres. But he 'uz smart 'nough t'figure, well, he could earn a better wage up north. So a'stead a'goin' on back when he'uz s'posed ta, he brung up 'is family from Sonora an' lit out north. Up inta Missouri. Worked's a farm hand in the Delta. Near Cape G'rardieu, I believe. Anyways, Tildie, she got'er schoolin'ar. Learnt 'er English jus' fine. Spoke it better'n me, she did."

Katie waited, knowing not to press him too much. But finally she nudged him with, "So you moved back to the Ozarks?"

Shadrack nodded, reminiscing. "That we done. M' uncle's farm is whar. Needed us'n t'help run it by then. M'aunt, she 'uz not well. M'cousin Orville got kilt in th' war. M'other cousins'd all ran off. But I'll tell ya, Tildie knew her farmin', she did. Oh my, yes. From back down Sonora way, I reckon, she learn't it good. An' she worked hard's any man."

And so they drove, Shadrack beginning to unspool his story in bits and pieces. Dribs and drabs. She prompted him at times, but knew not to press him. And he would tell her what he wanted to tell, but no more. And that was alright with her. She found his tale fascinating. And it eased the passing of the long dusty road.

They stopped more frequently now. For a bite to eat. To stretch their legs. But mostly because Shadrack could endure only so much social intercourse at one time. The stops allowed Katie to change rides. For her it was like shuttling between alien worlds.

KATIE WAS RIDING with her father when she checked her cell phone for service. "We've got bars!"

"Well . . . that's something. Must be getting close to Winnemucca."

"Do you think we should call Mom?"

"See if there're any messages first."

Katie checked the screen. "Two messages. Both from Mom. You think I should listen to them?"

"Why wouldn't you?"

Katie frowned. "Shadrack doesn't think we should, you know, be using these phones. He says they can triangulate your location by the towers."

"Just who is this '*they*' who've got Shadrack so spooked?"

"He didn't say."

"Well . . . nobody's looking for *us*. And it's only your mother calling, for heaven's sake."

Katie still looked dubious. "What if he . . . you know . . . finds out?"

"Shadrack? He's not going to find out. Just check the massages, will you?"

Katie used her thumbs with a dexterity incomprehensible to Elan. She held the phone to her ear, then turned to her father with her brows knit in concern. "Mom's coming home. She's got her travel permit."

"When?"

"She's not sure. Probably the day after tomorrow. Or maybe the next day. She's, like, having trouble booking a flight."

"Well . . . that's good news, isn't it?"

"Yeah . . . I guess so, but . . . does it mean we have to turn around?"

"Did you listen to the second message?"

"No." Her thumbs flew over the tiny keyboard. Her face brightened. "She can't get out until Wednesday."

"That gives us . . ."

"Three more days."

"More like four, actually." Elan smiled. "That ought to give us enough time to see the bristlecone pines and get back to pick her up."

The bus rattled and fishtailed as the washboard surface began to climb a knoll. Elan slowed and sought out the least-corrugated path. At the crest the road smoothed out again.

"So . . . what's so special about bristlecone pines?" Katie asked.

"They're the oldest living things on earth. Oldest living trees, anyway. Bristlecone pines. Some are five thousand years old."

"Wow. And they just grow out here in the desert?"

"No. No. They grow up high. Twelve or thirteen thousand feet. Up at timberline on Wheeler Peak. That's in the Great Basin National Park, where we're headed. They may be the oldest living trees anywhere on earth, right there."

"How do they know how old they are?"

"They count the tree rings. Each ring equals one year."

Katie thought about it. "You mean they have to, like, cut them down to find out how old they are?"

"No. They drill out a small core and count the rings in it. But there is a story about some Ph.D. student who broke his core drill and asked the forest service ranger for permission to cut down one old living tree. Just to see how old it was. Turned out to be one of the oldest. Maybe *the* oldest. Five thousand years old."

"And they let him *do* that?"

"They sure did. Someone had named it 'Methuselah,' as I recall the story."

Katie shook her head. "Maybe . . . maybe *that*'s who Shadrack's so worried about. The '*they*' you asked about."

"The bureaucrats, huh? Well . . . might just be a nugget of truth in that."

She pondered for a long time as the bus bumped along, throwing up a rooster tail of dust. Then she said, "Kind of reminds me of Shadrack."

"What does?"

"The bristlecones."

"Why?" Elan grinned. "Because he's so bristly?"

"No." Katie was serious. "Did you know, he doesn't even know how old he is."

"He doesn't? Doesn't he know when his birthday is?"

"Nope. He's like those trees. No birth certificate. He never knew his father or his mother. Grew up in an orphanage somewhere in Missouri. Until he was taken in by his foster parents."

"They adopted him?"

"No. I don't think so. But he took their last name. Smithers. Shadrack refers to them as his 'aunt' and his 'uncle.' His 'cousins,' I think, are their children. But none of them are related to him."

"So . . . you think we're going to have to cut down old Shadrack to find out how old he is?"

Katie cringed. She was not amused.

Elan thought about it. "You're growing fond of old Shadrack, aren't you?"

"He's . . . well . . . you know . . . he's had a hard life. But he's endured. Like the trees. I like listening to his stories. He's really a sweet man under all that gruffness and whiskers. He has a good heart. He grew up in a whole different world. And now he's, like, all alone."

Far ahead brake lights flashed through the clouds of dust. "Look!" Katie said. "I think he's stopping."

"Well, you'd better quick call you're mother and tell her we got her message. And that we'll pick her up when she flies in. I'll drive real slow."

ELAN CLIMBED OUT, slowly straightening his stiff, aching legs and back, and crabbed forward to where Shadrack stood leaning against the front fender of the pickup and gazing into the valley below.

"What's up?" Elan asked.

"Don' like this drivin' in daylight. 'Spesh'ly not through a city big's 'at one ."

There in the distance the City of Winnemucca was laid out like dull dominoes glued down in a series of bone-dry grids. Amid the surrounding ridge spines and streaks of alkali desert, incongruous green crop circles were randomly pasted like felt stickers on a dusty chalkboard. The sluggish flow of the Humboldt River wound in tight coils between railroad tracks on the near bank and Interstate 80 on the far one. Flashes of sunshine sparkled off the water and from windshields and chrome in the steady streams of traffic moving both ways along the freeway. The faint hum of distant traffic assailed their ears.

"Well . . . isn't there a . . . some sort of back way around it?"

"No, sir. Not thut I knows 'bout. Gotta get across the river, an' the only bridges're right'char. Right downtown. On 'a other side a' them railroad tracks."

Elan glanced around. "Well, we sure as hell can't camp out here. It's too open. And hot."

"I know a railroad crossin' off'n a road near the sewer ponds. Jungo Road 'ey calls it. An' if'n I got any luck a'tall, they's a summer bridge crossin' the Humboldt jus' b'yon'. An ol' flat car, if'n it's still there. An' then, b'yon 'at, a cattle pass 'neath the Interstate, a ways west. But I don't reckon I know whether we can get t'any a' it. 'Spesh'ly sportin' these 'ere California plates. We' be taking a mighty chance, jus' a'goin' down there a'tall." He turned to look Elan in the eye. "Jus' wanted ya t'know tha's how she stands."

Elan nodded. "What alternatives do we have?"

"Well . . . you an' that young'n a'yourn can turn back ri' now. Y'unnerstan'?"

Elan nodded again. "What about you?"

"Me? I ain't got me no choice, I reckon. I'm a'goin' on through."

Elan gazed off silently for a while, evaluating the landscape. Considering the options. "Well . . . I'll go back and talk it over with Katie."

Katie, of course, would not consider abandoning their quest, especially now that her father had seeded her imagination with his tales of bristlecone pine. She just *had* to see them. And after two uneventful days on the road, Elan was beginning to suspect that Shadrack's paranoia might lack sound foundation in reality. So he walked back and told him they would be coming along.

Shadrack squinted into his face. "You sure 'bout 'at?"

"Yup. Katie wants to see the bristlecones."

Shadrack drew a deep breath. "A'right. Reckon it's yer choice. Le's stop an' fill up the tanks long's we're down 'ere."

"Won't the gas stations want to see our travel permits?"

"'Ey don't in Cedarville."

So Elan and Katie followed Shadrack down the long slope into the valley, keeping a distance from his dust until the pickup entered a narrow, crumbling macadamized road. They caught up, but still lay back several blocks as the city traffic grew heavier. The bus and the pickup pulled up at separate pumps of a run-down Biz-Y-Fuel on the outskirts of town and topped off their tanks. Elan payed at the diesel pump with his credit card. Shadrack paid inside with cash for the gas. Everyone took their time using the dingy restrooms before they all climbed back aboard, Katie still riding with her father. No one asked them any questions.

Shadrack led them along a circuitous route to a well traveled highway, over an unsignaled crossing of the railroad tracks, and down a rocky road to a gravel pit where they found an old railroad flatcar on blocks spanning the narrow, meandering green flow of the Humboldt River. On the other side Shadrack followed a dusty gravel alley along the river back westward, which, after a seemingly endless traverse, curved abruptly south through a wire gate into a cow pasture and through a narrow cow tunnel beneath the Interstate. No one stopped them.

"Guess this was his lucky day," Elan observed.

"Nobody seems to care about us," Katie responded. "Shadrack may be, you know, overdoing this caution a bit."

Katie tried following their route, but most of roads were not signed or on her map. Narrow Grass Valley Road ran smoothly south, but soon ran out of pavement and reverted to the same rough gravel they had been driving for days. Shadrack led them southward through the stirring dust, then turned east at an intersection marked "Golconda Road", where they began a long winding climb up into the junipers and over the pass. Along the way two sandblasted pickups passed them coming the other way, the drivers in cowboy hats each raising a hand in silent greeting. The road wound down the other side of the mountain, where Shadrack turned south, and then east, and then south again, and east again along dusty unmarked valley roads, until Katie was utterly lost. Shadrack finally pulled off at the base of a low ridge. Before them in the basin of a wide north-south valley lay a paved highway.

"That looks like a pretty good road," Elan said.

"'S Highway 305," Shadrack responded. "Runs down t'Austin."

Katie perused her map. "Austin is on Highway 50," she said. "That's where we want to be, isn't it?"

Shadrack grunted, "Me'be."

"You planning on taking it?" Elan asked.

"Might," Shadrack said. "Like t'watch'er first. See who's a'drivin' on it."

So while Katie prepared peanut-butter-and-jelly sandwiches, the two men set up folding chairs in the shade of an old cottonwood beside a dry wash and watched the road. A single white pickup lumbered north, then nothing for a long while, until suddenly a convoy of a half-dozen big commercial eighteen-wheelers roared past heading south. A few more pickups passed while the ate their sandwiches and drank cool water to unstick their pallets. Then nothing.

"I knows a campground," Shadrack muttered at last. "M'be twenny miles east a' Austin on 50. We could make by afte'noon. We could hole up there an' get us some sleep 'til after the sun goes down. Then start a'driven 'gin after she comes on full dark."

"Drive at night. That's what you want to do now?"

"Be a moon a'risin' early. Mos'ly full."

Elan considered the proposal for a while, then sighed. "Sounds like a plan." He turned to his daughter. "Katie?"

"Sounds good to me," she agreed.

They encountered no roadblocks and little traffic as they sped down Highway 305, keeping a mile distance between the vehicles. Austin was little more than a historic mountain relic, inhabited by 200 souls where ten thousand once lived and worked and gambled and prospected before the silver mining all played out. There they turned left onto Highway 50 in broad daylight and no one gave them a second glance. Elan pulled closer behind the pickup so as not to lose it as they wound through the mountain passes and ravines to the east.

A half hour later Shadrack's turn signal flashed and Elan followed the pickup up a single-lane gravel road to a sturdy wooden campground sign that read: "Hickison Petroglyph Campground." It displayed a map of the campsite loop, trails, and petroglyphs. At an elevation of 6500 feet, the temperature was mild in the high-desert forest. They parked the vehicles in the shade of pinon pines and gnarly junipers at a secluded campsite well out of sight of the highway. Shadrack advised them to catch some sleep and climbed into the camper shell with his shotgun.

"But I want to see the petroglyphs," Katie told her father back at the bus. "And hike all the trails. It's *so* beautiful here."

"Well . . . we ought to get some rest," Elan mused. "Shadrack wants to eat a late supper and be back on the road by ten."

"But . . . I want to *see* them," she whined. "For sure. I . . . you know . . . may never be here again. Or get another chance to explore. Isn't this what we told Mom we were doing?"

Elan looked around at the clustered trees and slabs of soft beige rock. He had seen some squiggles and marks scratched into their faces behind fenced off areas near the sign. "Well, maybe later, but we have to—"

"I'll cook dinner," Katie cajoled. "I promise. And be ready to go when you are. I won't have to do any driving, so . . . so I can sleep along the way if I get tired. And it'll be dark outside anyway. Just let me look around here for awhile first. You go ahead and take your nap. *Please!*"

Reluctantly, Elan nodded. "Okay. I'll be lying down in the bus.

Wake me up if you need anything, okay?"

"Yes, sir." She snapped off a smart salute. "Oh . . . and I wanted to ask you . . . can I ride with Shadrack when we get going again?"

"You'll have to ask him, honey."

ELAN WAS ENJOYING the dark solitude and quiet of the lonely paved highway. He felt rested and fed. The moon hovered high above the eastern horizon, almost-full and bright enough to light the road even with duct tape constricting the headlight beams. He missed the company of his daughter, but the faint glow of the taillights ahead comforted him. Shadrack felt the mile interval would be a good idea in case anything happened. Checkpoints was what the old fellow had been talking about, Elan surmised, though he hadn't asked. Shadrack's reasoning was sometimes a little hard to follow, but usually reasonable. And Elan had grown to like the old farmer. Had grown to trust him. He was holding to the speed limit, as he had promised to do as long as Katie was on board. Elan smiled and wondered what the two might be chatting about. If anything.

A convoy of big eighteen-wheelers appeared as a string of bright beads descending the mountain far ahead and grew and grew and finally blazed past with blinding headlights and shuddering wake streams, the running lights of the trailers shrinking like Christmas-trees in the rearview mirror. It took them a long time to disappear over the foothills far behind. The road became quiet and empty again and straight as an arrow in the silver-white moonlight. No one was traveling their direction. East. Elan cracked the window to breath in the sharp tang of the cooling desert.

Then two things happened in quick succession. A vehicle spun onto the road behind him with flashing roof-bar emergency lights and blinding high beams, and a moment later the taillights ahead winked out and the pickup seemed to disappear from the face of the earth. "Shit!" Elan cursed. He reached for the walkie-talkie on the empty passenger seat and thumbed the button. "Shadrack, come in. This is Elan. I think I have a cop on my tail."

No response came. He checked the volume. It was all the way up. "Shadrack. Do you read me?"

No answer.

"Shadrack, are you there, come back?"

No answer.

"Shit!' he repeated, and began to slowly ease his foot off the accelerator, wondering what in hell he was going to say the cops. He spotted a wide, flat gravel stretch of shoulder near a dirt crossroad and crunched to a slow stop, hoping the cruiser would blow by him on a more vital mission. But the flashing lights pulled in behind him, the headlights blazing through the rear windows. Elan tried the radio one more time, without success, then let it slip through his fingers onto the floor and waited.

It was a long wait.

Finally the silhouette of a man in a smokey-bear hat climbed out of the patrol car and ambled up his long shadow toward the door. Elan rolled the window down the rest of the way and leaned out. "What's the matter officer? I don't think I was speeding."

The man wore a brown uniform and hat with a Highway Patrol patch in the shape of Nevada on the shoulder. He was tall and lanky, his face long and drawn beneath the brim. He appeared to be a bit older than Elan, slim, solid, and a little weary of making these late-night traffic stops. His right thumb was hooked in his belt just ahead of his holstered service weapon. He flashed the light he held in his left hand briefly across Elan's face, then swept the floor and passenger seat with it. "Are you carrying any firearms, sir?" The voice was slow and confident, almost a drawl.

"No, sir. I don't own any."

"May I see your driver's license and travel permit?"

Elan fumbled his license out of his wallet and handed it out the window. "Here's my driver's license."

"Where you headed?"

"Great Basin National Park. My daughter wants to see—" He bit his tongue. "I want to see the bristlecone pines . . . I mean . . . I'm just out scouting the route for later."

The trooper swung his flashlight beam into the back of the bus. "All by yourself?"

Elan drew a breath and considered the ramifications. The image of the old double-barreled shotgun Shadrack had stuck behind the front seat of the pickup haunted him. For "rabbits an' squirr'ls mos'ly." But Elan hadn't been convinced. Nor was he now. "Yes, sir. I'm . . . trying out this new camper bus I converted. See if it's seaworthy."

"You with the other vehicle?"

"What other vehicle?"

"The pickup ahead of you?"

"Oh . . . was that a pickup? I was just . . . following the taillights. Helps me follow the road at night. For safety."

The trooper nodded. "Well, it won't do you much good, going to Great Basin. The park's been closed for a month. Homeland Security's taken it over as an operations center and staging area and temporary detainment camp. National Guard soldiers are bivouacked there. I can't even get in without an invitation." He inspected Elan's driver's license. "Cedarville."

"Yes sir."

"You know a fellow name of Tollitson?"

"In Cedarville? Sure I do. Teddy Tollitson. Owns a big spread out near Eagleville. We used to teach together at the college in Alturas. But we can't get back there now, either of us. He teaches agriculture. Or used to."

The officer nodded and smiled for the first time. "My cousin married one of his sons. Warren. I've been over to his place for the wedding and a time or two since. Can I see your travel permit?"

"I . . . ah . . . didn't know I needed one. I live in this sector."

"You've got California plates," the trooper said.

"Yes, but I thought Cedarville was *in* this sector." He patiently explained the theory he and Shadrack had concocted at the kitchen table so long ago. About how they wouldn't let you drive to Alturas, where he worked, because the checkpoint was west of the Warners. So he supposed he was in the Nevada sector by default, and he didn't need a permit. Now it all sounded a little vacuous and flimsy

The officer listened, frowning. "That's a nice notion, but I'm not sure its right."

"Well . . . okay, then. You understand my predicament here. The question is, do I belong in this sector or the Alturas sector?"

"Did you bother to call Homeland Security for an answer before heading out?

Elan fidgeted. "No, sir. I just figured . . ."

The trooper considered for a while, then shook his head. "Don't know the answer to that one. But if you're coming from the California sector without a travel permit, then I've got no choice but to notify Homeland Security and hold you until they get here to pick you up."

The news shocked Elan like a live wire. "But . . . but . . . but what if I *do* live in the Nevada sector?"

"Then I can just turn you back. You're not supposed to come out this far."

"You'd send me back home?"

"If you live in this sector, yes, sir. But that's the best I can do for you. And I still better radio in and find out which sector Cedarville is in."

"Now hold on. Just wait a second. Your saying you'd have to lock me up . . . or just turn me around . . . depending on what they tell you on the radio? Now that's a pretty big toss of the dice for me, wouldn't you say? And how do we know *they* would know the right answer. Or what if you can't get through?"

The officer's smile turned sour. He did not look happy. "You see what I'm up against here?"

"And how come you didn't stop those big rigs going the other way?"

"They all had travel permits."

"How do you know that if you didn't stop them?"

"Transponders. Inside the windshields. Broadcasts who they are, where they're from, where they're going, cargo, tare weight, and commercial travel permit number."

"But . . . they were speeding."

"Everybody speeds out here. Can't stop them all."

"But *I* wasn't speeding. How come you stopped me?"

The trooper was silent for a moment, then grumbled, "Wish I hadn't."

Elan picked up on something in his voice. "You don't like this job you're doing for them, do you?"

"I'm not pleased with any of this state of emergency business, to tell you the truth. But the Highway Patrol's been nationalized, and I've got my job to do. And the way things are going, if I don't guess things right here, they damn well might lock *me* up with you." He fell silent and considered the stalemate. "You know Ted Tollitson, you say?"

"Yes, sir. I know him well. I taught with him. And I've done some accounting work for him in the past. Until he hired his own bookkeeper."

"All right. What I'm going to do here . . . is turn you around and let you head back home. And then, once you're on your way . . . after I see your taillights disappear over those hills back there . . . then I'm going to call into dispatch . . . and tell them how I disposed of this stop." He shook his head. "Since I already radioed in your plates, I'll have to think up something to radio in as a disposition."

"Thank you, officer. I guess I'll just head back home."

The trooper appeared vexed. He turned back toward the cruiser, thought for a moment, then leaned back in through the window. His voice was soft, confidential. "Your daughter is in that pickup?"

Elan stared at him. Bringing in Katie now could complicate matters. And Shadrack even more. Particularly that damned shotgun. But this fellow was sharp, and telling him lies might get himself locked up in some concentration camp, and that wasn't going to do anybody any good. The eyes that held his own also seemed to hold compassion. "Yes, she is," he said at last. "Her name is Katie. She's only fifteen. She'll be sixteen next week. And all I wanted to do was show her the bristlecone pines."

The trooper nodded. "Who's driving?"

Elan drew a deep breath. "A neighbor."

"What's his name?"

"Smithers. Shadrack Smithers." Elan was relieved the officer did not write anything down. "He's an older fellow. A farmer. His wife died just a few months ago, and he's having a hard time with it. We were bringing him along . . . to help get his mind off his loss."

"He from Cedarville?"

"Yes, sir. Owns a little farm there. Out near Tollitson, as a matter of fact. He's owned it for years."

The trooper straightened up. "Okay." He shined his flashlight onto the radio on the floor. "You better get on the horn there and tell them to turn around too. Homeland Security is not something any of you want to mess around with. Especially not here in Nevada. And especially not with your young daughter on board."

"You aren't going to talk to them?"

The trooper shook his head. "I never heard of 'em. You're trouble enough. This sort of thing is not what I hired on to be doing as a peace officer."

"Thank you, officer. By the way, what's your name? I'll be sure to tell Teddy I ran into you when I see him."

"I'd just as soon you didn't tell anybody you ever saw me." He crunched slowly back to the cruiser and switched off the emergency lights.

Elan started the bus and pulled a slow u-turn across the abandoned highway as he reached for the walkie-talkie on the floor.

SHADRACK'S ARMS and shoulders ached. He had been holding Katie's birding binoculars for too long, watching for something to happen. Now they hung from the strap around his neck. Katie sat in the ground beside him, hugging her knees and shivering, but she couldn't bring herself to drop back down to the pickup for her sweatshirt. She didn't want to miss anything. The truck was parked behind a grove of junipers on the back side of the low knoll they occupied. The flashing lights on the patrol car had dominated the vast empty desert for the better part of an hour. Chirping crickets serenaded them during the long wait.

Suddenly the lights went out.

Shadrack raised the glasses. "He's a'movin'. He's a'turnin' 'round the bus."

Katie jumped to her feet. "Oh my god, I wanna see."

"Looks like . . . they's a'lettin' 'im go."

"*Let me see!*" She reached up and fastened a fist onto the glasses. Shadrack reluctantly let the strap slip over his head. By the time she had focused, the radio in Shadrack's shirt pocket crackled.

"*Shadrack? Katie? Can you read me?*"

"Give me the radio!" Katie demanded.

"Cain't do it. Too dang'rous." When she reached toward his shirt pocket, he plucked it out. "I told ya before, they can back-trace these things—"

"Shadrack? Katie? Are you there?"

"We've got to let him know we're here! So we can meet up with him!" Katie felt her anger rising. A tantrum coming on. She wanted control of her own damned radio and her own damned life and was willing to fight for them. But Shadrack just held it high over his head while she jumped up and down in a rage, whacking him in the arm and ribs with her fists.

"Well," the radio voice continued. *"In case you are listening . . ."*

"Shush," Shadrack whispered.

"I'm turning around. I don't know if you can hear me. Or what you'll do if you can't. This is all a mess. Great Basin National Park has been taken over by the feds. They've got soldiers there. And a prison camp of some sort. Do not *go there! Do you understand? Do not—"* The transmission began to break up as the distance between them increased. *". . . Homeland Secur . . . meet you back . . . troglyph . . . stand? . . . camped . . . ternoon . . ."* And then it was all just static.

"Try calling him back! Let him know where we *are*!"

Shadrack just shook his head.

"Bastard!" she hissed. "Do you understand, like, what he's saying? I think he wants us to meet him back at that petroglyph campsite!" The fight seemed to have drained out of her, dampened by a new tingle of fear. But not the outrage nor the venom.

Shadrack nodded. "Seems like. Prob'ly a good idea . . . from 'is way a'lookin' at it. 'Cept fer one dang thing."

She glared up at him. *"What?"*

"It'd put us a'goin' back th' plumb wrong way."

"Wrong way?"

"Yes'm. I'm a'headed east, an' he's a'goin' back west."

"But . . . we've *got* to meet him. You've *got* to take me back to my father."

Shadrack shook his head. "Ain't *gotta* do nothin'. I knowed this here idea was a sour one. A'travelin' along t'gether with a girl. Yer pa shoulda knowed better. Shoulda jus' sold me that ol' pickup truck way back in Cedarville an' been done with it. Wouldn't a' ended up in this here pickle t' begin with."

"What are you going to *do* with me?"

"Don't reckon I know jus' yet." Shadrack reached out for the binoculars, and she let him take them.

"*Asshole!*" she muttered under her breath.

Shadrack appeared not to hear. He was focused on the patrol car, which still had not moved.

"No wonder they don't want anything to do with you," Katie growled.

"Who's'at?"

"*Your daughters.*"

With that, all conversation died. The moon seemed to have crystalized the landscape into a frozen pewter. There was no traffic on the highway below. No lights on the horizon. No sound, except for the crickets and the rumble of the cruiser's engine, which ebbed and flowed on the breeze. After a while the patrol car shifted into gear, turned with a sweep of high beams, and headed back west. Shadrack watched for a long while, until the taillights disappeared over the ridge that had swallowed the bus. Then he turned and began shuffling painfully down the gravel slope.

Katie found herself alone and confused. And afraid. She didn't want anything more to do with that selfish old sourpuss son-of-a bitch Shadrack. She felt like crying. Or running away. But she knew that was a crazy idea, since she couldn't get much more *away* than she already was. And if she wasn't careful, he might just leave her here. Shivering, she checked her cell phone again. Still no bars. She has no options. She could die out here alone in the cold. Or be eaten by . . . *something*. So she pouted for a while more, but not too long, before following his footsteps down the loose gravel slope. Neither spoke as she took her place in the blackness of the truck's cab and slammed the door.

Shadrack had trouble following his tire marks back down through the desert brush. Several times he switched on the low beams of the taped headlights to find the way. Just short of the black strip of highway he cut the lights and engine and climbed out. Saying nothing, he lurched up onto the blacktop. At the centerline he faced first one way, and then the other, mumbling to himself. Katie couldn't make out his words over the rush of blood in her ears from of her own thudding heart. But there was something terrifying about the set of his jaw. And suddenly she was too frightened to breathe.

ELAN WAS LOST. Lost in the moon-blanched landscape and lost in his own thoughts. His mind was racing. Spinning in circles. Reliving the panicky confusion of the traffic stop. Replaying his conversation with the trooper. Had the man really offered him only two choices? Turn around without your daughter or be turned over to Homeland Security? Could that be right? Shouldn't Elan have argued for Katie's safety? Made the man realize the danger she would be in if he turned tail and ran? And why was he still running away in the dark of night. What was Katie going to do? What *could* she do? How was she expected to get home by herself? Would Shadrack bring her back? Make sure she was safe? And what was Elan going to tell Bess? That he lost their daughter? That she ran off with old Shadrack Smithers? Could he fix things before she got back?

The dark-cloaked landscape rushed by without his notice. Elan hadn't paid all that much attention to the landmarks. Katie had been his navigator. That was her job. She had followed their route on the map, making notes. Now she was gone and nothing looked familiar. Especially in the dark. Heading in the opposite direction. And he was afraid to pull over and wait for them. If they were even coming this way. The trooper might not give him a second chance if he was caught stopped along the road.

By the time Elan thought to look for the turnoff to the petroglyph campground, he feared it was already behind him.

SHADRACK LIMPED down from the blacktop, climbed into the cab, and started the engine. He eased the front wheels up over the soft shoulder onto the pavement. Katie held her breath. With a grunt Shadrack spun the wheel left. Westward. Back the way they had come. Back the way her father had disappeared.

Katie breathed again. "Thank you," she said softly.

"Fer whut?"

"For taking me back to my father."

He nodded. "Ain't much of a choice, I reckon. Yer pa's been mighty good t'me. Ya both have. 'S time t'do wha's right."

"What about the Ozarks?"

"'Ey kin wait a li'l longer, I reckon. 'S already been nigh onto fifty years."

She smiled and felt like hugging the bony old man. A ridiculous notion, she had to admit. That would just scare him silly. Or rile him up.

Neither spoke as they lumbered down the long straightaway, without headlights, guided only by the moonlit center and fog lines. It took a long time before they crested the distant ridge, which had taken both bus and police car. The valley beyond opened slowly before them. It held no sign of light nor life.

A SIGN MATERIALIZED along the right shoulder, white and glaring and accusatory in the muted beams of Elan's headlights. *30 MPH Zone Ahead.* Elan knew with a sinking dread what that meant. He had arrived back in the ghost mining town of Austin. It was after midnight and the place was closed and empty and locked up tight. He allowed the bus to drift to the curb and roll to a stop. The diminishing velocity seemed to sap his energy and resolve.

Suddenly he felt faint and shaky and a little sick. He cursed his miserable fate. He cursed himself. For he knew it was not his stars, but himself that had gotten him into this mess. He alone was to blame for putting Katie in mortal danger. And for his inept negotiations with that Highway Patrol officer. But most of all for his craven blind flight through the night to save his own sorry ass.

Elan let his eyelids close. He couldn't remember ever feeling as weary as he did now. He didn't want to be where he was. Or who he was. And he had no clue about what he was going to do.

"THAR SHE BE," Shadrack proclaimed as a ghostly blue "Campground Ahead" sign slid past in the moonlight. "Thass where yer pa'll be."

"Thank you, Shadrack. Thank you, thank you, thank you. And I'm so sorry, you know, for what I said."

"'Bout whut?"

"About what I said back there. You know. About your daughters."

"You don't know nothin' 'bout them!" he snapped, staring straight ahead until he turned off onto the campground access road. After a while he drew a deep breath and sighed, then shrugged. "Ain't nothin' t'be sorry about, I reckon, when yer a'speakin' th' truth."

"No . . . I'm sorry . . . like I didn't mean . . . I shouldn't've said . . ."

"Hold on thar!" he barked suddenly, slowing the vehicle. A small red light on the dashboard pulsed on and off

"What's the matter? I didn't mean to—"

"Jus' shush up." He eased the pickup to a stop.

"What is it?"

"Don' reckon I know 's'yet. But 'er's som'thin' *wrong*."

"What is it? Is it the truck?"

"Up yonder . . . we's a'bein' watched."

"Watched? How do you know? I can't see anything."

"See that thar . . . thing . . . a'blinkin' in front'a ya?"

"Yeah. What is it?"

"'S'a warnin' us. I put 'er in m'self. She only flashes when somebody's a'watchin' with inf'red 'lumination. Night time vision."

"Oh my god . . . who'd be . . . ?" Katie stopped, a chill crawling up her spine. "You mean . . . ?"

"Shush!" He cranked down the window and stuck his head out into the crisp air while the engine idled.

Katie fixed her eyes on the blinking light. "Where on earth do you buy—"

"Shush!" Shadrack listened for a long moment, then drew back inside. "Army surplus . . . but neve' mine 'at. We got us a problem . . . an' what we gotta do is fig'er 'er out . . . what we're a'gonna do . . . righ'chere, an' now . . . an' mighty fast." For a long moment he stared blankly in thought, shaking his head. Then he nodded to himself. "Yup. No two ways 'bout it." He turned to face her squarely. "Yer a'gonna have ta git out."

"Out? Out of the *truck*?"

Shadrack jerked around and pulled his red plaid hunting jacket off the back seat and thrust it at her. "Here. Take 'is here coat. It'll keep ya plenty warm." He eased up on the clutch and the pickup began crawling forward.

"You mean . . . you want me out of the truck? *Out there?*"

"Yes'm. I'm a'gonna swing 'round 'at that thar clump a trees . . .

an' when I get 'er turned . . . you gotta jump out an' go hide in the brush thar."

"I don't *want* to get out of the truck. Not if somebody's watching—"

"Y'gotta. Only safe way." The pickup wheeled slowly off the road and began a wide, bumpy circle through the sage and rabbitbrush. "Try'n git behind one'a them big rocks. See 'em? 'S far from the road 's ya kin. But behind them rocks. Keep low. An' move slow. An' *stay thar!*"

Katie whirled around, looking for the unseen threat out there in the darkness. Over her shoulder, in the back seat, the pulsing red light reflected dully off the naked barrels of the unsheathed shotgun. "What are *you* gonna do?"

"Ne'er min' 'bout me. Your pa'll be along in time . . . least I'm a'hopin' so . . . if'n they ain't already got 'im. An' I'll be back t'check on ya . . . if'n I kin . . . elstwise . . . well . . . I reckon yer on yer own."

"But I don't want to—"

"*Ya gotta!* Now git ready . . . behin' 'em big rocks . . . ya see 'em? . . . ready? . . . open up 'at door!"

Katie pulled the handle and cracked the door a few inches as Shadrack slowed almost to a stop.

"Now *jump!*" He leaned over and gave her a rough shove.

Katie's shoulder pushed open the door and she threw herself out reflexively to keep from falling. The door slammed shut behind her as the wheels spun out bits of gravel. She stumbled on a rock and turned her ankle and fell sideways into a thicket of stiff brush. Shadrack's jacket helped cushion the fall, but her hands were scratched and poked by the brittle stems and branches. She lay where she had fallen, listening to the pickup rattle and bang back to the access road and accelerate down the gravel toward the highway. She lay still, listening, but hearing nothing but the receding hiss and growl of Shadrack's truck.

She was afraid. But her thudding fear was being eclipsed by a surging anger at Shadrack's impulsiveness. By the time she heard the squeal of his tires on the highway, Katie had convinced herself that the son-of-a-bitch was crazy. His was a madness born of a sick, incomprehensible, and incurable paranoia. And now she was left here in the desert on her own. And all for *nothing*.

She heard a cough in the distance. Katie froze and strained to listen as fear regained the upper hand. From up the hill above the campground she heard a voice. Then another. Soft at first, but rising. Agitated. Arguing. A sharp order was barked and a car door creaked open and was slammed. Bright headlights flared, winking as an engine started. Other doors slammed. A second big engine wound and caught and revved and a second set of blinding headlights blazed down on the rocks around her. She buried her face in the old man's jacket as two vehicles began crunching and rumbling down the gravel beyond the rocks, picking up speed. Something crawled down her neck, but she kept her face deep in the fabric until they both had passed. She lifted her head to see what and who they were. The first vehicle, in the headlights of the second, was a big truck with a brown canvass canopy over the bed and "U S Army" stenciled in white on the olive drab door. She couldn't read the markings on the second, but thought she saw a light bar across its rooftop. They accelerated toward the highway, kicking up dust and gravel. The first truck turned east at the highway and the second one headed west.

Katie knew where they were going. They were running down Shadrack. And he was luring them away from her.

She struggled to her feet and brushed off her clothes. This was her chance to explore the empty campground to see if their school bus was parked there. Exposed in the bright moonlight, she stumbled back toward the access road. If the bus was *not* there . . . well . . . then it probably meant that her father had intended to rendezvous somewhere else, and they had misinterpreted his message. Or else that he had simply missed the turnoff. But if it *was* there . . . and the thought made her shudder . . . if the bus *was* parked there in the campground, empty, then he had most likely already been taken into custody. And was bound for some Nazi-style concentration camp.

As she approached the campground grove, a bright light suddenly blazed from the moon shadow of the trees. *"Who goes there?"* a quivering voice demanded. *"Identify yourself and . . . and . . . state you purpose!"*

Katie stared into the light for only a second before shielding her eyes with her hand. Confused and terrified, she tried to collect herself. "I . . . I . . . I'm . . . my name is . . . Katie Groves ," she stammered. "And

I'm looking for my father . . . I got lost . . . I got . . . got separated from my father . . . hiking these trails . . . we were hiking . . . the petroglyph trail . . . looking at them . . ."

"Where's your father now?"

"*I don't know!* That's what I'm trying to *tell* you. We got *separated.*"

Private First Class Jerome DeSoto, Nevada National Guard, searched the girl with his flashlight beam. "That coat's too big for you."

"I know *that*. It's my dad's."

"Are you carrying any firearms?"

"No!" Katie opened Shadrack's heavy wool jacket to give him a better look at her.

"Okay. How old are you?"

"Eighteen," she lied. "Now, will you please get that light out of my eyes?"

Jerome lowered the beam to the gravel road between them and switched it off as he stepped out into the moonlight. "Y'don't look that old."

They stood evaluating at each other as their eyes re-acclimatized. Neither seemed to know what came next. He appeared to be a harmless enough young man. His military fatigues were a size too big for his slender build. His hair was long and black and tied back in a braid, not the standard military buzz cut. But his features were even and strong and dark. But young. "And you don't look old enough to be a soldier, either," she rejoined. "Like . . . where's your gun?"

Jerome blenched. He didn't need another critic. He was already under assault from the good old boy network in his company. A Paiute Indian by birth, brought up on the reservation where he graduated from high school, he had joined the National Guard to get away and qualify for some college credits in electronics. To make something of himself. But now he'd been called up to serve in this Army unit as a radio specialist. He was *in* the Army, but not really *of* it. Or the National Guard, either, for that matter. The other soldiers made sure he knew he was not a *real* soldier like them. He wasn't even allowed to carry a firearm except in supervised training.

Katie saw the hurt in his dark eyes her words had caused. Something unexpected seemed to pass between them. Something silent and tender. She had never in her life flirted with a complete stranger, but the instinct seemed to arise naturally as she let him look her over in the moonlight. "What are you doing out here, anyway?" she asked gently.

"Monitoring traffic. Checking permits. Unit's been called up to help with the national emergency. We've been assigned here."

"Why *here* for god's sake? Out . . ." she turned a slow circle, showing herself off ". . . out *nowhere*."

He shrugged. "I . . . don't know." The hint of a smile curled the corners of his mouth. "All that's above my pay grade."

She smiled back. "How come you didn't go out with the others just now?"

The hurt returned to his eyes. "Somebody had to stay and look after the bivouac. And the communications equipment. I'm a radio operator, so I stayed." He changed the subject. "Were you with the guy in the truck?"

"What truck?"

"That black pickup truck. You didn't see it?"

"No. It was, you know, too dark. I'm just trying to find my dad and go home. He has an old school bus. A short one. He did, like, a camper conversion on it. Have you seen it? It's kind of a . . . a spotty school-bus yellow color with patches of gray primer all over? Is it parked here at the campground?"

Jerome shook his head as a convoy of big rigs thundered past on the highway. When the noise subsided, he said, "No, haven't see any school buses, or anything much else. This campground's empty . . . except for us."

"And . . have you guys . . . have you taken any prisoners?"

"Not recently."

She shivered, but left the jacket hanging open and took a step closer. "I . . . I'm *scared*. I don't want to be here . . . when your friends come back."

"No, you don't. That wouldn't be good. These fellows . . . they can be . . . not very nice. They can get a little wild. A little . . . frisky. You know, rough."

"But . . . where can I *go*?"

He thought for a moment, then shook his head. "I don't know."

Katie stepped even closer. "I need my dad to pick me up. But I can't call him. My phone's got no bars. You don't happen to have a cell phone I could use, do you? One that works out here? "

"Yes . . . well . . . no . . . sorry."

She studied him. "But . . . you *are* the radioman, right?"

"This's all government equipment. No cell phones. Satcom stuff. Strictly regulated. And restricted."

"But . . . you *could* call out . . . if you wanted to?"

"Yes . . . well . . . but I'm not authorized to make calls, except for military use."

She eased right up next to him. "How about for search and rescue? The military does search and rescue, doesn't it?"

"Yes, of course. Sometimes, anyhow. In some circumstances, but not—"

"Hey, I'm, like, *lost! I'm a missing person!* " She managed an actual tear. "And I'm going to *freeze to death* out here in this wilderness if nobody finds me soon. I need search and rescue." She placed a hand on his arm and gazed into his eyes. "You can use that phone of yours for search and rescue, can't you? To prevent a civilian casualty?"

"I'd . . . I'd need authorization." His voice trembled. "Lieutenant Diesenwald isn't here . . . and—"

Katie stretched her face up toward the meek warrior's lips and brushed them with hers. Then she kissed him gently on the mouth.

His flashlight clattered to the ground. "Whoa." Jerome staggered back a step, surprised and a little dazed.

She smiled coquettishly. "Will that be authorization enough?"

ELAN HAD FALLEN into a crack in his childhood bathroom. Guilt-ridden, he was caught somehow between the cold porcelain toilet bowl and an unyielding metal wall. His neck was cricked and his left hand felt bloodlessly numb. Before him rose his mother, impossibly tall and odious in her black silk bathrobe, glaring fiercely down at him with terrible damning eyes. He flinched as an insect suddenly screamed beside him and those accusing eyes were no longer his mother's. They belonged to his wife. He and Beth were awaiting a phone call. Elan knew it would be from the Commandant of the concentration camp and he was going to tell them that they were holding Katie as a prisoner and were about to begin hurting her in unimaginable ways. Beth reached to pick up the phone. Elan tried to bat her hand away, but he couldn't move his arm. She was going to find out the terrible truth of what he had done with their daughter—.

The insect chirped again.

"Wha . . .?" Elan came more fully awake. The cell phone was chirping. He found himself slumped in the driver's seat of the school bus, which still sat idling at the curb in Austin, Nevada. He tried to straighten himself up and get his bearings. The phone chirped a third time, and foggily he rummaged through the utility box beside the seat. He managed to grasp the phone and flip it open. "Uh . . . 'lo?" He listened to a hollow, empty swishing and was about to hang up.

"Dad! It's Katie!"

"Katie? Where are you?" Again the swishing. *"Katie?"*

"At the petroglyph campground. Isn't that where . . . yes, it's Katie . . . I heard you . . . we have a delay in our signal here because, like, it's bouncing off a satellite . . . but isn't the petroglyphs where you wanted us to meet? Where the heck are *you*?"

He straightening the crick in his neck and searched for the right words as he gazed shamefully out at the empty streets beneath their dead amber lights.

"Dad?"

"Yes, honey. I'm here . . . I'm in . . . Austin."

He counted to four as he listened to the swishing nothingness. Then, "Can you come get me?"

"Can't . . .uh . . . can't Shadrack give you a ride?"

Four more seconds of emptiness. "Shadrack's gone."

"Gone? He's *gone*? Where's he gone to?"

Four seconds. "It's a long story. I don't have much time. The soldiers will be coming back—"

"Soldiers?"

Elan's interruption had put them out of sync. When the signal returned, another voice was speaking to Katie, muffled in the background, but Elan couldn't make out what it was saying. Then she spoke into the phone, "They're coming. Can you pick me up?"

"Who's with you?"

The next four seconds seemed to expand while Elan waited. "Pick me up on the highway!" Katie's voice was sharp with alarm. "Can you do that? A mile or so before you get to the turnoff, you know, for the campground. I'll be on the road. I gotta go."

And the line was dead. And the swishing of emptiness abandoned the phone to enter his heart.

LIEUTENANT DIESENWALD stepped down from the cab of the troop carrier, scruffy, grim and disgruntled. He surveyed the surrounding foothills, still frosted in moonlight. "You're still out there somewhere, aren't you?" he murmured to himself. "I can *feel* you watching."

"What's that, sir?" asked his first sergeant.

"Set up a perimeter," he snapped. "Live ammo. That fucker may be coming back."

"Yes, sir," Sergeant Dudly saluted. "I'll get right at it."

Diesenwald was not a happy man. His team had managed to lose the pickup truck which had penetrated so threateningly close to their position. He spat. So much for all the fancy electronics. He turned and almost stumbled over Jerome DeSoto. "What the hell do you want, soldier?"

Jerome saluted sharply. "We seem to have a problem, sir."

"Well . . . *do* we have a problem, private, or do we just *seem to* have one?"

"I don't know yet, sir."

"What *do* you know?"

"We seem to be picking up cross-talk on our sat phone, sir. Probably from a cell phone tower."

"I thought they shut 'em all down."

"Yes, sir. The cell towers were supposed to have been rendered inoperable. But we're still picking up cross-talk from civilian transmissions, sir."

"So?"

"That could compromise our security, sir."

"Well . . . shit . . . you're the radio tech . . . fix it."

"Yes, sir. But I'll need to take the humvee out to the road to track down the interfering signals. Triangulate them, sir."

"Okay . . . what are you bothering me for? Just do it."

"Yes, sir. I'll need your permission to take the humvee, sir."

"Didn't I just give it to you, goddammit?"

"Yes, sir."

"I suppose you'll need a driver?"

"No, sir. I can handle it myself."

"Then what the hell're you waiting for, private?"

"Sir, we'll have to suspend some surveillance until I'm finished."

"Everything?"

"No sir. Just the night vision."

"Why?"

"Interference, sir."

"How long?"

"Shouldn't be more than half an hour, sir."

"Then get to it, private. Chop, chop. Tell Sergeant Dudly what you're doing. And report back to me as soon as everything's back to nominal. You understand?"

"Yes, sir." Jerome snapped another sharp salute and turned on his heel.

ELAN CLIMBED OUT, stepped around the bus into its shadow to pee in the short grass, stretched his legs and back, then buckled himself back into the driver's seat. He racheted the shift into gear and was about to pull a U-turn, when a convoy of big-rigs approached from ahead, heading eastbound through the sleeping ghost town. They were all creeping along at precisely 30 MPH, the maximum speed allowed in Austin He counted eleven of them, big and brightly lit, their diesel engines vibrating the bus windows as they rumbled past. He figured that it might be wise to travel in their wake, just one of the herd, but another vehicle was following a couple of blocks behind the trucks. So he waited for it too to pass. As the automobile drew closer he saw the outline of an emergency bar on the roof and, as it passed, a "Lander County Sheriff" emblem on the door. Elan slid down in the seat, but the driver of the cruiser was focusing his attention on the trucks.

Hunkered down, he waited another minute or two, rethinking his strategy, until the tail lights all disappeared around a curve in the highway behind him. Elan made his silent turn and sedately followed them out of town toward the petroglyph campground and his daughter. Rather than trying to merge with them, he kept his speed down to let them all get as far ahead as possible and out of his world of concern.

At the edge of town the sheriff's cruiser had turned around and was parked by the left side of the road with its interior lights ablaze and the deputy recording his observations onto a clipboard. So damned much paperwork, Elan thought. Only a computer could digest it all. Elan figured he had reached safety, just before the lights of the cruiser winked on a mile behind him and swung a big semicircle heading his way. The headlights followed at a discrete, unvarying distance.

"Shit!" Evan muttered. "Shit! shit! shit! Now what have I gotten myself into?" He wondered just how far he would have to drive before he got out of Lander County. He doubted that this sheriff's deputy would be as cooperative as the state police officer who had already stopped him and let him go. This was, after all, the dead heart of hard-scrabble rural Nevada. He pressed down on the accelerator. The speedometer rotated up by ten miles per hour. He considered dousing his lights, like Shadrack had done, but that might enhance his pursuer's interest. "Shit, shit, shit." The last thing he wanted to do was lead law enforcement to Katie. It was feeling like deja vu all over again. "Shit, shit. shit."

THE HUMVEE SLOWED along the shoulder of the highway. "Get in!" Jerome called. "Hurry."

Katie scrambled aboard and the vehicle sped up as she closed the door. "How did you manage to—?"

"Long story. I'm supposed to be out looking for problems with our communications link. I only have about a half an hour to find your father and get back."

"Won't they know?"

"Hope not."

"Thank you for everything, you know, for what you're doing." Katie wanted to tell him everything about herself in the short time they would have together. She described her father. And Cedarville. And their fated camping trip. "After he brought the idea up, I was, like, Holy Cow, I wanna *do* that. Like, this is gonna be a whole new adventure and a lotta fun."

Jerome listened as he concentrated on the road ahead. "Guess you got more than you bargained for . . . what with this state of emergency business."

"Yeah. Like, what's it all about, anyway? I can't figure it out. The Internet is down, or so slow it might as well be. And the TV news only tells you, you know, what they want you to hear. Is there, like, some kind of a revolution going on out here?"

Oncoming headlight blazed from around a curve ahead, and Jerome dimmed his brights. They fell silent as a long convoy of trucks streaked past from the west, buffeting them in the wake stream.

"They don't tell us anything either," Jerome said. "Just enough to get our jobs done." He glanced over at her in the pale dashboard light and smiled. "Truth is . . . I don't think anybody around here has a clue. I . . . I just don't know. But I'll tell you this . . . something's not right about the whole mess."

They rounded a curve and abruptly entered an arena of flashing lights. On the left shoulder ahead was stopped a shadowy vehicle whose bright headlights nearly blinded them. Tucked behind it was the police cruiser which had pulled it over, its red and blue roof lights flashing like a misplaced pinball machine. As they closed the distance, the front vehicle revealed itself to be a stubby school bus spotted with yellow and gray paint.

"*That's my dad!*" Katie cried as they passed.

Jerome hit the brakes, reached over and activated the humvee's own emergency lights, squealed a U-turn, and pulled in behind the cruiser. He left his high beams blazing.

Katie squirmed. "What're you gonna *do*?"

Jerome held up a hand, sat up straight, and drew several deep breaths as he gazed blankly out the windshield.

"What are you *doing*?"

He took one final breath, then turned to her. "Getting into character." He reached back for a clipboard, then cranked open the door. "Stay in the car." He stepped out and tugged down the brim of his cap. "And keep your head down." He slammed the door and swaggered into the high beams like an actor entering the footlights, ignoring the deputy who stood beside the open window of the bus, watching him. Jerome bent down to study the cruiser's license plate and scribbled some notes on his clipboard.

Katie scrambled into the driver's seat for a better view and pulled down the visor to shield out the pulsing lights atop the cruiser. In that moment her eye caught a movement far up the road near the curve. A quarter mile ahead a dark vehicle without lights came to an abrupt stop in the distant psychedelic red and blue of the strobes.

Jerome straightened. "Hello," he called to the deputy.

The deputy made no reply, but walked back to meet Jerome, his body language sending the message that this was an unwelcome intrusion into his bailiwick. His face was young and plump and scarred by acne. Short-cropped blond hair covered his head like a shower cap. His pendulous belly swung over his belt buckle.

Katie watched as the dark vehicle reversed away up the road and swung off backwards into a drainage swale between two hillocks. Neither the deputy nor Jerome seemed to have noticed it.

"Jerome DeSoto, Nevada Air National Guard," Jerome reported. He pulled a laminated card from his pocket and held it out as the deputy approached. "I'm deployed with the Army Tactical Detail stationed up by Hickison."

The deputy glanced at the card. "Deputy Jay Fleegler. Lander County Sheriff's Department." He held out his hand.

"Got an ID?"

Fleegler grimaced, then pulled out his wallet and flipped it open.

Jerome studied it, adding notes on his clipboard. "Good to meet you, Fleegler." The two shook hands. "What've we got here?"

"White male. California plates. Driver by the name of . . ." he glanced down at the drivers license he held in his pudgy fingers.

"Groves, Elan," interrupted Jerome before the deputy could read it off.

The deputy looked surprised. "You know this guy?"

"Why do you think I'm here?" He held out his hand for the license. Confused, Fleegler handed it over.

"He alone?" Jerome asked.

"Seems to be."

"Firearms?"

"Not that I could see."

"You didn't pat him down?"

"Not yet."

"Good. He show you a travel permit?"

"Says he ain't got none."

"Ah," Jerome nodded, smiling. "That's good too. You radio it in yet?"

"Just about to . . . before you showed up."

"No need to now. I'll be taking over."

Fleegler frowned. "You sayin' you got jurisdiction here?"

"Absolutely. The Army's taken over tactical interdiction along this stretch of Highway 50."

Deputy Fleegler scratched his head. "I ain't heard nothin' about it."

"Well, you will. Just happened. Based on intel I cannot share with you at this time." Jerome grinned. "But it's gonna save you a heap of paperwork."

"I think I better call it in."

"I wouldn't do that if I were you." Jerome leaned closer and lowered his voice. "Just a word to the wise. Cop to cop." He nodded toward the bus. "Shouldn't be tellin' you this, but he's one of ours. Homeland Security. Undercover."

Fleegler looked concerned, but unconvinced.

Jerome lowered his voice further. "This is about to get ugly. *Real* ugly. Word's coming down direct from Central Command. They're looking for traitors infiltrating law enforcement here in Nevada. Moles. Anybody involved here, either side of the law, is gonna get sucked in. Might be under suspicion for the rest of his career. I'm giving you a chance to drive away. Pretend it was *me* made the stop. You had nothing to do with it. And I'll back you up, if it comes to that. You want to stay the hell out of this mess. Believe me. Okay?"

Fleegler stood in the bright high beams of the humvee and thought it over.

"Where you stationed?" Jerome asked, trying to close the deal.

"Substation in Austin."

"Oh boy," Jerome grunted and flipped to a page at the back of his clipboard.

"Why. What's the matter?"

"Fleegler . . ." Jerome placed a hand on the deputy's shoulder ". . . let me put it this way . . . I *know* things . . . I can't disclose 'em to you . . . sorry . . . but if I were you, I'd get the hell away from this mess as fast as I can. Your name is not on my list . . . not yet. You understand?"

Fleegler's jaw worked, but no words came out.

"You're messin' with national security here, Fleegler." He pulled a pen from his shirt pocket. "This is your last chance."

Fleegler looked into Jerome's eyes, then nodded. He climbed back into the cruiser and killed the flashers. Then he made a slow U-turn and headed back toward Austin.

Katie was out of the humvee as soon as he was gone. "What did you say to him?" she asked Jerome as she ran past to the driver's window of the bus. "*Dad!*"

"Katie?" Elan looked dazed. "What are you doing here?"

"Are you okay?" She leaned in and hugged him around the neck.

"I . . . I think so." He unbuckled his belt, pushed open the door, and found an unsteady footing in the gravel. "What are you wearing? Is that . . . Shadrack's?"

Katie was gazing up the road toward the curve. It seemed darker now, but she thought she could make out a figure holding something in his hands. Something long that reflected the lights. She blinked, but she couldn't focus properly. Couldn't be certain. It might have all been her imagination.

"Katie?"

Katie turned and smiled. "Yeah, dad?"

"Who's that fellow there . . . standing there by the hummer? He looks like a soldier?"

"He is . . . like . . . sort of."

"Do you *know* him?"

"He's my new friend. His name is Jerome. Come on, I want you to meet him." She led him by the arm. "Jerome, this is my father."

"Please to meet you, Mr. Groves." Jerome handed him back his driver's license.

"How . . . how did you . . . ?"

"It's a very long story, sir, and I've got to get back to Hickison before I get in more trouble than I'm already in. Katie can fill you in on most of it." He opened the door, leaned in, and switched off the hummer's emergency lights. "But maybe I can come visit you and Katie up in Cedarville sometime."

"I'd *love* that," Katie beamed. "Can he dad? *Please!*"

"But," Elan sputtered, "you're not . . . she's not . . . old enough . . . for . . . to have . . ."

"Maybe we can at least swap stories," Jerome said. He bent and kissed Katie on the cheek, then climbed into the driver's seat and buckled up. "Have a safe trip back home."

Katie stood on the centerline and watched the hummer's tail lights disappear around the bend. Back toward his unit. The moon was behind her now, low in the western sky. The long night would be coming to an end soon. A wave of melancholy swept over her.

"Come on, kiddo," Elan said. "Let's go home."

Wearily they trudged back to the bus and climbed aboard, shuffling things around, settling into their places. Evan revved the engine, cranked the wheel hard to the left, and eased out the clutch.

"Dad, wait . . . there's something I want you to see . . ."

"What honey?"

She pointed up the road toward the curve as the headlights swept across.

"What is it?"

She strained her eyes for a moment longer, then shook her head. "Nothing, I guess." Shadrack, or whoever she might have imagined there, was gone.

PART TWO

Kieferville, Missouri

November

THE BEWHISKERED OLD MAN balanced on one bony knee between two weather-worn headstones. His fingers were bleeding. He had torn away the weeds and long grass and blackberry briars with his bare hands to expose the time-blackened names he sought. *EZEKIAL SMITHERS* was chiseled into one. *RACHEL SMITHERS* into the other. Dates of birth and death were scratched beneath the names. His adoptive parents, they were. His first real family. But the world had moved on. The graveyard had long gone untended. It had taken him months to find these grave markers.

Shadrack cleared his throat. "Well . . . I's back," he said. "I know it's been a perty long spell . . . but not 'cause I ain't been a'thinkin' 'bout ya . . . all 'ese years . . . simple gone by." He lifted up his knee to clear a thorn branch under it. "Found me a space t'sleep, I did. In Diesler's bunkhouse up the road. Remember old Diesler? He's long dead now, a'course . . . an' his son Luther don't remember me, I guess . . . but he's a'givin' me a bunk an' three square meals a day fer helpin' out with the chickens an' the cows an' a little bit a'weedin' in the veg'tible patch." He bowed his head. "Feels good t'have somethin' t'do with m' hands ag'in."

He breathed in the scent of pinewood smoke and fresh-turned soil from the fields being readied for winter crops. A tractor droned in the distance. Clouds were building in the west and rain seemed likely sooner than later. Maybe even a snow flurry. He loved the outdoors, Shadrack did. He was going to sorely miss it.

He sighed and tugged the rag sweater tighter around his neck. It was time to get down to business. "I made up m' mind, I have," he declared at last. "An' I'm here t'tell ya what I'm a'plannin' t'do." He lined up the words in his head before he spoke them. "Well . . . I'm a'bound an' determined t' go on an' turn m'self in. Yes'ir. Clear the slate 's best I kin. I gotta 'tone fer the worst one a' my sins. 'S th' only ways I's a'gonna ever have a chance t'see Tildie ag'in, I reckon . . . o'er on th' other side."

He searched for the words that had to be said. Words that would embarrass him mightily. "I jus' want you t' know. A'forehand. Both a' ya. 'Cause ya likely ain't a'gonna like it much. But I want ya t' hear it from me first." He drew a shaking breath. "An' here's th' truth. I's th' one done shot an' kilt that drifter name a' Lupic Mufel. We was both drunk and a'arguin' out in th' woods behind that old honky-tonk. Shot 'im with that ol' shotgun ya give me fer squirr'ls. Way back then . . . jus' a'fore I lit out fer St. Louie . . . when that drifter went a'missin'. Only, truth is, he weren't never a'missin' a'tall. He was plumb dead an' buried. An' I know where 'is body's a'buried. So . . . I'm a fixin' t' turn m'self in fer it. Take th'punishment I's due. An' me'be . . . jus' me'be . . . I'll be blessed t'see Tildie ag'in. In the hereafter. If'n they be such a place a'tall."

Shadrack rose stiffly and bent backwards. His spine crackled. Stiffly he knelt back down on the other knee to finish this business. "This 'ere ain't got nothin' t' do with you . . . or the way y' brung me up. Ya done jus' fine. This was all m' own doin', curse a' devil. An' tha's the sure truth. Forgive me if'n ya kin. I's woeful sorry t've let y'down." He paused a final time, then rose to his feet. "Jus' a'wanted ya t'know."

THE POSTMAN DROPPED an envelope into the Groves' mailbox in Cedarville. Five months had passed since Bess's return flight from Portland had arrived on time. She had taken a cab to the checkpoint just north of Alturas, where they met her. As they drove back, her husband and daughter regaled her with an enthusiastic, though sanitized, version of their camping trip. No mention was made of Shadrack Smithers. Nor of the Nevada police. Nor of the Army National Guard. Bess accepted the account with good cheer and few questions.

Travel restrictions had been gradually eased for those who were gainfully employed and without criminal records. The Groves were on the list of upstanding citizens. So Bess had visited Ginger in Portland one more time in the intervening days, all without incident.

But the national state of emergency had not been lifted. Communications were more restricted than ever. Facebook and Twitter were things of the past. News outlets were all censored. Reliable information was scarce. No one knew what was happening out there. In Washington. In the heartland of America. In the hinterlands. It began to feel like they were living in some fascist third-world country. The real horror was the ease with which they were growing accustomed to it.

At least Elan had been allowed to return to his teaching, and for him life in Cedarville fell back into its time-worn rhythm of uneventfulness. He had even managed to lease Shadrack's farm to a young Polish couple from Stockton who had taken out a seed loan from Tollitson. Tollitson vouched for them, and somehow they were managing to make their monthly payments on time. Elan had no desire to probe more deeply into their circumstances.

Katie's sixteenth birthday had come and gone. It seemed to Elan that his daughter had blossomed into an attractive, self-confident, and independent young woman. Annoyingly independent. Like her mother. Whether it was a result of her turning sixteen, or of unspoken events which may have occurred during their strange camping trip, he could not say. He had no desire to inquire further. But it made him uncomfortable. Katie's new friend Jerome had telephoned her twice, but to Elan's relief, he had not come around for a visit. She said he had been reassigned to a unit in New Mexico. Elan hoped it would all just fade away.

Elan removed the unfamiliar envelope from the mailbox and held it up to the sunlight. It was addressed to him in childish block pencil letters, but bore no return address. The postmark was Kieferville, Missouri. He brought it inside and showed it to his daughter. Together they looked up Kieferville in the atlas. It was a tiny dot on a secondary road in the remote pine forests of the Ozark Mountains.

"Open it," she enthused.

Elan nodded and picked up the letter opener. The envelope contained no letter, but only a postal money order payable to Elan Groves in the sum of nineteen-hundred-sixty-two dollars.

Elan grunted and handed it to his daughter.

Katie was beaming. "At least there's one old bristlecone still standing," she told him.

IN THE DECADES SHADRACK WAS AWAY, a new Kieferville City Hall had been built across the abandoned railroad tracks from the roller rink and park. The sprawling one-story structure was no longer new.

Shadrack parked his pickup on the cracking asphalt, leaving the keys in the ignition, and minced his way to the front door. He was carrying his shotgun, broken open and without shells, in the crook of his left arm as he limped inside. A plump young woman looked up from her computer and smiled. "I'm sorry," she said, "but we don't sell hunting licenses here."

"Ain't what I's a'here for," Shadrack grunted. "I come t'see the chief a' police on important business."

The clerk shook her head. "We don't have a police department anymore," she explained, rising and approaching the counter. "We contract with the Sheriff's Department now. But Sergeant Wiederman is on duty today, and I think he's in. I'll see if he has time to see you. Can I tell him what this is about?"

"Yes, ma'am. Tell 'im I's here t'confess a murder I done."

The smile disappeared from her face. She glanced uneasily at the shotgun. "I'll . . . just . . . be right back." She hurried around the counter and disappeared down a hallway.

Shadrack bided his time, breathing deeply, hardly believing that he was really doing this. After all these years. He watched it all unfold as if from a distance. Like the rerun of an old TV show. Doubts still scurried like black rats in the shadows of his thoughts, but he tried his best to ignore them. He had made up his mind, he had. And that was that.

A short, muscular man in a blue uniform peered around the hallway corner to give Shadrack a cautious appraisal, then stepped warily into the hall. He looked to be in his forties, with a bushy black moustache cascading over his upper lip. In his fist he gripped an automatic pistol, pointed at the floor. "Sir, I'll have to ask you to place that shotgun on the counter and step away from it."

Shadrack grunted and complied.

Sergeant Wiederman approached, confirmed the shotgun was unloaded, and asked the clerk to take it to the storage room. He slid his service weapon back into its holster. "You wanted to see me?"

"Yes, sir."

"About a . . . a confession?"

"Yes, sir."

"All right. Come on back to my office." He gestured for Shadrack to lead, and he followed. The city clerk kept her distance as they passed. "Turn right here. My office is the first door on the left there." He offered Shadrack a chair and sat behind a desk with stacks of papers surrounding a laptop computer. "What's your name, sir?"

"Shadrack Smithers."

Wiederman clicked on the keyboard. "Smithers. Smithers. Didn't a family name of Smithers . . . used to own a farm out by the Scale Road?"

"Yes, sir. M' Ma an' Pa. Zeke an' Rachel Smithers. They's long dead now."

"Sorry to hear that. Do you have a driver's license?"

Shadrack peeled his license out of his wallet and handed it to him. "California."

Shadrack nodded.

"Cedarville?"

"Tha's in California. Up in th' corner near Nevada."

"Is this your current address?"

"I ain't a'livin' there no more."

"Where are you living now?"

"Up at Diesler's. In the bunkhouse."

"Luther Diesler?"

"Tha's right."

"I know where his place is. Do you happen to know the address?"

"No, I do not."

"Okay. How long have you been living up there?"

Shadrack considered. "Got here four . . . me'be five months ago."

"Have you got your travel permit with you?"

Shadrack bristled. "No, I ain't got no dang travel permit with me. An' I ain't come in here t' talk about 'em. I'm sick t' death with them travel permits. Fed up an' done with 'em."

Wiederman stared at him. "How'd you . . . um . . . " he glanced at his wrist watch ". . . never mind that now." He leaned back and managed a wan smile. "What can I do for you this morning, Mr. Smithers?"

"Shadrack."

"Okay. Shadrack."

"I come to confess a crime I done."

"What kind of a crime?"

"A cold blooded murder, it war."

Wiederman blinked. "When did this happen, sir?"

"Shadrack. Oh . . . long 'bout . . . me'be . . . say . . . fifty year ago, I reckon."

"*Fifty* years?"

"More 'r less."

"Here in Kieferville?"

"Yes, sir. Well . . . me'be. Might be jus' outta town. In the Nash'nal Forest."

Wiederman typed in the information. "Who did you kill?"

"Drifter name a' Lupic Mufel."

"How do you spell that?"

"Got no idea."

Sergeant Wiederman drew a deep breath and puffed it up through his moustache as he pushed away from his desk. It had grown darker outside, and a light sleet rattled against the window. Winter was nearly here. Too soon. Too much to do. He leaned back in his chair. He did not have time for this. But he couldn't ignore it. And if he *was* going to handle it, he needed to do it properly right from the get-go. There were procedures to follow. Evidence to be preserved. He sighed and picked up the phone. "Angel, I need you to call the sheriff's office and get a detective out here. Right now." He listened. "Murder investigation." He listened again. "We'll have to see. Somebody's going to have to do a records search." Pause. "Okay. Do what you can. I'll get it started."

"You's busy," Shadrack observed.

"You don't know the half of it, Mr. Smithers—"

"Shadrack."

"Shadrack. You and I are going to have to start all over again. This time in the interview room. I'll have to record all this on video camera. Is that okay with you?"

"Seems like." Shadrack flashed his gap-toothed smile. "I reckon I got time."

The interview room was small and empty except for two straight-back chairs surrounding a small wooden table. Fluorescent ceiling lights blazed, leaving no shadows. Two cameras peered down from separate walls. It took Wiederman a while to get the equipment up and running. Once the cameras were rolling, he recited the time and place and the names of the parties present. He advised Shadrack of his Miranda rights, which Shadrack waived, consenting to being interrogated. Wiederman followed the notes he had made on his laptop and reproduced everything that had already been asked and answered. Up to Lupic Mufel. "Do you know how to spell his name," he asked again for the cameras.

"No, sir, I do not," Shadrack replied. "Never see'd it writ down."

"Where did you hear the name?"

"In the parkin' lot a' the Rip-N-Roar. M'cousin Dolf pointed this fellow out t'me and tol' me 'is name. Lupic Mufel, it war."

"Okay." Wiederman held up his hand like a traffic cop. "I think we're going to have to continue a little differently now, Mr. . . . ah . . . Shadrack. I want you to tell me *when* . . . and *where* . . . and *how* this . . . this alleged murder took place. In your own words. As succinctly as possible. Can you do that for me?"

"I reckon so," said Shadrack. "It's kinda a long story."

Wiederman grimaced, glanced at his watch, puffed through his moustache, then nodded. "Take your time. I'll jump in if I have any questions. Okay?"

"A'right."

"Go ahead."

"Well . . . it all started down at th' Rip-N-Roar. You remember the Rip-N-Roar? Honky-tonk out by the crossroads?"

"I've heard about it. But that was before my time."

"Jus's well. A wild an' devilish place, it war. Deserved t'be bulldozed down. Now she's just a field a' weeds. Wished I'd a' never set foot in 'er." Shadrack shook his head. "Anyways . . . I was out thar at the Rip-N-Roar a'drinking beer and a'shootin' pool with m'cousin Dolf. We was both a'gettin' pretty drunk. I jus' finished up a tricky shot, 's best's I kin remember, when Dolf pulls on m'sleeve an' says, 'At's yer coat, ain't it?' He was a'pointin' at m'coat hangin' on a hook by the Wurlitzer jukebox. I nodded, an' he say's, 'I jus' saw that big fella take somethin' outta yer pocket.' 'Tha's m'money roll,' I says, an' heads over t' m'coat. Sure 'nough, my money clip's a'missin'. . . . the silver one my

Pa give me . . . with my initials on it . . . an' the fellow who took it sees what I'm a'doin' an' scoots out the door. I go right after 'im inta th' parkin' lot. Dolf's a'followin' and points to this big round-shouldered fellow walkin' away. 'Hey!' I shouts and starts after 'im, but he picks up a couple a' chunks a' broken concrete and chucks one a' 'em at us, jus' missin' Dolf's head. He turns an' keeps on a'walkin' faster away into the woods, still a'holdin' the other chunk in his hand." Shadrack fell into a muse. "Guess I shouldn't a'never followed 'im."

"You did follow him then?" Wiederman prompted.

"Why, a'course I followed 'im. He stole m'money. An' he still had it. First I asks Dolf whut's the fellow's name. 'Lupic Mufel,' he says. I'll never forget it. That's how I knowed 'is name. I tol' Dolf t'stay put whar 'e was. Didn't want 'im a'getting 'is head busted open on my account. An' I followed that slump-shouldered thief fellow's track inta the woods."

"You had him in sight the whole time?"

"Naw. I tracked him. Like trackin' a squirr'l. Had lots a' practice a'doin' that."

"It was still light out?"

"Evenin', 's I recollect. Summer. Twilight. Made it easy t' track a big, sloppy galoot like that."

"Go on."

"Well, sir, I tracks him t'is camp, I done. 'Bout a half a mile. Jus' off 'a the road. He was a'campin' dry . . . un'er th' trees . . . jus' a bedroll . . . an' a knapsack . . .'e wuz jus' a'lightin' a fire' . . . that chunk a' concrete on the ground next t'im."

"Did you confront him?"

"No sir. Not right 'en, nohow. I may a'been young, but I warn't born stupid. I walked back t'im' truck and pulled out that ol' shotgun. Th' one y'had me lay on the counter out thar. Both barrels was a'loaded with buckshot Put a couple extra shells in m' pocket an' headed on back. He had that campfire a'blazin' an' he was jus' a'sitting with 'is back plopped up agin' a tree keepin' warm. I could see that chunk a' concrete sittin' right next t'im. He was keepin' it close by. He seed me right away an' scratches t'is feet. 'Whadda you want?' he hollers at me, a'wavin' that concrete chunk around like 'e's jus' a'achin' t'fling 'er at me."

"Did you consider yourself to be in danger?"

"Naw. I's across the clearin'. But I holler's back, 'Ya done stole m'money. An' I want it back.'"

"Were you pointing the gun at him?"

"No, sir. Not yet. I yells, 'Gimme back m'money, an' I'll jus' let'er go.' An 'e hollers back, 'I ain't got no money a'yourn.' So I takes a step closer, an' 'e pulls back 'is arm t' throw. So I raise the gun an' shoots 'im dead center in the gut. Blam. Loud as the dickens."

"Both barrels?"

"Lordy, no. One 'uz loud 'nough. An' all it took. He doubles over a'screamin' an' I watches 'im fall an' writhe around all gut-shot an' a'bleedin' as 'e war. Made me kinda sick an' then I gets a'scart an' runs away."

"Where did you go."

"Back to m'truck. That gunshot was powerful loud an' sobered me right up. I 'uz so a'scart an' shakin' 'bout what I done . . . I didn't rightly know what t'do."

"So you don't really know if you actually killed him?"

"Oh, yes, sir. I kilt 'im dead alright."

"How do you know?"

"Well . . . I drove t' m' Ma an' Pa's house an' found a diggin' spade we kept in the shed. An' I drove on back. The fella was doubled up by the dyin' fire an' a'dyin' hisself. I added some branches and built the fire back up sos I could see. Never knew a fella could hold so much blood. I found m'money clip in 'is coat pocket, but m'money was all a'soaked with 'is blood. I ended up a'tossin' it all in the hole I dug fer 'im. Kept the money clip, a'course. Had m'nitials on it."

"You're sure he was dead?"

"Yes, sir. By the time I got the grave dug."

"How did you know?"

"Well, sir . . . 'e'd a'stopped a'breathin' . . . an' 'e was stiff . . . an' cold . . . an' I watched 'im fer a while. He war dead aw'right."

"So you dug him a grave?"

"Yes, sir. Dug most a' the night, I did, scared as th' dickens. Worst night a' m'life."

"What did you do with his rucksack and blankets?"

"Tossed ever'thin' down in the hole a'fore I filled 'er up. Didn't want nobody t' find it."

Wiederman thought for a moment. Puffed through his moustache. "Do you think you can locate that grave site now?"

"Don' rightly know." Shadrack shook his head. "I been a'lookin', but them roads out thar ain't whar they used t'be. Been moved around an' paved over some. Somebody's a'cut down th' old trees an' new ones've growed up. Nothin' don't look much the same no more."

Wiederman puffed through his moustache. "Is that cousin of yours . . . Dolf . . . is he still around?"

"No, sir. Died in th' war."

"Have you told anyone else about this?"

"No, sir. Not 'til you."

"Are you married?"

"She's a'passed, rest 'er soul."

"I'm sorry." Wiederman sighed. "Why are you coming forth with this just now, Shadrack? Can you explain that to me?"

Shadrack considered where to draw the line. "'S a personal matter. An' that's that."

Wiederman nodded. "So . . . other than yourself . . . we've got no witness . . . and no *corpus delicti*—"

"Wha's that?"

"No dead body."

"Uh. Prob'ly not."

"No missing person report."

"Don't know nothin' 'bout that."

"All we have is your own testimony."

Shadrack frowned. "M'word's good."

"I'm not saying it's not. But we have certain . . . legal . . . evidence standards to meet before we can commence a prosecution. I'll have a detective at the sheriff's department review this interview and search the missing person's records. Then we'll have to send a report over to the district attorney's office. Oh, and I'm going to have to impound that shotgun of yours for now."

"'Spected y'would."

"In the meantime, I'm ordering you not to leave the county. Just stay up there at Diesler's place until you hear from us."

"What? You ain't a gonna lock me up ri'chere an' now? After all I jus' done tol' ya?"

"We'll be looking into it, Shadrack." Sergeant Wiederman rose and stuck out his hand.

"How come ya cain't lock me up?"

"For one thing, all we have here is a daytime holding cell. And the cells over at county are already pretty full up, mostly with detainees for Homeland Security. We don't have anyplace to put you."

"But . . . Can'cha *make* room? I's a *murderer*!"

"Well . . . that all remains to be seen. We'll be looking into it, I can promise you that. You just stick around Diesler's, and we'll get back in touch as soon as we can."

"This ain't right!" Shadrack grumbled as he rose and turned, refusing to shake the peace officer's outstretched hand.

KATIE PUSHED OPEN THE DOOR to her father's study. He sat reading and scratching at the lesson plan he would be using for the next day's accounting class, and really didn't want to be disturbed. She could read that in his body language. But she needed to talk to him anyway. "Dad . . . I've been wondering about something."

"Not now, sweetheart," he said without glancing up.

"But I think it's important. Maybe urgent. We need to talk."

Elan sighed and laid down his pen, placing it carefully on the page to mark where he had stopped. He looked up and even managed a thin smile. "What is it, Kiddo? You have my full attention. What's going on at school? Are you having some sort of problem?"

"No. Nothing like that. It's just that . . . well . . . I'm worried about Shadrack."

"Shadrack?" He gestured for her to step in and close the door. No need for Bess to hear this. He lowered his voice. "Now why would you be worrying about Shadrack?"

"Because of that check he sent you yesterday. That was supposed to be a payment on the truck, wasn't it?"

"That's the way I figure it."

"Was that the balance he owed?"

"Well, no. I sold it to him for . . . twenty-four hundred, as I recall. And he paid three-hundred cash down. So he still owed me . . . twenty-one hundred."

"Was there any interest?"

"No. But I was glad to get what he sent. Actually, I was about ready to write the whole thing off as a bad debt. And bad judgment on my part."

"And how much did he send you?"

Elan opened a drawer and took out the money order. "Nineteen-hundred-sixty-two dollars."

Katie frowned. "Why do you think he sent you *that* strange amount?"

Elan shook his head. "I don't know. Maybe it was the amount he won at some casino. At the blackjack table, maybe."

"I don't think he gambles."

"Well . . . maybe he got a job. Maybe this was his first paycheck. I don't know. Nobody knows what that old man is thinking."

Katie shook her head. "And maybe he sent you all the money he had left in the world."

Elan considered the notion. "Okay. Could be. But why would he do that?"

"That's what I've been worrying about."

THE REVEREND DOCTOR MARTIN BLYTHE was scratching at the leaves drifted against the foundation of the church. Time and again he paused to pull a clot of them from the rusting tines of the parish's old metal rake. Rusty oak. Pale yellow box elder. But he was in no hurry. The doctor had emphasized *moderate* exercise. And he was feeling better today. Enjoying the outdoors again. The sleet had stopped and the sun had broken through a crease in the storm clouds to the west. Sunlight blazed down, rekindling that glowing ember deep inside him. That ember that had grown cool and forgotten during his bouts of depression. With the shortening days and the long dark nights of doubt. With the prospect of the church closing. But now the sunlight filled him. Rekindling that special ember inside which knew for certain that salvation was possible.

It was, after all, almost that season again. The season to string up the Christmas lights. And for the smell of fresh-brewed coffee in the rectory hall as those parishioners, many unseen for a year, flocked back for Christmas services. It was the season for renewal. And hope. He stopped his raking and drew a few deep breaths, his face upturned serenely to the sun.

And as he did so often now, he prayed for a *sign*.

When he returned to his task, he was smiling. He sang Hark the Herald brightly to himself as he raked.

"*. . . Peace on earth and mercy mild . . .*"

The rake lifted and dipped and scraped back the leaves in time with the tune.

"*. . . God and sinner reconciled . . .*"

A crunch of gravel in the parking area behind him brought him to a halt. The minister turned. A dull black Toyota pickup had arrived.

Shadrack Smithers rolled down his window and gazed up at the tall white steeple crowning the church he used to attend. So many years ago. Where he and his parents and his cousins and his friends and neighbors had all sung The Old Rugged Cross together on Sunday mornings. When everything was so much simpler. And surer. The old church was still standing. A kind of miracle in itself, in this world where everything else seemed to have changed. The pastor in a black frock had turned to face him. He was leaning on a rake and smiling at him, almost as if he was expecting him.

So Shadrack shouldered open the door and stepped out just as a dark cloud swallowed the sunlight. He had not intended to tarry here, but he didn't want to be unneighborly. "Howdy," he called as he limped toward the man of the cloth. "Used t'tend church 'ere m'self when I was a boy. Back when ol' Pastor Mather was a'doin' the preachin' here. Name is Smithers. Shadrack Smithers." He stuck out his hand.

"How do you do, Mr. Smithers—"

"Shadrack's good 'nough."

"Shadrack." The cleric took the proffered hand into both of his as if receiving an offering. "I'm Reverend Martin Blythe. I never met Reverend Mather personally, but I understand he was a fine man."

"Yes, sir," Shadrack said, wondering what was the polite way to retrieve his hand. "'At 'e war. 'E could spout out a mighty sermon that'd bring home th' spirit a' th' Lord an' get'cha all fired up."

Up close Shadrack could see that the black vestment Reverend
Blythe wore was not a robe at all, but an old black trench coat, frayed and
threadbare at the cuffs. His cheeks were sallow and sunken. His hair had
grown patchy and thin. In spite of his bright smile, the man appeared
unwell.

"Might I ask," the preacher inquired, relinquishing his grip on
Shadrack's hand, "are you still a practicing Methodist, Shadrack?"

"Well . . . no, sir . . . I's a jack Methodist. Truth is, I ain't a'been
inside no church fer nigh on . . . a'most fifty year now."

"So . . . might I be so bold as to ask you something else?"

"Go on an' ask away."

"Why not?"

"Why not whut?"

"Why haven't you returned to the church?"

Shadrack's first impulse was to turn and stomp back to the truck, the
way he always would do when folks asked questions that were none of
their business.   But he restrained himself. He thought it over. A few
flakes of snow began to spiral down. This preacher here, he seemed like
a decent enough fellow. And he really deserved a fair answer, didn't he,
now that everything had changed? Now that the cat was out of the bag.
Now that Shadrack himself had changed. Or wanted to, anyhow. Now
that he had nothing left to hide. He shook his head. "'Cause . . . well,
'cause . . . 'cause I become a sinner, I did . . . m'self . . . yes, sir . . . years
ago . . . an' I's damned fer all eternity . . . is why, I reckon."

The snow was falling thicker. Beginning to stick. "Why don't we
go inside the parsonage, Shadrack? Will you share a cup of tea with me?"

"Well . . . I don' know . . ."

"Please? You see, I've got a . . . a problem here . . . with attendance . . . and an *outsider's* viewpoint might be exactly what I need.
Won't you help me out?"

THE TELEPHONE RANG on line one. All the other buttons were dark.
The city clerk glanced over at the clock. The big hand had inched to
within one minute to five, and she was already zipping up her down
jacket. Light snow was spiraling down in the premature gloom outside.

It was a good night to get home early. But she set down her mittens and picked up the handset. "Kieferville City Hall. Angel speaking."

"Hello?" spoke a tentative, unfamiliar female voice. "Is this the Kieferville City Hall."

"Yes, it is. How can I help you?"

"Well . . . I'm calling from California . . . and I'm trying to locate a . . . a friend . . . who just sent us a letter from the post office in your town. Would you happen to know if an elderly man with a bushy beard and a limp has showed up there recently. Say in the last few months?"

"What is the gentleman's name?"

"Smithers. Shadrack Smithers."

The clerk blinked. *Smithers.* Small world. "Well, a Mr. Smithers was in here earlier today. He brought his shotgun with him."

"He did?" Pause. "Do you happen to know how I can reach him? Do you have his telephone number? Or his address?"

"No, I'm sorry. He talked to Sergeant Wiederman. But he's gone now."

"Shadrack, or the sergeant?"

"Mr. Smithers left several hours ago. I believe Sergeant Wiederman is still back in his office, but he has a detective with him now. I can leave a message for him to call you back."

"Well . . . I don't know . . . I don't want to be a bother . . . but yes. My name is Katie Groves. Catherine, actually." She spelled her name and recited her phone number.

The clerk wrote it down. "And this is about . . . Shadrack Smithers. Fine. I will leave the message for Sergeant Wiederman."

"Thank you."

SHADRACK EASED HIMSELF into the padded rocking chair by the fireplace while he waited for his cup of herbal tea. Rocking a bit seemed to ease the pain in his hips. A fresh log had begun to crackle behind the screen. Flakes of snow stuck and melted and ran down the western window panes. The sun had set. It was growing dark outside. He looked around the small parlor. It was comfortable. Cozy. The colors were subdued. The worn Persian rug was clean and the well-used furniture was neat and tidy. The way Tildie used to like to keep things. It reminded him of her. Even the smell was familiar. The fragrance of . . .

"Here's the pot of chamomile tea, Shadrack," Reverend Blythe smiled, setting a tray on the coffee table by the sofa. He wore a white shirt and black trousers held up by black suspenders. Without his trench coat, he appeared skinny enough to justify the need for suspenders.

Shadrack leaned forward.

"Don't get up. I can pour. Now, that's no milk. No sugar."

Shadrack nodded, a strange sense of disorientation growing over him.

The preacher handed him a large white cup with a saucer underneath. "Just the way you ordered it."

Shadrack balanced them together on his knee, but words of thanks would not come. He had lost his voice.

"I'll go slice some pound cake and be right back."

Shadrack sniffed at the steaming cup. It smelled like the tea Tildie used to serve him. His throat tightened as he breathed in the aroma. It smelled like Tildie. Carefully he lifted the cup and took a sip. Tasted it. The cup began to rattle against the saucer in his hands. It was all familiar. Too familiar. And suddenly he was overwhelmed and the cup was rattling and the tea was sloshing and he was bawling like a baby. His eyes were blinded with tears. The cup and saucer shook with his sobs. Splashes of tea spilled to the floor.

And then there was a hand on his shoulder. "I'll take that." And the cup and saucer were gone.

Shadrack tried to say, "I's sorry," but it came out all wrong in snorts and coughs and groans.

The hand was on his shoulder again as he wept deeply and shook and sobbed and snorted for breath. Paroxysm of grief and loss and yearning and, yes, relief, went on and on for a long time, and did not so much end, as exhausted themselves with his strength. Then Shadrack felt shame rising to replace it. Through streaming eyes the room slowly melted back into view. He tugged an old bandana from his back pocket and wiped his eyes and blew his nose. "I's so sorry . . . 'bout all the mess . . . an' . . ."

"Nothing to be sorry about, Shadrack. I am honored to be of service. To serve as witness to a man who seems to have found himself.

But tell me . . . how long have you been holding that in?"

Shadrack blushed and sniffled and thought about it some. "Seems like . . . all m'life."

The preacher said nothing, but continued gently kneading his shoulders.

"I . . . I miss m'Tildie, I do. Tha's m'wife. She . . . died. In the spring. An' I ain't been right since." He sneezed into the bandana. "An' they's more," Shadrack added woefully. "Th' part I confessed t' th' *po*lice 'is afternoon. It be th' part 'bout me committin' a . . . a terr'ble, terr'ble sin."

"Would you like to talk about it?" The clergyman stepped across the fireplace and eased himself down into the recliner on the opposite side. "That's what I do for a calling, you know. I listen."

So Shadrack told him everything. His words effervesced like spume from a bottle of champagne kept corked for too long. He shambled through the confession he had given to Sergeant Wiederman. But unlike Wiederman, Reverend Blyth received it all with patience and compassion.

"So the police let you go?"

"Yes, sir. Said they ain't got no cell available. Told me they'd look inta it. Git back t'me."

"And your wife . . . Tildie, is it? . . . your wife Tildie never knew?"

"No, sir. An' it war . . . like a burr under m'saddle th' whole time . . . an' I reckon even she could feel it . . . not even a'knowin' what it war. An' now I see . . . I see me'be I shoulda tol' her all along. Righ' from th' beginnin'." He thought some more. "That woulda been tricky . . . Tildie bein' brung up Catholic an' all." He nodded to himself. "But now I reckon all this confessin' today war really . . . well . . . it war really a'confessin' t' *her* anyhow, rest 'er soul."

"And to God, might I suggest."

"Oh, I don't know nothin' 'bout that. We ain't much on speakin' terms. I's jus' a lowly sinner."

"We're *all* sinners, Shadrack. But that's how it works. Confession. Forgiveness. Reconciliation. Grace. From God all blessings flow."

Shadrack chewed on it. "So . . . are you a'sayin' . . . I'm a'gwine' t' ha'f t'confess this here criminal sin all *over* ag'in . . . t' the Lord?"

Reverend Blythe laughed. "No, sir. No you do not, Shadrack. He has heard you. And he knew the whole thing all along anyway. He was just waiting for you to . . . to come to him . . . or at least to come to yourself . . . to open yourself up to the truth." He spanked his hands on his thighs and stood up abruptly. "Now, it's time to eat, don't you think? This confessing's hungry work, I warrant, and Mrs. McMoran just brought me over a tuna casserole yesterday afternoon that was way more than I could eat by myself. A fine lady, she is, trying her best to keep up my spirits. You see, I've been goin' through a . . . a period of darkness of my own lately."

"Well . . . I oughta git a'goin' . . ."

"Nonsense. You'll have to stay for dinner. We haven't even begun to talk about *my* problems."

SERGEANT WIEDERMAN DIALED the number on the message. It rang for a long minute without anyone picking up, and he was about to hang up and call it a day. It would be nice to get home before the roads got slick.

"Hello?" a man's voice answered.

"Hello . . . I'm calling for a . . . Catherine Groves."

A long pause. "Who's calling?"

"This is Sergeant Albert Wiederman, Sheriff's Deputy, Kieferville substation."

Another pause. "Missouri?"

"That's correct. Is Catherine Groves available?"

"What do you want with her?"

"I'm returning her phone call from . . . five o'clock this afternoon. Is she available?"

Pause. "What was she calling *you* about?"

"I don't know. I haven't spoken with her yet."

Pause. "I don't think we want to get involved." The line clicked dead.

The house in Cedarville was silent for a heartbeat. Then Katie stepped around the corner from the livingroom. "Was that for me?" she confronted her father.

"Wrong number," he muttered without meeting her eyes.

"That was from Kieferville, wasn't it?"

"Didn't say."

"Yes they did. I heard you ask about Missouri."

Elan rounded on her. "Okay. It was some sheriff from Kieferville saying he was returning a call from you."

"And you hung up!" Her eyes flashed. "I knew I should have called on my own phone."

"You make calls like that on your cell phone?"

"I make lots of calls on my own phone that you don't know about."

"To who?"

"None of your business."

"It *is* my business. I'm your father. And you're still a minor and living in my house. I have a right to know everyone you're calling as long as you're living here."

"No," she told him. "You don't. And if you don't like it . . . I can move out."

That stopped him cold. Elan stared at her, suddenly on shaky ground. She had never spoken back to him this way. Everything seemed upside down. "What's . . . gotten into you, sweetheart?" A light dawned in his eyes. "You haven't been . . . talking to that . . . to that Army fellow in the humvee—"

"His name is Jerome."

"You've been talking to him?"

"That is, like, none of your business."

"Are you . . . seeing him?"

"Don't be ridiculous." She turned on her heel and disappeared around the corner.

Bess stuck her head out of the kitchen doorway. "What was *that* all about?"

"Oh . . . I . . . don't know. I . . . I have to go . . . grade some papers."

"Who's Jerome?"

Elan shambled down the hallway and into his study as if he hadn't heard.

THEY FINISHED THE TUNA CASSEROLE. All of it, to the surprise of them both. It looked like more than two skinny old men would be able to eat in one sitting, but their appetites were unusually hardy that evening.

Reverend Blythe talked while they ate. About the dwindling attendance at the church. How the young folks were moving away. Old families were dying out. About how the District Superintendent had talked to him about beginning the process of discontinuing the church forever. And he talked about his own bouts of depression and doubt. Shadrack grunted some, but said little. Mostly he listened. Nothing was resolved, but Shadrack's quiet, nonjudgmental attendance seemed to balm the minister's troubled spirit.

Afterwards, Shadrack stood at the sink drying the dishes and turned the conversation back to his own mortal sin. "So . . . you's a'sayin' . . . I don't *need* t' go t' jail for my sinnin'?"

"The Bible says, 'Render unto Caesar the things that are Caesar's, and unto God the things that are God's.'"

Shadrack grunted. "Never rightly figured out whut that meant."

"Well, you have already made your peace with God. Right? So whether or not you go on through the criminal court process of crime and punishment is no longer relevant to Him."

"He don't care?"

"That's the way I see it."

"An' you's the preacher."

"That's right."

Shadrack grunted and hung the dish towel on its peg. "Well . . . I ain't a'gonna be able t'pay ya nothin' . . . fer this fine supper an' all yer hospitality an' advice . . . 'cause I give all m'money away th' other day . . . but I thank 'ee fer ever'thin' . . ."

"You owe me nothing, Shadrack. If anything, it's the other way around. I am indebted to you."

"Fer whut?"

"For opening your heart up to me. And for listening to mine."

"Warn't nothin'. But I reckon it's gettin' on time fer me t' git along. Gotta git a fire lit in that bunkhouse stove a'fore the pipes freeze up." He tugged on his rag sweater and pulled his slouch hat down to his ears as he limped toward the front door.

The minister opened the door and stepped out onto the porch. The snow had stopped, but an icy breeze rattled the leaves. "Can I count on you at Sunday's worship service?"

Shadrack tested the top step for ice, found none, then turned. "Like as not . . . I's a'gonna be'n jail. But if'n y'got any more a'em holy words fer me, I'd favor t'hear 'em now a'fore I git a'going."

Reverend Blythe considered the challenge. Then he spread his arms above the congregation of a single old gap-toothed parishioner standing on the step below. "May the Lord bless you and keep you. May the Lord make his face to shine upon you, and be gracious unto you. May the Lord lift up his countenance upon you, and give you peace."

"Amen," Shadrack nodded. "Mighty fine words. I done heard 'em a'fore. Never did know 'xactly whut 'ey meant. But she's a mighty fine way a' wrappin' things up, ain't she?"

THE NEXT MORNING Katie wrapped herself in Shadrack's oversized coat and slipped out into the cold back yard. Beneath the nearly leafless locust tree she punched the number for the Kieferville City Hall into her cell phone. The sun had just risen in Cedarville, so it had already been up more than two hours in Missouri.

"Kieferville City Hall. Angel speaking."

"This is Katie Groves. I spoke to you yesterday. I was wondering if Sergeant Wiederman was in?"

"Looks like he's on the other line. But he asked me to let him know if you called again. I'll go hand him a message. Can you hold?"

"Yes, I can." Time passed slowly. Katie's phone was a pre-paid plan, so she was paying for the silence while she waited. It looked like it was going to be a warm, clear Indian summer day. *What was taking him so long?* She thought about hanging up and calling back later. But she ground her teeth and waited on hold.

"Wiederman here," a solid male voice spoke at last.

"Sergeant Wiederman, this is Katie Groves. I left a message for you to call me yesterday."

"Yes. The person I talked to didn't want to call you to the phone."

"That was my father."

"Said he didn't want to get involved."

"Yes. I heard him."

"Involved in what?"

Katie could think of no response.

Wiederman broke the silence. "You wanted to talk to me about Shadrack Smithers?"

"Well, yes, but I only wanted a telephone number where I could reach him. If it's not too much trouble. You've talked to him?"

"I have. I interviewed him yesterday."

Pause. "Is he in some sort of trouble?"

"That's . . . yet to be determined. But maybe you can tell me how you know him."

"Well . . . we went on a camping trip together this summer. Shadrack and me and my father." She gave him a skeleton outline of their adventure, omitting the lack of travel permits and encounters with law enforcement. She made it brief, because her minutes were costly.

"When did this take place?"

"June. Beginning of June."

"Did you know him before that trip?"

"No. Well . . . I knew who he was. His wife taught a Spanish class in grade school."

"That's . . . Tildie?"

"Yes. That's right. Did he talk to you about her?"

"And she passed away this spring, is that right?"

"Yes. He told you?"

A long pause. "Did he ever mention to you a man named Lupic Mufel?"

"Who? Is that a person's name?"

"According to Shadrack."

"How do you spell it?"

A sigh passed as the sergeant blew through his moustache. "I'm not sure. Did he mention to you anyone with a name sounding anything like that?"

"I don't think so. No. Is that what he was talking to you about?"

"I can't really . . . it's a pending investigation . . . Shadrack claims he and this Mufel character . . . or whatever his name is . . . had a . . . a conflict . . . about fifty years ago. We're looking into it."

"Fifty years!"

"Yes, ma'am."

"Is he . . . under arrest?"

"Not at this time. But I reviewed it with a detective from the department, and he's going to look into it further."

Katie was stunned.

"So let me give you this before I forget." Wiederman read off the address and telephone number for Luther Diesler's farmhouse. "I don't know if there's a telephone in the bunkhouse where Shadrack's staying, though."

"Thank you. I'll give it a try, I guess."

"Why did you say you wanted to get in touch with him?"

Katie thought for a moment. She knew what she wanted to say, but she didn't want to sound like a silly little girl. "I'm worried about him."

"Worried? How so?"

She told Wiederman about Shadrack's debt to her father for the purchase of the truck and the check that came in the mail in such a strange amount. "I just thought . . . maybe he'd sent us the last of his money. All of it. And I wondered why. It made me worry."

The line was silent. Then Wiederman said, "He wanted us to lock him up. He expected we would. So I guess he figured he wouldn't be needing the money behind bars."

"In jail?"

"Prison, actually."

"For what?"

"I can't tell you that. It might jeopardize a pending investigation. But . . . why don't you ask him? I think it would do him good to hear from you. He needs a friend. And give me a call back if you learn anything that can help us . . . straighten this matter out. Will you do that?"

Katie wondered how much her father knew about this. He had said he didn't want to *get involved*. In what? "We'll see," she said, and punched the end call button.

ELAN GROVES LEFT EARLY for the morning drive into Alturas and the accounting class he was teaching at the college there, figuring he would arrive in plenty of time to answer student questions before they got started. As he drove up the steep, winding road toward Cedar Pass, he glanced in the rearview mirror. The alkali lakes and playas and barren hills of the Great Basin stretched out behind him. He always enjoyed this view. It contrasted so starkly with its counterpart on the western downslope beyond the pass. There the agricultural fields and farms of the Pitt River valley lay like a lush green patchwork carpet and water flowed freely away toward the distant ocean.

But something was not right this morning. There was too much slow traffic for this lonely highway. He rounded a bend and saw a line of vehicles stopped at some sort of checkpoint up at the turnoff for the ski park. *Why?* There wasn't any snow on the ground yet. Maybe up at the higher peaks of the Warners, but not down here at the rope tow and chair lifts. He came to a stop behind a big Fredoner Grocers truck. The traffic inched forward in jerks and spurts. An occasional semi or pickup passed by heading the other direction.

He was going to be late for his class!

Below him to the left was a drop off to Cedar Creek and the mixed conifers of the Modoc National Forest. Here rain and snow fell aplenty. Quaking aspens shivered with a few golden leaves which had not yet fallen. To his right rose a sheer stone cliff capped high above with slickrock peaks and perilously balanced boulders. There was no way through but straight ahead.

He swung his left wheels out into the oncoming lane and peered through the windshield. Maybe a quarter mile ahead a taut white canopy arched over the roadway, across both lanes. Every few hundred feet speed signs stepped down the limit to 50, 40, 30, 25, and 15 mph just before the checkpoint stop sign. They inched forward incrementally. The big rigs were not being delayed, and each one gained him fifty feet as it passed through. Occasionally a passenger car or a pickup was sent down the narrow road leading to the ski area. Impatiently Elan counted down the speed limit signs. Now he could make out a banner flapping from the canopy. It had a forest green background with the initials *PCN* printed in bright yellow letters.

What the hell is that?

The big rig driver ahead handed something down, took it back, and was waved through with both stacks belching black fumes. Elan crept up to the stop sign. A half dozen soldiers were observing under the margins of the canopy. Two of them were monitoring eastbound traffic, which was light. All wore standard issue M-16 rifles strapped over their arms and PCN patches on their shoulders. A young black soldier in forest camo fatigues and short hair stepped up to his window. "Where ya headed?" he asked with a warm, toothy grin.

"Alturas. I teach at the college. And this is making me late for the class."

"Travel visa?"

Elan had already removed his papers from the glove box and handed one over.

"This is a Homeland Security permit. Won't do you no good here."

"What? Why not? I live in Cedarville. Which is in California."

"Used t'be, maybe. But not anymore, it ain't. There ain't no more California. Nor Washington 'r Oregon, neither. Now it's all the Pacific Coast Nation."

Elan was dumbfounded. "That's what PCN stands for?"

"Yes, sir. Though some folks jus' like ta call it the Jefferson Nation."

"When . . . how . . . did *this* happen? I never heard anything about it."

"If ya got questions, ya kin aks 'em over at the administration office." He pointed down the narrow paved road that led to the ski lifts. "Now I can't have ya blockin' this here highway no more. I'll have t'aks ya ta either turn around or go on into the administration office an' apply for a Jefferson travel visa. Yer holdin' up the traffic where yer at."

"Has California seceded from the union? Is that what's— "

"Sir! You have to move along! Now!" He gestured to two idle soldiers for help.

"Okay. Okay. I'm going."

The ski area had been commandeered by Jefferson Nation troops. The administration office was a huge olive-drab circus tent that looked to be surplus from some forgotten war. It rose at the edge of the ski parking area, with a few passenger cars and pickup trucks parked in front. No big rigs. Behind the tent soldiers were spray painting olive-drab over the words "California National Guard" on trucks and humvees. Another was stenciling on "PCN" in yellow. Back by the ski tow two bulldozers scraped the ground for what looked like the foundation of a more permanent building. It looked like they were planning to stay.

Inside the tent, the ancient fabric gave off that oily, mildewy, old-canvas, olive-drab smell. A dozen electric space heaters tried to warm the place, without much success. Four folding tables faced the door, with a soldier in military fatigues behind each one and a short line in front. Three were women, and one a young male officer. All wore camo fatigues with PCN patches on their shoulders. Elan would have preferred to speak to the man, but his line was the longest. That figured. He glanced at his watch. *Shit!* His class was about to start . . . without him. He settled for the shortest line. The lights flickered and someone shouted, "Turn off some of those damn heaters." In a few minutes Elan was face to face with a stocky, tar-black woman with short nappy hair and a no-nonsense attitude. She reached out and he handed her his travel permit.

"This here won't do you no good. You need a Jefferson Nation travel visa."

"I've already been told that. I'd like to apply for one of your visas right now. I'm already late for a class I'm teaching at the college."

She shook her head. "Ain't gonna get it today. I can assure ya that." She handed him a stapled packet. "You fill this here out and send it in. Or bring it back yourself if you're in a hurryin' mood. And if I was you I'd attach a copy of my drivers' license and that Homeland Security permit to make it slide along a little smoother."

"When will I get my permit?"

"*If* you get a visa, it'll show up in the mail in about a week."

"A week!"

"Yessir. At the earliest."

Elan paused in thought, calculating lost wages. He leaned closer. "Will they issue me one, do you think?"

She studied his travel permit and handed it back to him. "Prob'ly. But it's not for me to say."

"But I live in *California*. Just down the road. In Cedarville."

"Ain't no more California here. You got to get rid of that old thinkin' and get with the new program now."

Elan felt he had hit a wall. "Can I fill this out while I'm here?"

"Go ahead. You can use one of them tables over there." She pointed. "But now you got to get out the way for the next person in line."

"What the hell is happening here?"

"Not for me to say."

"I want to talk to your supervisor."

"Ain't none here," she chuckled. "The lieutenant and the captain are out supervisin' the construction." She turned in her chair. "Wait . . . ya see that tall skinny fella there. That's Colonel Wolfson. He's here this mornin' inspectin' the operation. Maybe he'll talk with you, if you aks him nice. But don' hold your breath. Now please step aside for the next customer."

The Colonel stood ramrod straight in his green dress uniform and cap, complete with white shirt and black tie, studying a thin sheaf of papers in his pale hands. Only his neck bent as he read. He looked to be in his fifties, with graying hair and worry lines etched around his eyes and at the corners of his mouth. Medals and ribbons spangled his chest like a living billboard, leaving scant room for his name tag, which read "Wolfson". He glanced up as Elan approached.

"What's going on here?" Elan demanded. "I need to get to my job in Alturas."

The Colonel studied him closely. "You a reporter?"

"No, I'm a teacher. At the junior college in Alturas. And they won't let me through to my job."

"What do you teach?"

"Accounting. Why?"

Wolfson barked a laugh and shook the papers. "I wish to hell someone would teach my quartermaster accounting. His damn columns don't seem to add up."

"Mind if I take a look?"

"Why not?" He handed the papers to Elan and turned to summon the only other man in garrison dress uniform across the tent. "Major! Can you come over here a sec?"

The Major stepped smartly and snapped a sharp salute. "Yes, sir."

"Can you take these ledgers back to Staff Sergeant Wanamaker and find out why the hell they don't add up."

"I think I found your problem," Elan interjected, showing him the first sheet. "These two columns differ in the same amounts. This one has too much. This one too little. Something got included here that should have been there . . . in the amount of . . . approximately . . . eleven-thousand dollars. Throws the whole tally off."

"Is that right?" Wolfson studied the page, then nodded. Then he handed the pages to the Major. "You tell Wanamaker he screwed up these two columns and I want him to fix it right now. And tell him don't ever let it happen again."

"Yes, sir." The Major saluted again, snapped his heels together, and headed off toward the back corner of the tent.

"What exactly is going on here, sir?" Elan asked again in a more respectful tone.

"This? It's a fiasco. But what you see is what you get."

"California seceding from the Union? Won't this just bring on another Civil War?"

"I hope to Christ not. Actually, it's an accommodation designed to *prevent* a civil war."

Elan was stunned. "A breakup of the nation?"

"A reshuffling. Temporary I hope. At least that's how it's planned. Temporary. Just a restructuring of the hierarchy."

"But . . . don't the voters get to weigh in on it?"

"Not while the state of emergency is in place. We'll see about all that later."

"So . . . this is all something Congress has approved?"

"As far as I know, Congress hasn't convened in half a year. This is coming down from the top."

"The top? Meaning the President? And the military?"

"More of a coalition, as far as I know. Something much larger."

"Corporations? They're involved?"

"Contractors."

"Then . . . there's been a coup?"

The Colonel squared on Elan and squinted. "Nobody uses that word. I'd be careful with it, if I were you. You're sure you're not a reporter?"

"No sir. I teach accounting."

The old soldier smiled with his mouth, but not his eyes. "Now, I'm in a good mood today, Mr. Groves. And I don't want you to put me out of sorts, okay? If I were you, I wouldn't spend any more of my time going around asking the kinds of questions you are asking. Okay? It is what it is. And we're all trying to work this thing out without tearing the country apart any more than it already is." He lowered his voice. "And I caution you . . . you didn't hear anything from me. Understood?"

"Ah . . . yes . . . I guess so," Elan grunted his submission. "But . . . can I get my travel visa today? Right now?"

"Not from me, you can't. I don't issue them. You'll have to follow procedures like everyone else." Colonel Wolfson turned brusquely. "Good day, sir."

LATE IN THE AFTERNOON Detective Kringle stopped by the substation in Kieferville to see Sergeant Wiederman. "Where the hell did you pick up this Shadrack Smithers character, anyway?"

"He just walked in. Wanted to make his confession. Why, did you find anything on him?"

"Nothing at all. Not even a birth certificate."

"He says he was adopted. Smithers is his adoptive family."

"Birth name?"

"He didn't say. I don't think he knew."

"Agency or private adoption?"

"He didn't say."

"Well," Kringle groused, "don't matter anyhow. They didn't keep records back then the way we do now. And even if they did, we'd probably need a court order to get them unsealed. All the damn' Smithers around here seem to be long gone or dead by now. Except for your fellow Shadrack."

Wiederman took a deep breath and puffed through his moustache. "I suppose you didn't find anything about this Lupic Mufel."

"Nothing. No record he even existed. I checked the national data base. But he seems like a pretty nasty fellow, anyway. Probably better off dead."

"And nothing about a missing person's report."

"Records don't go back that far. None that I could find, anyhow. And if they did, they'd be old papers moldering in a storage box in some rat infested warehouse."

"No report of anything in the newspaper?"

"I looked at a few microfiche, but I really don't have time for this shit. We don't even know exactly when this was supposed to have happened."

Wiederman puffed through his moustache again. "So . . . what do you want to do?"

Kringle leaned forward. "I talked to Clarence."

"The new DA?"

"Yup. Caught him on his way back from the courthouse. Told him what we've got here. And he said we ain't got nothin'."

Wiederman chuckled. "Guess he's smarter than I thought he was."

"He says a good attorney would get Smithers off on self-defense. No way he intends to prosecute this mess unless we come up with something more."

"Like what?"

"Shit. *Anything!*"

Wiederman thought about it. "He have any ideas?"

"Matter of fact, he did." Kringle lowered his voice. "Clarence thinks we ought to turn this Shadrack fellow over to Homeland Security. For traveling without a permit, you know? Get it out of our hands."

"But . . . wouldn't they just house him back in our jail?"

"No. No. That's the thing. They've got that new detention camp over by Springfield up and running now. They're already taking some of our surplus out of the jail. We could forget about all this murder stuff while he's in federal custody. Which might be forever, the way things are going."

"So . . . we would just . . . keep the file open and hope he never comes back?"

"That what Clarence thinks we ought to do. Let him die in federal custody. Problem solved."

Wiederman leaned back and gazed out the window. The sun would be setting soon. He didn't like it.

"You still there?" Kringle asked.

"Yeah. I'm here." He puffed through his moustache. "It's just that . . . I know this'll sound funny to you . . . but I kinda liked that old fellow."

"Smithers?"

"Yeah. Reminded me some of my grandfather."

"*Jesus!* And you're going to let that influence how you enforce the law?"

"No. No. I suppose you and the DA are right about this."

"Of course we are. Can't let the newspapers get wind that we aren't going to prosecute a confessed murderer."

"Alright . . . but . . . do me a favor, will you?"

"What's that?"

"Can you go pick him up? He's staying out at Luther Diesler's place. I told him not to leave town."

A pause. "Alright. But I'm on my way back to an interview in town now. I won't be able to get back out here 'til tomorrow afternoon."

"That's fine. He's not going anywhere. He *wants* to be picked up."

Kringle sighed as he stood. "Alright. But you owe me one."

NEXT MORNING KATIE PHONED the Diesler farm in Kieferville from her cell phone. Luther himself answered. "Howdy," he said.

"I'm . . . calling from California . . . for Shadrack Smithers . . . is he . . . available?"

"Nope. Sorry miss. Say . . . are you that girl name 'a Katie?"

"Yes. Katie Groves. That's my name."

"Well tha's jus' fine. Pleased t'meetcha. Ol' Shadrack, he talked plenty 'bout you. Had lots a nice things t'say. The way you been helpin' him out. You an' yer father."

"Well . . . thank you . . . can I leave a message for him to call me back?"

"Nope. He ain't a'comin' back, I don't reckon."

"He's not?"

"Nope. He done borrowed near forty gallons o' gas and two hundred bucks offa me an' says he wouldn't be comin' back."

"Where is he going?"

"Back home, he says."

"Home?" Katie was confused, and then it registered. "Can I . . . how much does he owe you?"

"Aw, don't concern y'self none, miss. I trust ol' Shadrack. He'll make it good. The work he done fer me, he prob'ly earned it anyhow."

PART THREE

Bristlecone

Late November

HORACE KEARNS, DIRECTOR OF THE SURPRISE VALLEY Senior Center, called the emergency meeting to order at precisely twelve o'clock noon. This was an unusual time for them all, since most of those in attendance worked day jobs, and the seniors met in the evening. But not today. With the new travel restrictions severing Cedarville from the rest of Modoc County, everyone seemed to be in town, available, and in a surly mood.

"I see a lot of familiar faces here today," Director Kearns croaked. He was recovering from the surgical removal of a polyp on his larynx. He was a tall, flinty, stoop-shouldered farmer in his late fifties with a freckled face and a ruddy complexion, except for the white band across his forehead where he usually wore his hat. "Plenty of ya from Cedarville. An' I see Teddy Tollitson and his crew up from Eagleville. An' Tom Ramirez down from Ft. Bidwell way. An' some a'ya I don't know yer names, but I seen ya before. Well . . . yer all welcome here today."

Heads nodded among the restless citizens who filled the folding chairs or watched standing from the back of the senior center conference room. Kearns waved to the clusters of townsfolk who stood beyond hearing on the sidewalk outside, gazing in through the latticed panes like children at a Christmas department store window. They were the perpetually uncommited, whose curiosity was alloyed with the fear of getting involved with something that might someday come back to bite them on the ass.

"As y'all know," Kearns continued to those who could hear him inside, "Cedarville ain't got no City Council to take care of this mess for us, since the town ain't incorporated. The only incorporated city in the entire county is Alturas, and that's now behind the Khaki Curtain, as my wife calls it."

Smiles and a murmur of appreciation ran through the room.

"Anyhow, the State of California seems to of dried up an' blown away on us. She's gone. Done disappeared." He paused for effect. "Which leaves us with a bona fide dire emergency that this here community's gotta take care of. By ourselves, looks like. There's decisions we gotta make. An' work to be done. So let's us git right down to business."

Heads nodded again. A few grunted assent.

"Now . . . I had me a talk on the telephone this mornin' with the county attorney over in Alturas. Pearworth is 'is name. Deputy County Counsel. Anyhow, even *he* don't have much of a notion about just what's a'goin' on here or what our legal status is just yet. A'course, he can't get through the blockade himself t'talk with ya here directly, man ta man."

"What's he say?" Honus Cribs called impatiently from the back. "What's this Pear . . . Blossom say?"

"Yeah," crowed a heavy lump of a woman in the second row. "Are we still in California, er ain't we?"

A number of others shuffled to be heard, but Kearns raised his hands for silence. "*Listen up!*" he croaked. "Now y'all jus' listen up. Y'all gonna get your chance to talk. Ever'body. But we got to do it in an orderly manner, or nobdy'll get heard. I'll make a quick presentation to get the discussion goin'. Then I'll open her up to y'all's comments an' questions as soon as we get our feet here on solid groun'. Is 'at okay with ever'body?"

"What about us in Eagleville?" called one of Tollitson's hands. "We in this here too?"

"An' Fort Bidwell?" asked Tom Ramirez.

"Ever'body's gonna get heard," Kearns replied hoarsely. "We're all in this together, fer better er worst."

There was some cross-talk and grumbling before the folks settled down to hear what Director Kearns had to say. He started by explaining that nobody but commercial truckers could get through Cedar Pass without a Pacific Coast Nation visa. The semblance of order broke down into angry comments and shouted questions. Kearns quieted them with raised arms and pressed on. The problem was, he slowly made it clear, that the State of California had ceased to exist. The new border for the Pacific Coast Nation stopped at the militarily defensible position of Cedar Pass, leaving them all on a sliver of no-man's land caught between the high peaks of the Warner Mountains on the west and the western boundary of the State of Nevada some twenty miles to the east, where the paved, striped two-lane highway degenerated, as if randomly, into a badly-graded gravel Nevada road. That sliver ran from below Eagleville all the way up the Surprise Valley, through Ft. Bidwell, to Oregon in the north. None of it was any longer a part of the State of California. Nor any other state of the union.

"Ya mean we done seceded?" someone shouted from the back. "Why'd we do *that*?"

"No," Kearns grunted, the pain in his throat worsening, "it's more like *they* done seceded from *us'n*. An' for the time being, we're on our own. An independent sovereign realm with a whole lotta work to do."

The sobering reality quieted down the crowd. No one could figure out who to blame, which was what many of them had come here for in the first place. Not to do any *work*.

"Now . . . one of the first things we're gonna need is a Minister of Finance to figure out whether we got any money," Kearns rumbled. He was staring straight at Elan Groves, who sat in the front row beside his daughter Katie. "How 'bout you, Elan?"

"Now hold on—" Elan began.

"No, you listen up, Elan. You're about the only one of us can read a spreadsheet proper. And you know all them folks over in the tax collector's office, don't ya? We're gonna need money to run this place. This realm. This sovereign nation. Whatever it is. Now how much of our money do ya think California's holdin'?" He was betting Elan couldn't resist showing off his expertise in government fund accounting.

Elan took the bait. "Well . . . there's . . . the real property taxes . . . then there's sales tax . . . both of those are general funds . . . and the gas tax, for roads . . . and the transient occupancy tax they collect for us . . . that's general funds too . . . and they collect the Fire District's bond tax money . . . and the Health Care District tax . . . and the School District's money, some of which is local taxes and some state money . . . and—"

"So you'll take the job, Mr. Finance Minister?" Kearns lifted his hands like a preacher to draw acclamation from the assembly.

"Wait a minute!" Elan rose. "Finance Minister of *what*?" He gazed around at the mostly familiar faces. "Who do you think we're supposed to *be* here, anyway?"

"We do need a name for ourselves," Kearns conceded. He turned to the assembly. "Any ideas?"

"Sure," piped up Moray Willits, owner of the Cedarville general store. "Why'n't we jus' call the country 'Cedarville'."

"Now jus' hold on," Ted Tollitson rejoined. "How's about callin' it 'Eagleville'?"

"No way," interjected Tom Ramirez. "That leaves Ft. Bidwell out in the cold. And all the ranches up north."

"Naw," called somebody from the back, "you tractor guys're all thinkin' too parochial . . . how about jus' callin' ourselves the 'Surprise Valley Nation'?"

"Or 'East Modoc'—"

"Or how about 'East California'—"

The volume rose as everyone advocated for his own regional preference, while a single slim arm waved to be recognized.

Kearns pounded a fist on the table. He couldn't remember ever having to do *that* before. "*Order!*" he bleated. "Let's do this orderly. One at a time. Katie, you got your hand up."

The group fell silent as slender Katie Groves rose to face them. "Well . . . I've got an idea. How about . . . 'Bristlecone'," she said.

Everyone seemed to blink, as if they hadn't heard right.

"What was that?" Scooter Thompson asked from the back.

"Bristlecone," she repeated with more force.

"Wha's'at suppose' t'mean?"

"Bristlecone pines are the oldest living trees on earth. They're strong . . . and they're proud . . . and they endure with majesty right where they are, while the whole world changes all around them. The bristlecone stands as a symbol for the kind of nation we need to build right here. Together. Right now."

"How do you know so much about 'em, young lady?" asked Peachy Watkins, who cooked for one of the three café owners in town.

"Well . . . I'm doing my term paper on bristlecone pines. They're magnificent. Stately. Enduring. Like we can be, if we all stop arguing with each other and start pulling together."

A bemused silence settled over them until Leonard Kline, owner of the new Gas Mart, broke it with, "We're gonna need ourselves a bank, too. T'put all that money Elan's gonna bring in."

"You volunteerin' t'run the bank, Leonard?" Ted Tollitson gibed.

"Ya could do worse, Teddy."

"Bristlecone Bank," someone else called out. "Now I like the sound a' *that*."

"Ain't we gonna hafta hold some kinda election t'let the people vote on this?" asked Moray Willits.

Everyone turned to Director Kearns, who threw up his hands. "I sure don't have a clue what we gotta do. This ain't never happened before. At least as far as I know. Maybe Sherry at the library can look it up fer us. Or Michael over at the bookstore. They could serve as our historians to figure out what we gotta do. But in the meantime, we gotta get started . . . today . . . right here an' now. We got no funds, an' time's a'wastin'."

The meeting plowed on as Kearns loosened the reins and allowed people to talk about whatever they felt was important. Most issues found little resolution. Kearns simply jotted them down on a yellow pad and for the most part kept quiet. This was just as he had intended. This was the prelude. The warm up. The symphony would come tomorrow. Or the next day. Or next month. But he wanted those assembled to feel free to discuss anything that troubled them. To let the cream of the ideas rise to the top. He wanted everyone to feel a buy-in. Feel a part of a team effort.

Hour after hour, like the roll of great waves, the discussion surged and ebbed between heated oratory and tepid ignorance. The congregation agreed they needed a police force, but haggled over who the chief should be. Or the minister of defense. Or the public works director. They were all in agreement to retain the current fire chief and the department hierarchy. And the school board, too. Without objection they appointed Wiley Baxter, the only lawyer in town, as Chief Justice of the Supreme Court. Someone wanted a new dog catcher and an enforceable leash law. Others wanted their dogs to run free. They argued over that for half an hour. Issues of parking and downtown development and water quality and sewer leach field permits fluttered in the breeze and were forgotten or steamrollered by a louder voice. As the afternoon wore on folks began to drift away. Few reinforcements came through the doors to replace them. The metal folding chairs were now half empty. A few stood or paced slowly in the back of the room. November shadows lengthened outside, and the clock hands approached four.

Katie couldn't sit still any longer. Her butt was sore from the brutal metal chair. The stuffy room cloyed with a locker-room odor of stale sweat and tobacco breath. She stood and stretched her legs at the refreshment table and discovered the delicate little home-baked pfeffernusse cookies Mrs. Banke had baked and brought in to share. Katie closed her eyes and slowly savored one of the sugar-dusted confections, then stepped away from the table. But she returned to taste another, and then another, swearing that each one would be her last. By her fourth cookie, her stomach began to feel heavy and unsettled. She decided to step outside and maybe take a walk around the block to wake up.

"Okay," Director Kearns was croaking as Katie closed the door, "that's probably just about enough for our first day. But there is one last thing I'd like you all to be thinking about. We'll be needin' a head of state for this new . . . empire. Anyone interested in running for president?"

"Ain't you gonna do it?" Moray Willits asked.

Kearns shook his head. "Not with this here throat a' mine. An' I don't want the responsibility. I'm too old. Now . . . who wants to volunteer?"

Dead silence.

"As prime minister then. Any nominations."

"Wha'za diff'rence 'tween a prime min'ster an' a pres'dent?" Willits wanted to know.

Kearns' laugh became a barking cough. "Darn if I know, Moray. You wanna try it out an' let us all know?"

"Wha'chur really lookin' for is a figurehead, t'stand up an' take it on the chin for our country. Am I right?" Willits pressed.

"Yeah," Ted Tollitson grinned. "An' t'take all the blame when the Homeland Security agents show up an' haul him off to prison."

"Or worse," Hiram Atwater piped in. "I heard stories'd turn yer hair white--"

"Yours's already white, Hiram—"

"Yeah, but who'd be fool enough to take on a job like *that*?"

A swell of mumbling and quipping rose and fell and ended again in dead silence.

"No volunteers? No nominations? Elan, you been mighty quiet." Kearns voice was no more than a raspy whisper. "You a'hankerin' for the job, maybe?"

"No way," Katie's father shook his head vehemently. "Finance is the limit of my skills. And, you know what, the more I think about it, I'm not so comfortable with this 'Minister' business. I believe 'Financial Consultant' would suit me just fine."

"But ya got that look on your face," Kearns persisted. "Y'must have yourself an idea of who might serve as our head of state. Am I right?"

"I . . . I just might have." He turned and his eyes flicked across the room looking for his daughter. He had last seen her on the sidewalk outside the windows. Elan turned back to Kearns. "Yes, sir. I just might have a candidate in mind. He's a long-time resident. A fine, upstanding citizen. Most of you know him. Anyway, he's a landowner here in the valley. Owns a farm on the way down to Eagleville. But . . . he happens to be *gone* right now. And . . . he's not planning on coming back in the near future. Which may be his greatest recommendation."

Kearns raised his hands. "But if he's *gone* . . . how can he accept the nomination?"

"Well . . . that's just it," Elan grinned. "I happen to hold a general power of attorney over his affairs. As his agent in fact, I guess *I* could accept on his behalf."

"Well," Kearns rasped, playing to the crowd. "'Jus' who you got in mind, Elan?"

Elan rose and faced the audience just as Katie was reentering the front door. "I hereby nominate . . . *Shadrack Smithers* . . . to be Emperor of the Bristlecone Empire."

"Smithers?"

"Who's Shadrack Smithers?"

"Tha's Tildie's husban', ain't it?"

"Yeah. Ain't seen 'im about much lately. Since she passed— "

"Don't really know the fella—"

"This'll save us all a lotta grief—"

"Dad, no!" Katie was trying to find her way back to the front, but curious onlookers blocked her path. No one paid her any attention.

Elan still held the floor. "And . . . because he's not here . . . and probably won't be coming back . . . as his agent in fact . . . I hereby *accept* the nomination on behalf of Shadrack Smithers."

"Dad, *no!*"

An irrational enthusiasm fired the noisy crowd.

"I call for a vote," someone shouted.

Kearns raised his hands. "Any other nominations?"

"No, let's vote on 'this'un!"

"Yeah, this Smithers sounds like the man—"

"I think he's coming back!" Katie shouted fecklessly.

"All right," croaked Kearns, "I move that we appoint Shadrack Smithers by acclamation to be . . . what was it?"

"Emperor of Bristlecone," Elan said.

"Emperor of Bristlecone!"

The crowd, on its feet now, confirmed the appointment with its boisterous assent and considerable relief.

BY THE TIME BESS SET THE SERVING BOWL of chicken stew on the dining table, Katie had still not come home. "Where is she?" she asked her husband.

Elan explained that Katie had been with him for most of the meeting at the senior center, but after he finished helping put away the folding chairs, she was nowhere to be found. He assumed she had decided to walk home by herself. "Or," he smiled, "more likely, jog."

"Without telling you? Well then, where is she? Have you tried to call her?"

"Cell phones are still not working."

Bess shook her head. "This is not like her."

"I know," Elan agreed. "She's been acting kind of peculiar lately."

Bess thought about it. "Did something happen at the meeting to upset her?"

Elan finished spooning stew into the first of three bowls beside him, then reached it over to his wife. "Hard to tell anymore. She seems to be getting more headstrong every day. Haven't you noticed?" Into the second bowl he dipped out his own portion and tasted it. The third bowl sat as empty as a memorial urn.

"That's it?" Bess prompted.

Elan carefully spread butter on his roll. "Well, she did seem a little upset when the convention appointed someone to . . . to lead this . . . this new empire we're trying to get organized—"

"Who was appointed?"

He raised the spoon to his lips. "Shadrack Smithers."

"Shadrack? Tildie's husband? He's back in town?"

Elan held up a hand until he finished chewing. "Not that I know of."

"But . . . how could they appoint him if he's not here?"

"Well . . . it's kind of a . . . it's a technical deal. No one else wanted the job, actually."

"I can understand why not," Bess clucked. "But why on earth did they pick old Mr. Smithers? Why—"

They heard the back door whisk open and click shut.

"Katie?" Bess was on her feet. "Is that you? Come and have supper."

"I'm not hungry," came a muffled reply.

"Come into the dining room, honey. We'd like to talk to you."

The sullen-faced teenager appeared in the doorway. Her gray hoodie was damp and disheveled from a passing evening shower. The liner beneath her dark eyes was smudged. "What?"

"You walked home in the rain? In the dark? Why didn't you wait for your father to give you a ride?"

Katie glowered at him, then turned back to her mother. "I wanted to be alone."

"What's wrong?" Bess moved over to help her take off the damp sweatshirt, but Katie stepped back. "What is it, honey?"

"*He* knows." She glared at her father. "Why don't you ask *him*."

"Now hold on there—" Elan rose.

"He's coming back!" Katie snapped. "Didn't you know that?"

"Who's coming back?" Bess asked.

"What makes you think he's coming back?" Elan wore a false smile.

"Because I talked to that farmer he was staying with. Diesler.

That's how I know."

"Who's coming back?" Bess repeated.

"In Kieferville? You called Kieferville again? What'd this Diesler say?"

"Shadrack Smithers, Mom."

Anger appeared in Elan's eyes. "Why didn't you tell me?"

"Because we weren't, like, *talking* that much, were we, Dad?"

"What in earth is going on here?" Bess demanded, glancing from one to the other. "What does Mr. Smithers have to do—"

"Shadrack, Mother. He likes to be called 'Shadrack'." Katie faced her father. "And you were making *fun* of him. I saw you!"

"No I wasn't. You weren't even there to hear my whole presentation—"

"No, but I heard enough of it. You were making a big joke out of Shadrack. And putting him in harms way. Just for a laugh."

"No, I—"

"*Emperor of Bristlecone!* Oh my god! What kind of a joke is *that* supposed to be? Like, give me a break!"

He reached to take his daughter by the shoulders. "Now you listen to me, young lady—"

Katie jerked free and pushed her hands against his chest. "Leave me alone." She took a step toward her room, then pivoted, snatched a key off the peg by the back door, and fled out into the dewy darkness.

"What's going on between the two of you?"

Elan started to turn away, "I'll go talk to her—"

"*No!*" Bess caught his wrist. "What the *hell* is going on here? Talk to *me*, Elan. This has been going on ever since I got back from Portland. But now it's getting worse. Don't you see? We're losing our daughter? You've got to *talk to me*. What happened while I was away? Tell me! And this time I want the truth!"

They both heard the car start.

"That's my car," Bess yelped. "She's not supposed to be driving by herself." Bess hurried through the laundry room and pulled open the back door in time to see the taillights disappearing up the driveway. "Especially not at night. Her provisional permit doesn't allow—"

Elan snorted. "Her instruction permit was issued by the State of

California. Guess she doesn't figure she needs a permit to drive here in Bristlecone."

CRISSY WOLSKI STARTLED AWAKE and sat up in bed. Had she heard the sound of a car door slam? She thought maybe she had. She glanced at the red numerals of the bedside clock. It was 2:32 in the morning and all was quiet except for Michal's husky breathing. Maybe she had dreamed the sound. But she had to pee anyway, so it wouldn't hurt to go downstairs and check it out. As she swung her feet onto the cold wooden floor, Michal stirred and rolled onto his back, but continued snoring lightly beneath the down comforter. Crissy wiggled her feet into wooly moccasins, wrapped herself in her heavy robe, and padded over to the window. In the moonlit yard outside everything appeared still and peaceful. And perfectly in order.

She slid her hand down the thick banister as she descended the stairs toward the hallway. Halfway down, a shadow moved across the pebbled glass window of the front door. She froze between steps. A key tick-ticked against the front door lock, then rattled inside. She held her breath, her heart suddenly hammering. The lock clicked and the door swung open to silhouette the shape of a man against the pale glow of moonlight. The form was bent and featureless and moved in slow jerks like a zombie. He lurched into the house.

Crissy screamed.

The man in the doorway jerked upright and squealed something incoherent.

Crissy turned and pounded her way back up the stairs, but she tripped on the last riser and ended up crawling into the bedroom. "Turn on the light," she panted as she slammed the door shut with her feet. "There's a man in our house!"

Michal fumbled on the lamp and stood befuddled beside the bed, blinking between dream and wakefulness. His mussed dirty-blond hair stood out on his scalp as if in confusion. "A man . . . wha . . .?"

"A man. Yes. And I don't know who the hell he is." She dumped his clothes from the straight-back chair and tried to wrestle it beneath the doorknob.

"Was that *you* . . . that *scream*?"

"*Yes, it was me.* Call 911!"

"911?" Michal fumbled up the phone and held it to his ear. "Still dead," he pronounced. "Ever since the roadblock. Remember?"

"Where's your cell phone?"

"There." He pointed to his pants which she had dumped onto the floor.

She dug the phone out of a pocket and flipped it open and punched in the three numbers. There was a long silence before a pattern of beeps dissolved into a mechanical voice that said, "I'm sorry, but the number you have dialed is no longer in service. If you feel you have reached this message in—"

Crissy snapped it shut and moaned, "What're we gonna do?"

Downstairs in the foyer the Emperor of Bristlecone, uncoronated and unadvised, fumbled for the light switch, but his fingers didn't recognize the rotary knob which had replaced the old-fashion toggle switch they were feeling for. Finally he managed to punch on the hall light, but everything looked different in the multiple glows of a candela-bra fixture where a bare 40-watt bulb used to hang. The walls had been papered over with a dull cream-and-yellow pattern of repeating haystacks. And the floor . . . new speckled linoleum now covered the bare boards beneath his feet. His nose wrinkled at the sweet, flowery aroma of clothes-drier sheets which perfumed the air. Fatigued and irritated from the long drive, he was sorely perplexed and annoyed. *Who're these folks in m' house?* Shadrack wanted to know. *An' whut've they done?*

The bedroom door upstairs creaked open and a man's faux-bold voice demanded, "Who are you?"

"Who am I? Who'm *I*? That ain't the real question now, is it? Who're *you*?"

"This is our house. Go away before I call the police."

Shadrack snorted. "Go'wan an' call 'em. This here's *my* house, an' you's a'trespassin' on my prop'ty."

The voice upstairs was silent for a moment, then asked, "Smithers?"

"Shadrack, if'n y'please."

"Well . . . ah . . . we rented your farm," Michal Wolski announced sheepishly. He stepped out onto the landing in his red flannel pajamas. "Didn't you know?"

"*Rented!* From *who*?"

"Well . . . it was . . . we leased it from that accountant fella in town. Graves, I think, is his name."

"Groves," came an angry female voice behind Michal. "Elan Groves." Crissy squeezed her husband aside. Her dark brown tresses flowed down the shoulders of her robe, and her striking green eyes blazed angrily. "Don't you even know when your own farm's been rented out? And we been payin' our good money for rent. You near scared me to death jus' now. Now you get outta here and leave us be before we call the police."

Shadrack stood stunned in the foyer. He seemed to deflate, to collapse in upon himself, mumbling, "He rented it out? Elan done rented out m'farm? Now what'm I 'sposed t'do?"

Michal eased himself halfway down the steps. "Have you come far?" he asked gently.

"Been a'drivin' . . . two days . . . me'be more like three . . . an' I ain't slept much a'tall." He began to tremble. "He *rented* it to ya, y'say?"

"Yes, sir. Where do you plan to stay tonight?"

Shadrack just shook his head.

"Have you eaten?"

"*Michal!*" Crissy snapped. "What are you doing? This man *frightened* me."

"Come on, Chrissy. Lighten up. He didn't know we were here." He descended the rest of the stairway.

"How long y'got it rented fur?" Shadrack asked.

"The lease is for one year," Michal replied.

"Uh."

"August first to August first."

"Uh."

"But Mr. Groves led us to believe that we'd be able to renew it from year to year. He said you weren't planning on coming back."

"I wuddn't."

"But you did."

"Uh."

"Would you care for something to eat, Mr. Smithers?"

"Shadrack."

"How about a bowl of oatmeal, Shadrack . . . or maybe some toast or yogurt?"

"Michal! He nearly scared me to death!"

Michal turned and asked softly, "Do you remember what we were reading about last week? In that little Zen book of yours? Do you?"

Chrissy sniffed. "Compassion?"

He nodded and seemed to relax. "Now come along, Shadrack. I'll show you how we've fixed up the kitchen and find you something to eat." He took the old man gently by the arm. "We can set you up for tonight in the guest room. It's still being remodeled, but it's clean, and Crissy can put sheets on the bed." He nodded to his wife, then turned back to the old man. "I know we've got us a bit of a problem here . . . but I think we'll work it out. Don't you?"

As Michal was putting water on to boil, the doorbell chimed.

"Whu'zat?" Shadrack wanted to know.

"The doorbell," Michal told him.

"I ain't got no doorbell."

"You do now. Crissy and I put one in."

Crissy hurried into the kitchen. "Who'd be ringing our doorbell at this time of night?"

Michal shook his head. "Let's go and find out."

On the front stoop Katie Groves stood abashed, bedraggled, and shivering. "I'm sorry to bother you . . . but I saw that pickup truck pull in and park outside . . . and I saw your lights come on . . . and . . . and I was wondering—"

"Katie?"

Katie looked past the somber couple confronting her. "Shadrack!"

"Well, as I live and breathe," the old man marveled. "What'er you a'doin' here?"

Katie pushed her way past the doorkeepers and threw her arms around the old man. "I came to see you. You made it back! Thank God for that!"

"Katie Groves, if I'm not mistaken," said Michal, extending his hand. "We met once at your father's place."

"Yes. Yes. I remember. How are you and your wife making out,

Mr. Wolski?"

"Why are you here?" Crissy demanded.

"Why? I . . . ah . . . need to talk to Shadrack. I was waiting for him out by your mailbox. It's important."

"*Now?*"

Michal intervened. "Shadrack was about to have a bowl of oatmeal. And he's tired from his long drive. It might be better if you came back in the morning."

Katie hung her head. "I've . . . got nowhere to go tonight."

"Why don't you just go back home?" Crissy snorted. "Come back in the morning?"

Katie shook her bent head. "I have a sleeping bag in the car. I guess I can finish the night out there—"

Crissy threw up her hands in exasperation. "Michal? Are there no limits to this compassion thing?"

Michael grinned. "You read it yourself. True compassion is limitless." He turned to Katie. "The sofa downstairs is available. You look like you could use a bite to eat too, young lady. Guess I could mix up a batch of pancakes. Whadda ya think, Crissy?"

NOT NEARLY AS MANY TOWNSFOLK showed up for the second noon meeting the following day. So they decided to set up folding tables in a rectangular configuration for those who wanted to participate eye to eye, with chairs behind for the spectators and kibitzers. A group of farm workers from the valley, many of them undocumented, asked for and received a seat at the table. They selected Raul Gutierrez to represent them.

Director Horace Kearns called the adjourned meeting to order. "Now," he croaked, coughed, cleared his throat, and spat into a wad of tissue. "Now . . . let's see here. We got ourselves a number a' things on the agenda. Let's see. Ted Tollitson wants t'talk about settin' up a farmer's co-op t'grow what we can for the folks in this valley. Mr. Gutierrez will prob'ly want t'be a part a' that discussion." He shuffled his notes. "An' we're gonna need some kinda board t'regulate prices on near-abouts everythin' folks need, with authority t'enforce price regula-tions." He glanced up and found Moray Willits' face in the audience.

"But I think the first item of business has got to be all the complaints we've been getting about the prices at the grocery store. Seems like they been going way up the last few days. Elan, I'm gonna let you take over this inquiry as Finance Minister. Before my voice gives out for good."

"Thank you, Mr. Director," Elan replied. "Moray, you might want to join us up here at the table to explain exactly what's going on?"

Scooter Thompson called from the chairs in back, "He's been jackin' up his prices 'cause we got no place else t'shop, is what's a'goin' on."

"They're getting pretty steep," Mrs. Banke agreed.

Several others chimed in with grunts and nods.

Looking uncomfortable, Moray Willits found an empty chair across from Director Kearns. He was a plump man in his late forties with shiny skin and a bald head. He was still wearing his dark blue grocer's apron over Levis and a gray sweater. "It's a supply problem," he mumbled. "Not really your business, I guess."

Kearns interrupted, "We'll be the one's t'decide if it's any a our business, Moray—" but he froze in mid-sentence, staring the length of the room.

Everyone turned to follow his gaze. Through the front door stepped Bess Groves, who most everyone knew from teaching their children, followed by her daughter Katie. Katie was holding the door for a skinny old ghost of a man in an oversize pair of clean overalls, bewhiskered and limping behind her.

"Well I'll be . . ." Kearns croaked. He turned a questioning eye toward Elan, who was staring at his hands in his lap. Kearns managed a twisted smile as he stood. "Shadrack! Welcome back. Good t'see ya made it home."

"Howdy, Horace." Shadrack minced his way up the aisle toward the front table, with Katie in his wake. Bess hung back and found a chair.

" I guess you heard about yer being appointed yeste'day, have ya?" Kearns asked.

"Yes, sir. Katie tol' me all 'bout it jus' this mornin'. An' ya kin jus' fancy my surprise."

"Why, I guess so." Kearns forced a hoarse laugh as he steadied himself against the table. "Now . . . I imagine . . . now that yer back . . .

an' with all that farm work ya gotta catch up on . . . well . . . I imagine yer prob'ly gonna tell us . . . yer gonna have to . . . well . . . refuse the appointment . . . am I right? But we'll all un'erstan' . . . under the circumstances . . . a'course we will."

"No, sir." Shadrack announced proudly as he reached the table. "I's mighty proud a you all bestowin' this honor on me. An' I accept it. I got the time. An' I got the spirit. An' I got an advisor." He nodded at Katie. "So I's a'gonna take it on. Now, where do I sit?"

Bewildered, Kearns offered Shadrack his seat and took another one further down the side.

"Much obliged, Horace. An' kin one a'ya make a space fer Miss Katie Groves t'sit b'side me. Thank ya. Now y'all go on where y'was a'fore I come in. I'll jus' follow along 'til I catch the drift." Katie whispered something in Shadrack's ear. Sheepishly he grinned his gap-toothed smile when he asked, "Say, Horace, what's this here job a'payin' me?"

"Well . . . we ain't figgered that out yet." He looked to Elan for help.

But Elan just shrugged. "All the phones are still dead, and I haven't received my travel visa yet, so I haven't been able to talk to anyone at the county or at the bank to see how much money we've got. Or how much we've got coming. But I guess I'd like to know the answer to Shadrack's question myself."

"I reckon yer workin' fer free fer now," Kearns said to Shadrack. "Y'wanna quit, maybe?"

"No, sir," Shadrack shook his head.

"Well, I guess we'll work us up a budget later on. But ain't you gettin' social security, anyhow?"

The old man shrugged. "Don' rightly know. Haven't checked m'bank account o'er'n Alturas fer all the months I been gone."

The long silence that followed was broken by Elan Groves. "Anyway, it's nice to see you, Shadrack. I look forward to hearing about your trip." He glanced down at a sheet of paper. "In my capacity of Finance Minister, I was about to ask Mr. Willits some questions about the sharp rise in prices at his grocery store."

"Howdy, Shadrack," Willits grinned. "Good t'see ya back. I was jus' a'tellin' Horace here I got a supply problem, an' it's not really anybody's business but my own."

Elan spoke to Shadrack. "May I continue?"

Shadrack bowed his head, embarrassed by the formality. "Go on. Don' min' me."

Elan turned to Willits. "Maybe it *is* our business, Mr. Willits. Now, a number of folks saw you unloading crates of food from that General Services trailer truck this morning. The big semi, I understand. Didn't that come outta Alturas?"

"Might of. But there's still a lotta other stuff I still gotta buy and bring in . . ." Willits' voice trailed off.

"Are the wholesalers charging you higher prices now, compared to what they were charging before the blockade?" Elan asked.

Willits paused. "Some of 'em might be. I'd have ta check the invoices, I guess."

"You don't know right offhand?"

"Well, not exactly . . ."

"But you know enough to substantially increase your own retail prices. Is that right?"

"Y'don' unnerstan'. It's complicated—"

"Moray," Kearns broke in, "If I was you I'd stop talkin' right now before y'make a whole lotta other good folks in this room mad. We can have our Finance Minister look over your books—"

"Now you jus' hold on," Willits protested. "You got no right t'look at my books. I got rights."

Kearns smiled. "Under what law, Moray?"

"Well," Willits sputtered. "I got a fundamental right t'make me a livin'—"

"A *fair* living, Moray. Now just stop talkin' an' listen up a minute. We ain't disputin' yer right t'make a livin' for yourself. We all want that, don't we folks?"

There were a few ambiguous grunts from the assemblage.

"But ever'body's gotta eat in this strange situation we fin' ourselves in. An' we gotta be fair to everybody. Ya unnerstan'?" He coughed and spat into his tissue before nodding to Elan to take back the reins.

"Mr. Willits," Elan said, "no one's disputing your right to enjoy a fair return on your business investment and labor. It benefits the community as well as yourself. But we need to assure the community that your return *is* a fair one, and to do that we will need to examine your ledger of costs and expenses—"

"*Over my dead body!*"

Katie felt Shadrack shudder at the image.

Elan watched the grocer silently for a moment. "You understand that if you don't cooperate, our first option would be to open a community store to compete with yours. Selling the same commodities, and probably more, with open books and fair prices. I understand the Cressler & Bonner building might be available."

"You can't do that! An' steal my good customers? That's communism!"

"The hell we can't," growled Director Kearns. "There ain't no law around here no more, 'cept what this convention says there is. Bristlecone law."

"Your customers will shop where the values are best for them," Elan continued. "Now, we want to work *with* you, Mr. Willits, and we want you to have a *reasonable* profit to live on. We would prefer to continue using your suppliers and wholesalers, as long as their charges are fair. They've already got free passage through the checkpoints. But if we can't work this out with you, with full and open disclosure to my department and the public, then we, as a community, will have to arrange to supply the public with what they need and demand. That's what government does."

A sputtering of applause rose from the audience.

"Shadrack!" Willits pleaded, sweating. "They can't *do* this! You're the man they put in charge here. An' you're a businessman. A farmer. Tell 'em they gotta stop interferein' with m'private business right here an' now!"

All eyes turned to the grizzled old man with the wild bushy salt-and-pepper beard and unkempt hair. The man whom they had bizarrely appointed emperor. Whatever that meant. Shadrack glanced at Katie beside him. She smiled and nodded encouragement. He wrestled over the situation in his mind for so long that a few people began to wonder if he had even heard. Finally he drew himself up, took a breath, pursed his lips, and turned toward Moray Willits. "I seen enough dead bodies in my time, Moray," he said.   "An' you sure don't want t'be one of 'em." People exchanged puzzled looks. Shadrack continued, "I been a'doin' business with ya fer a long time . . . an' I can bear witness ta yer bein' a good man at heart." He paused to let the words sink in. "But I think ya oughta go on an' roll back yer prices t'what they was last week. Right now. All by y'self." He nodded finality. "An' if y'be needin' t'*up* any of 'em . . . well . . . you just talk ta Elan Groves here, an' show 'im *why* y'gotta do it."

"An' what if he don't agree?" Willits demanded.

"Well . . . ," Shadrack considered the problem seriously, "well . . . the two of ya can bring it t'me, an' I'll take a look." Again he nodded, then thought some more. "Things's gonna be a'changin' perty fast, I reckon." He looked Willits in the eye. "Right now you's one a'us. But ever'body gotta eat, like Horace says. An' you sure don't wanna be on the wrong side a' this if'n she gets worse." He sat back in his chair, finished.

A ripple of applause rose again, this time joined by those seated around the tables.

ELAN HAD GOTTEN THERE EARLY and was waiting on the front steps of Wiley Baxter's office when the lawyer arrived the next morning. Elan wanted to go over some things before the others showed up. "Morning, Wiley."

"Oh . . . Elan. You startled me."

"Didn't mean to. You know, don't you, that you've been appointed Chief Justice of the Bristlecone Court."

Baxter shook his head. He was a stocky fireplug of a man, energetic, shorter than Elan, gray at the temples, but not as pale as his nearing-retirement years deserved. He looked to have a lot of career left in him. "That's what old Horace Kearns told me when he stopped by the other day."

"What did you say to it?"

"I told him I'druther serve as Attorney General."

"Attorney General? Huh . . . well . . . who'd take the job of Chief Justice then?"

"I suggested Marty Hoover's name to him. He's been retired up on his ranch for years. Up near Fort Bidwell. Put in fifty years before the bar, he did, and he was a damn good lawyer in his day."

"I never met him, but . . . isn't he kind of old now?"

"In his eighties, I guess, but he's still sharp as a razor. I drove up and talked to him day before yesterday." Baxter nodded gravely. "Said he'd do it, of course. Didn't really want to, but he's been following the situation, and, I can say this for him, he's still got a strong sense of civic duty. Doesn't expect many cases to come before him anytime soon."

"So . . . you're going to be Attorney General?"

"Horace says he'll bring it up before the convention next time. And you're Finance Minister, I hear."

"Last I heard."

"Mornin' Margaret." Baxter stepped aside to let his secretary unlock the front door.

"Morning," Elan nodded.

"You boys can come on inside, you know. Looks like we might be getting some snow pretty soon."

Baxter lowered his voice to Elan after the door shut behind her. "Are any of us going to get paid?"

"I hope so. I just got my Pacific Coast visa in the mail, so I was planning to drive over to Alturas when we get finished with this meeting. Try and find out whether we've got any money." Baxter reached for the door handle, but Elan caught his arm. "About this meeting . . . I just wanted to give you a heads-up before everyone shows up—"

Molly's car swung around the corner and whisked up to the curb. Katie was in the driver's seat, and Shadrack rode shotgun. The Wolskis were in back. Molly was not aboard.

"They're early," Elan grumbled as they climbed out.

"Let's just play 'er by ear when they get inside." Baxter slapped Elan on the shoulder and turned to greet the new arrivals. "Howdy Katie," he waved. He held open his office door and one by one welcomed his clients inside.

The conference room was small and windowless. It had room for only four at the narrow trestle table, so Shadrack, Michal and Crissy Wolski, and the lawyer sat, while Katie and her father remained standing on opposite sides of the doorway. After they had settled in and orders for coffee were tallied by Margaret, Crissy Wolski seized the initiative. She explained that the existing lease, as written and executed, was not going to work out. She and Michal had put a lot of work and money into remodeling the farmhouse and installing a new irrigation system and planting fruit trees and grape vines on the agent's representation and their good-faith belief that they would be able to stay there for a lot longer than one lousy year. And then Shadrack had showed up out of the blue, needing a place to stay.

The lawyer put down the copy of the lease he had been perusing. "So, what do you have in mind?"

"We want to buy the farm," Crissy told him.

Michal lay his hand on her arm. "Actually, it's a little more complicated than that. You see, we want to live there . . . and to work the farm . . . and at the same time provide Shadrack with a place to stay."

"At the farm, you mean?"

"Yes, sir. For as long as he wants to. And we want to work the land together. All of us. And share the fruits of our labors."

Baxter glanced over at Elan. "You signed the original lease as Shadrack's attorney-in-fact. Do you approve of this?"

"This is the first I've heard of it." Elan took his time. "Sounds a lot to me like one of those old hippie commune pipe dreams."

"That's about what I thought you'd say," Katie scolded from across the empty doorway.

"So you've been helping them figure out this . . . this goofy . . . this scam?" Elan's voice was rising.

Baxter quickly intervened between the two. "Let's just see what the *clients* want to do, okay? If you two want to fight a personal battle, you can take it outside. We'll wait."

Father and daughter hung their heads. "Sorry," Elan said. "Go ahead."

Baxter eased himself back down in his chair. He picked up his pen and turned to Shadrack. "Now . . . how much do you plan on selling the place for?"

"How much?" Shadrack fidgeted. "Ain't really thought 'bout it."

"Okay. How would you value the lodging you will be receiving?"

"Unh. Don' guess I know. Reckon we'll figger somethin' out."

"And what about board? Will you all be eating together?"

"Hadn't much thought 'bout it."

"Well . . . how about working the farm? How do you plan to divide the profits?"

Shadrack glanced uncomfortably towards Elan, who offered no help. "Unh. Don' rightly know. They's got 'emselves these . . . on their computer . . . some kinda sheets —"

"Spreadsheets," Michal supplied.

"Arr . . . showed me a couple of 'em . . . tells 'em what to plant an' jus' when. Now, I's jus' a ordinary ol' time dirt farmer . . . but I knows the soil out thar . . . an' I reckon if'n they got somethin' they want planted . . . well . . . I kin make it grow."

"And the profits?"

"Ain't never been much a'that."

Baxter dropped his pen and exhaled. With a wry smile he turned to Michal and Crissy. "How about just adopting this old fella as a surrogate grandfather? Might save us all a whole lotta paperwork."

"Can we do that?" Crissy asked.

"He's joking," Michal explained.

They talked the whole morning long. The lawyer asked questions, offered suggestions, and made notes on his yellow pad. Katie and her father, without making eye contact with the other, would occasionally make a comment or ask a question. But Shadrack and the Wolskis did their own bargaining. At Baxter's prompting, they considered a lease-option, an enhanced power of attorney, a conditional sale contract, a grant deed with reservation of a life estate, limited liability partnerships, a mutual operating agreement, living trusts, and a simple irrevocable will. Elan grew restless from all the legalize. He wanted to be on his way to Alturas and resolve what he considered more important issues, but he stayed on until a preliminary understanding was reached and the next meeting was scheduled to review the documents the lawyer would draft.

"You're probably going to want to draft a revocation of my power of attorney, too," Elan told the lawyer as he pulled on his overcoat.

"Not likely," Shadrack objected. "Who's gonna look after my side a'things fer me if'n ya quit on me now?"

"Looks like you already got another advisor." Elan tilted his head toward his daughter.

"Yeah I do," Shadrack said. "But I'm a'gonna need *both* a'ya, So's we kin work like a team t'gether."

An uncomfortable silence passed before Katie said, "I'd like that."

"Alright then," Elan agreed. "But I've got to get over to Alturas right now. Got a lot to do there."

THEY CAME TO TAKE HIM AWAY five days before Christmas. Two inches of snow had fallen on the long driveway leading down to Shadrack's farmhouse, but recent muddy tire tracks marked the way. The two men climbed out of an SUV, which was unmarked except for the faint shadow of Border Patrol lettering bleeding through the new paint job. Both wore gray uniforms under heavy brown open parkas with Homeland Security patches on the shoulders and pistols in holsters on their service belts. A third man, in back behind the security screen, did not attempt to join them.

On the way to the front door Agent Vince Blaylock, the shorter, stouter, and older of the two, pulled from an inside coat pocket the booking photographs of their quarry and handed it to his lanky junior partner. "Butch," he said, "keep your eyes open. He shouldn't be too tough to spot. Now you step over there and give me cover."

Vince waited until his partner was in place, then rang the doorbell and waited some more. After a while the door opened and he was confronted by an attractive, brown-haired, green-eyed young woman in navy blue warmups and a dirty apron. "Yes?" she asked, annoyed.

"Morning, ma'am. We're looking for Shadrack Smithers," Vince said.

"He's not home."

"Where's he at?" Vince pressed.

Crissy studied the two men for a moment. Registered their shoulder patches and holstered firearms. Pursed her lips. Turned to call her husband, then remembered he was out with the cows. She grimaced. "He might be over at the Senior Center."

"Where's that, Ma'am? In Cedarville?"

She nodded.

"Where in Cedarville? Downtown?"

Again she nodded, brusquely.

"Mind if we have a look around inside?"

"Matter of fact, I *do*." She slammed the door in his face.

"What're we gonna do now, Vince? Y'think she's telling us the truth?"

Vince shrugged and stepped down off the porch. "Probably. Don't matter all that much. We already bagged our main target. This guy's just a TWP."

"'Traveling Without Permit'?" Butch asked as they crossed the ripples of drifted snow.

"You got it. You're picking up the lingo, kid. Just takes time. Don't worry about it."

"So . . . we're going over to this Senior Center?"

"Might as well, long as we're here. If we can find it. Then we'll head on back, one way or the other. And even if we don't nab this Smithers," Vince added with a nasty smirk, "word'll get out and put the fear of God into the sucker for the rest of his days."

The Senior Center was not hard to find. The low, square building had a sign and stood on Main Street at the far corner of the first commercial block. But parking appeared to be a challenge. They wanted the SUV close at hand. So Vince double-parked until a pickup backed out of one of the diagonal spaces in front of the market a half-block farther down, then wheeled the SUV into the vacated space. Both men glanced at each other, nodded, grunted, and climbed out.

"Hey, man," said the prisoner in back, "I gotta take a piss. How about—"

They slammed their doors without bothering to respond, then walked slowly back up the sidewalk, getting their bearings, trying not to draw attention, and stood outside the Senior Center searching the crowd inside through the latticed windows. "See anything?" Vince asked.

"No . . . ," Butch replied. ". . . no . . . wait . . . that's *him*."

"Where?"

"There. Sitting at the big table. Right in the middle. That's Smithers, isn't it? See him?"

It took Vince a moment to spot him. "That's him alright. Good job."

"How're we gonna get him outta there, Vince?"

Vince thought for a while. "We go in together. I'll wait inside the door and cover you. You walk on up to Smithers, flash your badge, and tell him we want to talk with him outside right now. Right now. Don't let him balk. Make it quick. Before these rubes figure out what's going on."

Butch considered the plan. Nodded. "You gonna draw your firearm?"

"Only if I have to. Once we get him outside, we shouldn't have a problem."

They glanced around. Faced each other again. Each drew a deep breath and exhaled. "Let's go get him," Vince said.

Shadrack was not surprised. Not really. It was he who had started the ball rolling, back there in Kieferville, and deep down inside he figured they would come for him sooner or later. It was just the timing of it all that unsettled him. He was of course prepared to go with them. That was what he wanted all along. Or what he *had* wanted anyway. At least before he had received absolution from the good Reverend Martin Blythe. And before he had been vouchsafed his commission and his charge from this Bristlecone convention to perform the good deeds necessary to help save a foundering community. So now he was suddenly conflicted. But he rose anyway and went willingly with this stranger holding the Homeland Security badge, in order to buy a little time to think things through. Things that were happening so fast.

They made it through the silent mob of stunned conventioneers without objection. Vince led them out the front door. Onto the sidewalk. Vince's face shone with perspiration. "Turn around and put your hands behind your back," he ordered.

Shadrack thought about it for a moment as onlookers began to file out behind them. "Wha'chou plannin' on arrestin' me fur?" he asked.

Vince grabbed his upper arm with a pincer grip and twisted his shoulder back. "I told you to turn around."

"Hey!" somebody hollered, "stop that!"

"That's police brutality!" another growled.

"Stay back!" Vince warned, one hand on his holster and the other on Shadrack's arm. His eyes scanned the gawkers as if he were taking names.

"I don't like the drift of this," Horace Kearns croaked to Elan Groves as they crossed the lawn together. "Look. Over by the market. That must be their car."

"I didn't know he was coming back," Elan said. "I honestly *did not know*."

"It ain't your fault. We all did this together—" Suddenly Kearns spotted the snowplow coming up the highway. "Delbert!" he shouted to his cousin and waved for him to stop. For years his cousin had run the snowplow for the county, when there was a county to run it for. It was just a big hydraulic-powered steel plow blade bolted to the front of a county ten-ton dump truck filled with cinders and salt. He was just bringing it down from the county equipment barn in anticipation of the first big snow of the season. Kearns stepped up on the running board and pointed at the erstwhile Border Patrol SUV by the market. "They're tryin' t'take Shadrack away. We're prob'ly gonna need your plow."

Delbert didn't have to ask why. He shifted gears and the rig growled around the corner to circle the block and turn around.

In the meantime Wiley Baxter had pushed through to the front of the growing throng. "Have you got a warrant to extradite this man?"

Vince ignored him, bending and strapping the plastic flex cuffs around Shadrack's crossed wrists. He angily jerked them secure.

"Ow! Tha's too tight—"

"I'm Attorney General of this—"

"Shut the fuck up! You're interfering with an arrest." Vince turned his back and began frog-marching his prisoner toward the SUV, while keeping a wary eye on the surly, growing crowd.

"You've got no authority here," Baxter persisted, pressing close behind him. "Zero. This is an independent nation and you cannot . . . *cannot . . . rendition* our President like this. Or anybody else. It's a violation of international law." He raised his voice. *"Do you hear me? You're violating our law!"*

Vince ignored him. "Butch! Get the door open! An' keep an eye on Rodriguez."

"What's your name, officer?" Baxter demanded. "And what

authority do you claim to have here?"

Butch opened the rear door and waited until Vince pushed Shadrack roughly inside with a mumbled "Watch your head." Then Vince pulled his pistol and spun on Baxter. "Does *this* look like authority enough for you, buster?"

The crowd fell silent. A few people edged back in fright. Others pressed defiantly closer, filling the air with indignant epithets. But a few of the farmers started for their pickups to get their shotguns. And their rifles. And their handguns.

"Stay back!" Vince ordered, brandishing the pistol and squeezing around the front to the driver-side door. "You're all interfering with a lawful arrest." He pulled open the driver's door, climbed inside, and with trembling fingers managed to start the engine.

"There's folks behind you," Butch cautioned. "Want me t'get out and shoo'em away?"

"Stay where you are. I've got this." In the rearview mirror Vince saw people milling around behind the vehicle. He revved the engine a few times in warning, then eased the shift into reverse. The SUV began to inch backward at a slow crawl, nudging legs and bodies away behind the bumper. Vince's face glistened with sweat. He sure as hell didn't want to run anyone over. Way too much paperwork in that. And an investigation. Probably loss of pay. But he was making a slow progress. Suddenly the people behind began to open a path. "They're givin' up," he smirked.

Emergency lights flashed and bright high beams glared in his mirror. Vince couldn't see what it was. With a clunk the snowplow engaged the rear bumper, lifting and pushing the SUV back to its original place against the high concrete curb.

"Shit," Vince barked and thumped the steering wheel. "They can't *do* that. We can have all their asses tossed in jail."

A long silence followed as their situation began to sink in.

"Should I radio in for backup?" Butch asked his partner.

Vince grimaced. "Nobody's gonna send backup way out here unless we're dead. And even then they might not." He shook his head. "No, we're gonna have to get outta this jam on our own. Any ideas?"

Silence again.

A jolt of relief shot through Shadrack, who had not been able to keep his mind from toying with the mechanics of escape. But escape from *what*? From this ridiculous car? From the absurd conflict between the things he felt obliged to do and the things he no longer wanted to do? Something odd was going on in his mind. His hands had gone numb and his wrists burned where the plastic ties bit the flesh. He felt the pain, yes, but it no longer seemed to be *his* pain. It haunted him from a distance. Far away, as if from tilted, intersecting planes. A convergence of valley floors, where separate rivers merged. A whole geography of vast intersecting planes of intention and meaning. Shadrack began to chuckle. Slowly at first, from deep in his belly, then higher in his chest, and finally in his throat. Because he saw Tildie laughing. She was always so quick to laugh and to bring sunlight and singing into his life. She was laughing at him now, without a hint of malice, for the ridiculous situation he had gotten himself into. They were laughing together. It was such a beautiful laughter. In that moment he no longer felt the grief nor the guilt nor the sadness of her loss, but something joyful and enduring. And suddenly, after all those years, he understood the *meaning* of her laughter.

The prisoner beside him had drawn back warily into the corner. "Yo . . . *Viejo* . . . chou okay? " he asked.

Shadrack shifted his gaze to his companion for the first time. The man was in his late twenties or early thirties. Brown skin. Stubble of beard. Tattoo on his wiry neck. Mexican probably. Shadrack was flashing him one of his rare gap-toothed grins. When the laughter had subsided enough for him to catch his breath, he replied, "*Creo que si.*"

"*Ta bueno,*" the man grinned back. "You laughin' or cryin', *amigo*?"

Shadrack waggled his head,. "Cain't say, I reckon. *Lo mismo.*"

The prisoner nodded knowingly.

"Wha's yer name?" Shadrack asked.

The Mexican frowned, examining Shadrack up and down before his expression relaxed. "Rodriguez."

"Where'd they pick you up."

Rodriguez nodded southward. "Gerlach."

"Wha' for?"

The man showed a span of white teeth. "Chou ask a lotta questions,

Viejo."

"Sorry," Shadrack said, still grinning.

"*Esta bien.* 'S'all right. They claim I sellin' guns."

"Keep it down back there," Vince snapped. "We're tryin' t'think." He turned to his partner. "I think we might be able to climb over that curb."

Butch looked out the window. "It's pretty high."

Vince shrugged. "What've we got to loose?" He switched the transmission into four-wheel drive and downshifted to low low. "Hold on, here we go." The engine roared, the carriage strained, and the right front wheel began to climb.

Blam! The SUV jumped and settled onto the rim of its shredded right rear tire.

"Jesus!" growled Vince. "Now we're really fucked." He swung around and yelled at Shadrack. "Tell your pals to stop damaging government property. Or they're all gonna be shot." He buzzed down Shadrack's window a few inches.

Shadrack met his eyes with the goofy grin still on his face. "Don' see as how y'gonna manage t'shoot 'em all. Folks out thar, they all got shotguns a'their own, y'know. An' huntin' rifles. Matter a'fac', Chamber puts on a big squirr'l roundup ever' spring, so they got a lotta practice usin'em."

Muscles stood out on Vince's jaw as he ground his teeth. "Well, how about I just shoot *you* then."

Shadrack's grin widened. "G'won ahead. An' see whut happens."

Blam! The other rear tire was gone.

Shadrack pressed his face to the window opening. "*Hey!* Stop a'shootin' out them tires!" he yelled. "An' somebody call Gunter over at the tire shop. He's gonna have t'change 'em."

Horace Kearns lanky figure emerged from the cluster. "Y'mean ya want *us* to replace the tires? Why would we do that?"

"How else ya gonna send these fellas on their way, Horace?"

Kearns spat into a tissue and nodded. "Good point."

"Have 'im change the tires soon's they let me go."

"They gonna let ya go?"

"I reckon. If they wanna drive away from here, they is."

"An' whose gonna pay for them tires?" Kearns asked.

"Bristlecone," Shadrack pronounced. "We'll spend some'a that money Elan's 'bout t'bring in. Gunter'll take a IOU."

"You gonna sign it?"

"I reckon I kin."

Vince buzzed down Butch's window and leaned over. "Go ahead and change the tires," he called, "and back that plow off . . . and we'll consider letting Mr. Smithers go."

"Shadrack," Shadrack muttered.

Kearns approached the front window. "Now you sure don't seem to have much respect for our intelligence, do ya? You go on an' let him go first, and *then* we'll consider changing your tires."

The bargaining didn't last long. The Homeland Security boys had no chips left to play, and they knew it. The town folks could bide their time all day long. All Vince and Butch could hope to win was their vehicle back in operating condition. At least they would have Rodriguez to show for their troubles. And, of course, their own freedom.

Butch cautiously cracked the passenger door, eased himself out, and sidled along the side of the SUV to unlatch the back door. Folks stepped back to make room. He pulled the door open and reached inside to help the wrist-bound Shadrack climb out. When Shadrack's feet were planted on solid ground, Butch bent to retrieve the bracelet cutters from a cargo pocket of his pants. Rodriguez seized his chance. With surprising agility and power he sprang forward, bolting out and into Shadrack's scrawny chest, caroming the old man into the half-open door, which flew back into Butch's face, toppling him backwards. Rodriguez dove out, crashed into the crowd and disappeared into the sea of onlookers.

"Stop that man!" Vince hollered, but without daring to open his own door. "He's a prisoner of the United States government."

No one made any effort to restrain Rodriguez or pursue him.

"What'd the poor guy do?" a ribald voice called from the crowd. "Look a'chew th'wrong way?"

Everyone seemed to enjoy the comment. Two bystanders helped Butch to his feet. His nose was bloodied and possibly broken, but he was still trying to fish the cutters out of his pocket. Ted Tollitson stepped up and pressed his bandanna against the man's bleeding nose. "Somebody see if Emma's still in back. She's got some medical training for the senior program. And help me get this man over there on the bench where she can take a look at him. I'll cut off Shadrack's cuffs." He pulled his lock-back knife from its scabbard on his belt and bent to saw through the restraints.

The restless crowd cleared the way and oversaw Gunter's ballet of quick tire change artistry. The citizens were riled and working themselves up into a frenzy, feeding on their own outrage and indignity. To them this was personal. When California had tossed them out like so much garbage, they had pulled together and elected their own leader. And now a couple of brazen armed thugs from who knows where had been dispatched to interfere in their local affairs. With their sacred right of self-determination. With their *sovereignty*. In the streets outside the Senior Center they watched as an armada of pickup trucks converged to escort their uninvited guests out of town and across the playa, and then, squinting into the distance, witnessed their banishment onto the rough gravel roads of western Nevada. Cheers arose and a couple of shotguns were discharged into the air.

Inside the Senior Center the mood was somber and edgy. Shadrack's wrists were being slathered with an antibiotic cream and yerba buena by Emma Hilt, the center's self-proclaimed medical technician, nurse, and sorceress.

"Ain't nothin," he kept reassuring her as she fawned over him like a baby and he squirmed to keep an eye on the crowd outside.

"Jus' hol' still," she ordered. "Y'never did know what fer yer own good. They should'a took more care with ya. Imagine. And at your age—"

"Now there ain't nothin' wrong with my age—"

"Jus' hol' still. Think I better wrap some gauze around 'em—"

"Don't want no *gauze*," Shadrack barked, jerking back both wrists. "*Thank* ya, Emma, but I's done here." He began to roll down the sleeves of his worn chambray work shirt.

"Lemme wipe that off, y'ol' coot, a'fore ya stain up yer dang clothes."

Shadrack submitted to the towel. "I surely do 'preciate what y'done fer me here. But we gotta get this 'ere convention back inta session."

"No need t'rush, Shadrack," said Horace Kearns, who had been hovering nearby. "Better to make sure you're okay before—"

"I's fine, Horace. But we need t'talk this thing over . . . all a'us . . . an' perty quick, I reckon . . . a'fore some a' them young bucks ou'char figure they kin take things inta their own hands. I know personal well what mischief a young'n kin do with a shotgun . . . an' make things a whole lot worse." He shook his head. "Fer *ever*'body."

IT HAD BEEN A BAD DAY for the Homeland Security team. They had managed to limp away without mortal damage and figured they could make their way back to Winnemucca on two bald, unbalanced, previously-owned rear tires, but without a single prisoner aboard. Butch's nose was not broken, at least by the primitive standards of the Cedarville first aide volunteer, and the bleeding was finally stopped by a roll of gauze protruding from each nostril. Oh well. A bad day. It had happened before. Maybe not *this* bad, but still . . . and now they had to cover their sorry asses. Vince would spend most of the long drive concocting the heroic fiction they would tell when they got back. "When you got a lemon, ya better make lemonade," he told his reluctant partner. They had no intention of returning to Cedarville. Either of them. Ever.

PART FOUR

Cedarville

Winter

WRAPPED IN A DOWN JACKET AND WOOL LAP BLANKET, Crissy Wolski hunched in the rocker on the veranda and sipped hot black coffee. She watched two slim figures bend and straighten in the morning mist, bend and straighten, as they worked their hoes and spades in the vegetable garden. Weak year-end sunlight touched the peaks of the Warner Mountains three-thousand feet above their heads and glistened off the fresh snow there. Perhaps the rays would strengthen enough to burn off the wisps and tendrils of valley fog before long. By then Katie would have run off to her morning classes, if this weren't the year-end holiday week. But Shadrack would keep on weeding and furrowing and planting and coaxing the seeds and sprouts. All day long if he took a mind to it. He was the hardest worker she had ever seen. Scrawny and hobbled, he was determined to grow things on his own terms. And the plants responded to the magic in his fingers. Leeks. Garlic. Kohlrabi. Winter cabbage and kale and chard and beets and carrots.

Another figure caught her eye, pushing a wheelbarrow into the garden through the gate in the deer fence. That would be Rodriguez, bless his heart. A former gun-runner, they say, but a gentle and sweet man who had found a home, at least for now, with Shadrack in the old bunkhouse they were restoring. He bent to collect another batch of weeds for silage that would feed the livestock as the long winter drew on.

Crissy sighed. Christmas had come and gone. Winter was settling in. And according to Michal, the extra hands might spell the difference between a meager yield and an abundant one come spring. Depending on the weather, of course. A good snow pack would be a mighty boon. But she had to admit that things were working out much better than she had ever imagined. She gulped the last tepid splash from her cup. It was time to put some eggs and flapjacks on the griddle for the hungry crew.

When the triangle finally clanged, they all assembled in the kitchen, where the breakfast nook wall had been removed and a new trestle table erected to accommodate them all in one shift. They left their shoes on the mud porch without having to be reminded. A wood fire crackled comfortably in the Wedgewood cookstove. Crissy started a pot of hot coffee around and set a special cup of honey chamomile tea at Shadrack's elbow. The work crew. Dirt farmers all. And, like an adopted family, Crissy was growing fond of them all.

The chair at the head of the table stood empty. "Where's Michal," Katie asked brightly, shaking her chestnut hair as she waited for the plate of scrambled eggs to make its rounds.

"Out looking for parts for the tractor," Crissy replied.

Shadrack looked up. "Wha's he need?"

"A shaft bracket. For the three-point."

"Uh. It war a bit wore down."

"My dad might have something—"

"That's where he headed first thing." Crissy passed the tray of bacon. "If he can't find something there, he'll have to drive over to Alturas."

"I can run the errand for him," Katie volunteered. "I've got mom's car. And my own travel visa."

They all heard a diesel engine growl to a stop outside. Everyone turned to the kitchen windows. Elan Groves and Horace Kearns were climbing down from Kearns' big one-ton pickup. They slammed the doors and crunched toward the house. Crissy made them remove their shoes before she let them inside. "Did Michal catch you?" she asked Elan.

"Couldn't help him. Sorry. He's headed on in to Alturas."

"Would either of you like some breakfast?"

"Jus' a cuppa coffee, if y'got any," Kearns said.

"I'm good," Elan replied.

Shadrack grinned his gap-toothed grin as they padded into the kitchen. "Howdy Elan, Horace."

"Morning, Shadrack," Kearns said.

"You were up early this morning," Elan said to his daughter.

"No school this week," she responded. "Mom said I could take her car."

"What's up?" Shadrack asked.

"Morning Shadrack," Elan said, turning to him. "Horace here heard something this morning that we thought you should hear."

Everyone stared at him in silence. Shadrack nodded encouragement.

"I'll let Horace update you."

Kearns cleared his throat, paused a moment for emphasis, then announced, "The State of California jus' might be comin' back."

"Coming *back*?" Crissy asked.

"Yessum."

"Where'd you hear *that*?"

"Gunter up at the tire shop. He heard it from one of them long-haul truckers. Rupert Holmsworthy, I think it was. You know him? No? Drives from outta Nevada somewheres near Winnemucca." Kearns coughed and spat into a tissue. "Anyhow, Rupert told him *he* heard it up at the checkpoint while they was doin' a inspection on his rig. They told him he needed new front tires or they weren't a'gonna let him come back in."

Everyone turned to Shadrack, who considered for a moment before asking, "He say when?"

"Perty soon now, I hear. Me'be the beginnin'a the year."

"We thought you better know right away," Elan added.

Shadrack thought some more, then pushed his plate away. "Kin 'ey *do* that?"

Elan shrugged. "Guess they can do whatever they damned well please. Probably you're gonna want to convene the council."

Rodriguez broke his silence for the first time. "*Bueno.* Prob'ly gonna need some more guns *tambien.*"

OUTSIDE THE SENIOR CENTER Riley Suggs, the newly-appointed public works director, and his crew of volunteers were busy epoxying a ceremonial bronze plaque to a flat slab of basalt. Horace Kearns' cousin Delbert had brought the rock down in the dump truck, snow plow raised, from an outcropping above Teddy Tollitson's ranch. Teddy had loaded it himself with the front-end bucket on his tractor. The volunteers had managed to dig a narrow trench and erect it without anybody getting seriously hurt. Now they all stood leaning on their shovels and lining bars admiring their work.

The plaque had been cast in a greensand mold by Elroy Jackson's daughter Belinda down at his blacksmith shop in Eagleville. She had lived for a while in an artist community over in Paisley, Oregon, before that state too had disappeared from the face of the earth. Belinda beamed with pride to see her new creation being placed on permanent historic display. No one mentioned to her that the tablet looked a little lopsided and insignificant against the massive black slab of gnarled stone. Or that she had misspelled the word "skirmish". The plaque commemorated the now-famous "Skermish at Cedarville" where local armed minutemen had fought off and defeated agents of an invading foreign army to save their appointed leader from capture. And everybody seemed to be feeling pretty damned good about it all.

The meeting convened inside with a robust attendance of ministers, advisors, citizens, and curious bystanders from the ceremony outside. Shadrack sat at the center of the extended main table like a wizened savior from a comic portrait of the last supper. Horace Kearns handed him a gavel he had borrowed from the high school debate department. Instead of banging it, Shadrack pushed it over in front of Katie Groves, who sat next to him, and waited until the familiar small-town palaver and joking settled down by itself. Finally, when he thought he could be heard, he announced, "We got some important news 'at gotta be took care of ri'chere an' now," and waited until the final few had quieted down.

"Tell'em what y'got, Shadrack," Kearns encouraged.

The room fell silent.

Shadrack cleared his throat. "Well . . . 'pears 'at the State a' California jus' might be a'plannin' t'start back up agin."

"Start back up?" asked Peachy Watkins from the restaurant across the street.

"'At's right."

"When?" she demanded. A rumble of other voices echoed her question.

"Don't rightly know as yet," Shadrack admitted. "But *we* oughta be a'gettin' ready fer it . . . a'fore it comes."

"What ch'all planning' on doin'?" asked Moray Willits.

"Ain't up t'me," Shadrack said. "This here's a democracy . . . an' *you* all gotta make the decision."

"What choices we got?" Leonard Kline wanted to know. "I'm jus' tryin' t'run m'gas mart here in town. Jus' like Peachy at the restaurant. An' Moray over there with the store."

"Well . . . tha's why we gonna wanna hear from y'all. I reckon we kin jus' . . . let'er happen. Let the reborn California jus' grab us back on in. Go back t'the old ways. Or . . . or . . . we kin try doin' somethin' else."

"Like whut?"

"Well . . . for one . . . like try'n t'form us our own state."

A stunned silence, followed by a rising murmur of conversation.

"State of Bristlecone?" Leonard asked.

"Might be," Shadrack nodded. "If'n 'at's the way y'wan' it ta be called."

"How we gonna do *that*?"

"Well . . . I's glad y'aksed. That's why Horace aksed Lawyer Baxter t'come on in an' talk t'ya about it. He's our new Attorney General, case any a'ya forgot."

Wiley Baxter pushed back his chair on cue and stood up with controlled energy, his blue pin-striped three-piece trial suit, now a little worn, still looking sharp from ten feet. His gray hair was neatly trimmed and combed. He always felt more comfortable being free to pace the room when facing a jury. Baxter looked over the throng, taking his time to make eye contact with most of his audience. "First of all . . . I want you to know that they're holding a lot of folks in detention camps over there in California . . . or whatever they want to call themselves now. Holding them against their will." A number of heads nodded. "Just because those folks tried t'speak out against what's going on over there." The nodding spread like a slow contagion. "Their legislature passed something called a *sedition law*, making it a crime to speak out the truth." He paused for the words to sink in. "There's a lot of people over there have never been accounted for." Baxter glanced from face to face. "A whole bunch of folks have just plumb *disappeared*." A rumble of discontent rose, but Baxter raised his hand. "And now . . . and *now* . . . they're planning to make *us* a part of California again. Bring us back into their fold. And force us to kowtow to them under their damned sedition law . . . or else face imprisonment ourselves for speaking the truth."

"No *way!*"

"We don't want no part a'that."

"Amen."

"Now, hold on," Baxter continued, raising his hand again. "There's maybe something we can do." He paused to let them think about it. "Now . . . when California joined up with Oregon and Washington to form the Pacific Coast Nation . . . without affording us an opportunity to *vote* on what they were doing . . . they did more than just cut us free." He shook his head. "They did more than *disrespect* us." He paused for effect, then spoke with a rising oratory. "They *broke the law.* And because they purported to secede from the Union without the consent of the people . . . all their acts were void . . . and everybody who adhered to it vacated their offices . . . and it was an act of revolution against the United States of America . . . and an act of insurrection that left *our* homeland here . . . this beautiful Bristlecone territory we all live in . . . without a state."

He had them riled up and their attention riveted on his lips.

"What kin we do about it?" shouted Elroy Jackson, standing in the back with feet splayed and blacksmith muscles bulging.

Baxter raised both arms to calm them. To keep them under control. "I'll tell you what we can do. We can petition to rejoin the Union as an *independent state.*"

"How do we do that?" Jackson wanted to know.

"Well . . . let's take a look at that. Now that the elected officers of California have disqualified themselves from office, the body to consent to the admission of Bristlecone to the Union is this here legislative body. You and me. The government of Bristlecone. *Us!* We'll have to hold an election first, of course. But that won't take long. Half the voters of the territory are already here in this room today. And then when *we* have the consent of the people . . . when *we* have complied with the law . . . then *we* can appeal directly to Congress for statehood. And if Congress isn't in session, or if they won't hear us, we can appeal directly to the President. Just like they did back in 1861 . . . during the Civil War . . . when West Virginia broke off from the Confederate State of Virginia."

"Who *is* the President now?" Scooter Thompson asked from the front row. "Is it still that . . . what's's name?" Several tentative guesses were called out, but no one knew for sure anymore.

"We can cross that bridge when we get to it," Baxter told them and sat down.

"Let's do it *now!*" Jackson called out. "Before them clowns over in California try to pull us back in with another land grab."

"What about us jus' a'joinin' up with Nevada?" Moray Willits countered. "Seems like that'd be a whole lot better fer business."

Peachy Watkins jumped up from the front row. "I for one don't by God wanna be no part of no *Nevada*," she cackled. "Not with all their gamblin' an' whorin' an' atom bomb testin'."

And so the flood gates sprung open for a good old-fashioned American hometown debate. The speakers were passionate in their views. No one had a very good grasp of the underlying facts. And everybody seemed to want to be heard first. Shadrack just leaned back and let them go at it. A shoving scuffle started to break out between Moray Willits and Elroy Jackson, but Varner Woolsey, the newly appointed Police Chief and Minister of Defense, fired a single bullet into the floorboards of the meeting hall and the belligerents all settled down to a noisy, enthusiastic, nonviolent discussion.

Moray Willits was finishing a long rant about the need for a stable and visitor-friendly business climate when he sensed the latticed window panes vibrating from a powerful engine outside. He turned his head to glance out front. "Well I'll be damned," he said. "Ain't seen one a those for a coon's age."

"What is it, Moray?"

"Damned if it ain't the CHP."

People flocked to the window where they saw a California Highway Patrol cruiser double-parked behind the diagonal vehicles at the curb, engine thrumming and vapor swirling out of its tailpipe. Two officers sat as immobile as mannequins inside. A moment later a dirty old Modoc County Sheriff's unit swung around them and pulled into the red zone by the fire hydrant. A big, stoop-shouldered deputy with hangdog jowls climbed out and lumbered over to shake hands with Riley Suggs, who had been buffing up the new bronze plaque. Suggs pointed inside.

"Why that's Drummond Buck," announced Chief Woolsey. "Dang! Haven't seen him since we worked together at the jail. Surprised he ain't retired by now."

"What's he want?" someone asked.

"Guess we're gonna find out," Woolsey responded. "Here he comes." The new Chief pressed his way to the front door. "Drum," he said as he greeted the deputy, "it's sure been a long time. Come on in. Doin' civil process now? I thought you plumb retired."

"I did. But they called me back. Lost a lot of good deputies during the shutdown, and now they're scramblin' t'hire some of us back. Got myself a nice signing bonus," he grinned. "Say, it smells like gunpowder in here. You folks havin' a celebration?"

"Naw, just a little housekeeping I took care of. What brings you out here to Bristlecone?"

"Bristlecone?"

"That's what we call this valley territory now that you boys in California dumped us. And, for your information, I've been appointed Chief of Police and Minister of Defense. Got a new uniform on order."

"Well, I guess I better be congratulatin' you right now, 'cause it ain't gonna last. And ya might wanna think about canceling that uniform order."

"Now why's that, Drum?"

Buck pulled a sheet of paper out of his satchel. "The Sheriff's Department'll be takin' over law enforcement again here in the valley. An' you'll be in California again. I've been sent out to serve and post this notice about it."

The mood around them changed from somber to hostile as he spoke.

"What?" the deputy asked. "I say something wrong?"

Wiley Baxter inserted himself between the two lawmen. "When is this takeover supposed to happen?" he asked genially.

"Who're you?"

"Name's Baxter. Wiley Baxter. I serve as Attorney General of Bristlecone. You can deliver that notice to me. Thank you. Now, when is this supposed to happen?"

"Well," Buck said uncomfortably, pointing to the sheet, "it says there, January first. Start a'the new year."

"That's in just over two days."

"Yup."

"I see," said Baxter, still cordial, still smiling. "There's only one problem."

"Oh?"

"And it's a big one."

"What's that?"

"Nobody asked *us* about it. And two days won't give us time to call an election."

Buck's eyes narrowed. "Now, we ain't gonna have no trouble from you, are we?" he asked as if addressing an unruly child.

A titter of amusement spread through the room.

Baxter took a breath, then continued in an even tone. "We're not a part of California. Am I right?"

"Not right now."

"California doesn't exist."

Buck nodded.

"Then you have no authority here, my friend. Nor do those CHP officers outside. California law does not apply here. Modoc ordinances do not apply. You can't even ticket a drunken jaywalker here." He smiled pleasantly and offered the deputy his hand. "Nonetheless, on behalf of the independent jurisdiction of Bristlecone, I am happy to receive your notice."

"*Jeeze!* An' I thought you folks were gonna be happy as pigs in mud t'have us take ya back in."

Chief Woolsey walked the Modoc County deputy back to his car trying to soothe his ruffled feathers. "Ya gotta see it from their point a' view, Drum. California jus' outright fucked 'em good an' then dumped 'em without s'much as a g'bye kiss. They're still mad's swarmin' hornets 'bout it all. But y'give 'em a little time'n you an' me're probably gonna be back a'workin' right side by side again." Both men ignored the haughty CHP escort and ended up shaking hands and pounding each other on the back in fraternal good will.

Inside Attorney General Baxter was trying to convince the commission that they needed to send a petition to Congress and the President *right now*, before California accomplished their land grab coup. "I can draft something up by tomorrow morning, if you pass a motion to authorize Shadrack here and the secretary to sign it."

"Who's the secretary?" Kearns stepped in. "We never appointed one."

"I don't know. How about Katie Groves? She seems to be doing it anyhow."

"I don't know. Katie, you willin'?"

"What? You want me to take the minutes, just because I'm the only female up here?" She shrugged. "I guess somebody has to do it."

"Better make that 'Bristlecone Territory *Clerk*'," Baxter corrected.

Katie shrugged. "Whatever."

"Well . . . is there a motion then?"

"About what?" Hiram Atwater asked from the back.

"*Hell's bells!* About Katie bein' elected secretary."

"Clerk," Shadrack corrected.

"Oh."

Silence, then Peachy Watkins spoke up, "I move t'appoint her. She'll do a fine job."

"Any more talkin'?" asked Shadrack.

Nobody had anything else to say.

"Alright. Everybody in favor, say 'Aye.'"

Most people mumbled, "Aye."

"Nays?"

No one said anything.

"The ayes've got'er," pronounced Shadrack. "Katie's our new clerk. Welcome aboard, young lady."

Kearns looked over at Baxter. "Now . . . we gotta have a motion about that other thing . . . how do ya wanna put it?"

"Well . . . two things, actually." He turned to address Shadrack. "I think we need a motion to petition for statehood right away . . . to both the Congress and the President . . . and we need to call for an election of the people to ratify it all."

Moray Willits was the first one to his feet.

"Moray?" Shadrack said.

"The voters don't know all the upshots a' this thing. An' I'm not so sure we ain't a'gettin' ahead a' ourselves here. What's t'hurt in waitin' an' seein' how things play out by 'emselves a'fore we all go jumpin' offa the cliff."

"Time is of the essence," Baxter reminded him. "If we don't act now, we may lose our standing to petition. We can always rescind it later."

"I know . . . .I know . . . but still . . . how're we gonna run our businesses here without the backin' a' the State a' California?"

"Good question. But we can talk about that as a part of the voting process."

Baxter himself made the motions, which were seconded by Elan Groves. Both passed on strong voice votes, but not unanimously.

Elan Groves cleared his throat. "How are we going to send these petitions off to Washington? There's no time for the mail to get through. Not in two days. And the Internet is still down for all practical purposes. Maybe we could fax them, but the phone lines and cells towers are not what you'd call reliable. And they're censored anyway. This is the sort of thing that would be noticed and blocked, is my guess. So . . . assuming you can get everything drafted and signed by tomorrow morning, how do you propose to get this petition out?"

Wiley Baxter sucked in his breath. He hadn't thought about that. Slowly he shook his head, thinking. "Anybody got a CB radio?"

"I got one," Honus Cribs offered, "but it won't do no good. They got the signals all scrambled perty much all 'a the time."

Katie Grove's hand shot up.

"Katie," Shadrack called on her, "you got a idea?"

"Satellite phone," she said. "We can fax the petitions in over a sat phone."

"Problem with that," her father pointed out patiently, "is we don't have access to a satellite phone."

Katie smiled. "I think I know somebody who can help us out."

PRIVATE FIRST CLASS JEROME DESOTO gazed out at the gray, barren mountain ranges surrounding Holloman Air Force Base like a prison wall. For what seemed like about the hundredth time he was contemplating the pros and cons of going AWOL. To him desertion was just one small step short of suicide, but things had been going from bad to worse since his transfer to this new unit in Alamogordo, New Mexico. His new company had no use for a full-blooded American Indian here, especially one who presumed to have expertise in radio electronics. The notion was laughable. And they already had more radiomen than they could keep busy, so Jerome was tasked with the jobs no one else would do.

Somewhere a telephone rang. A moment later a pit-faced soldier named Ringer slouched out of the com tent and called out to him, "Hey Chief, ya got a phone call." Ringer stared at him insolently, then laughed. "Thought you people used tom-toms. Ya better make it snappy. Y'got latrine duty again today."

Jerome pushed open the canvass flap of the tent and picked up an antique Bakelite handset as the duty officer slipped out to give him some privacy. "Hello?"

"Jerome, it's Katie." A long pause on the line. "Hello? Jerome? Are your there?"

"I'm here."

"I know we haven't talked much lately . . ."

"I wasn't sure I'd be hearing from you again. How are you?"

"I'm good, I guess. I know we have a lot to catch up on, but I need to ask you for another, like, favor. If you're not mad at me or anything, or, you know, if you're still my friend."

Another pause. Then Jerome sighed. "We're still friends. As far as I'm concerned. Things have just gotten . . . depressing here . . . what do you need?"

Katie told him.

TWENTY-FOUR HOURS LATER A DIRTY PLUM-COLORED SEDAN climbed the highway from Cedarville toward the Cedar Pass. Fresh snow clung to the white pines across Cedar Creek and clumps plopped down into the white powdered meadows. The blacktop was already free of snow and dry in all but the shady stretches. But Katie took it slow with her mother's car. In the back seat an exhausted Jerome DeSoto slumped with his eyes closed and head nodding. He was a fugitive now, traveling on forged credentials. His flight in a stolen Army humvee to the sanctuary of Bristlecone had exhausted him. Katie had urged him to take the morning off and sleep a few hours at the farmhouse, but Jerome insisted on being shuttled to the Modoc Electronic parts store in Alturas to find some transistors and a variable capacitor and hardware to jury-rig the purloined sat phone and make it invisible to prying surveillance. Time was running out.

Beside her in the passenger seat rode Shadrack Smithers, the chaperone her father had insisted on, humming a little country ditty to himself. "Sure is perty up 'ere," he said. "An' the mountain air . . . oh my!"

"You're in a cheery mood," Katie smiled. "Seems like you've been cheerful ever since you got back from Kieferville."

"Tha's a fac'," he grinned back at her. "I've found me some peace a'mind back thar, I reckon. Back in Kieferville."

"I'd love to hear about it," she prompted. "That is, if you feel like, you know, sharing."

Shadrack thought about it as the car approached the old ski lift turnoff just below the summit. The canopy had been removed from over the highway, and the checkpoint shed stood abandoned beside the road. Back by the ski lift they caught a glimpse of the gigantic empty tent flapping vacantly in the morning breeze. There were no vehicles anywhere to be seen.

"This war it?" he asked. "The bound'ry 'tween Bristlecone an' . . . an' whatever they a'callin' 'emselves now?"

"The Pacific Coast Nation," Katie replied. "Looks like a ghost town now, doesn't it? Kind of like, you know, a no-man's land . . . no . . . not '*land*' . . . it's more like a no-man's . . . '*time*.' You know, an . . . *interlude*. Lost here between the old Pacific Coast Nation and the new . . . what? . . . the new California? . . . the Bristlecone Nation?"

Shadrack nodded absently, apparently lost in his own thoughts. After a while, as they crested the summit and started down the long, winding slope into the Pitt River Valley, he opened up. "Don' min' a'talkin' t'you 'bout it at all, young lady. Kieferville, 'at is. I reckon I ain't got no secrets left in me no more. No ma'am." He sought out the right words. "Y'see . . . seems t'me like a . . . a *fear* . . . an' . . . an' a *cravin'* . . . yes'am, plain ol' fear an' cravin' . . . 'ey both had a stone cold grip on me . . ."

"That doesn't sound like you, Shadrack," Katie said, surprised. "I can't imagine *you* being afraid of anything."

"Well . . . I reckon I war . . . most a m'whole life long, seems."

"What would you be afraid of? If you don't mind my asking."

He drew a deep breath and sighed. "Mostly . . . jus' . . . a'losin' Tildie. Afeared a' her up an leavin' me, I reckon."

"But why would she want to do that?"

"Guess I never fig'ered I was worthy of 'er. I al'ays fig'ered she deserved better'n me." He thought about it. "An' mos'ly on account a'a secret I was a'keepin' from 'er. Sumpthin' I done a long time gone by . . . afore I ever met 'er." He nodded to himself. "Anyhow, o'er in Kieferville, I done shook off all 'at contrary thinkin'. Now I's at peace . . . mostly." He waited for the next words to come. "Y'see, if'n 'ere be a afterlife . . . well . . . I reckon now . . . I'll meet up with Tildie again thar, bless 'er soul . . . an' she'll know the truth . . . an' it won't trouble her none. An if'n thar *ain't* . . . no afterlife, 'at is . . . well . . . then I fig'er thar ain't nothing much t'trouble m'self 'bout no more. None of it don't matter nohow. Either way, I feel . . . I feel like somethin' bad's been scoured away inside me . . . I feel . . . I reckon I feel free inside . . . fer th'first time in most'a m'life."

Katie waited for more, but after a moment she prompted, "What happened in Kieferville?"

Shadrack told her. About the murder he committed as a young man, and his attempt to confess it to the mustached Sergeant Wiederman at the police station. And how the policeman turned him away. Just didn't want to be bothered with what a hobbling old man might have done nearly half a century ago. And as the highway grade began to flatten and straighten out, he told her about his encounter with Reverend Martin Blythe, and how the good minister had pointed out the error in his thinking. About how the true Christian path runs not through the civil authorities, but directly from a man's heart to God. All he had to do was confess his sin to the Lord, if he ever hoped to see Tildie again. Assuming there *was* an afterlife. And he had confessed and opened his heart. The police were not a part of it at all.

Katie turned left where the road t-boned into Highway 395 and followed the North Fork south past the old California agriculture inspection station, which stood unused and empty. "Looks like another ghost town," she smiled. "Another no-man's land."

Shadrack grinned. "'Nother 'no-man's *time*,' ya mean, don'cha, young lady?"

"So," Katie smiled as they slowed at the outskirts of Alturas, "So . . . in Kieferville you finally found yourself."

Shadrack thought about it. "Reckon 's'more like I got *rid* 'a myself thar."

ON THE FIRST DAY OF JANUARY two older gentlemen, neither of whom had bothered to stay up and ring in the New Year, were out walking their dogs as the sun rose. Nothing about the valley seemed to have changed. Meadowlarks warbled and trilled from the tall sagebrush as they always had. The alkali playa mirrored back the faded sunlight from its usual butterscotch-colored scrim of rainwater. White pine and juniper still scented the Cedar Creek canyon trail. Distant humps of black cattle grazed as always on the vetch and rye grass beneath the pewter cast of winter sky. And the crisp air itself, punctuated by plumes of steam from artesian hot water vents across the valley, still exuded that familiar Great Basin ambiance.

But the two men had been told that, while they slept, something would change in the invisible realm of human politics. Now they felt it in their bones. The State of California, they felt, had winked back into existence. As had the States of Washington and Oregon. All with the stroke of a pen in some far-off chamber of secrets. As if by magic, the pads of the dogs' feet and the soles of the mens' boots now trod the soil and grass and concrete sidewalks once again claimed by the State of California. The Pacific Coast Nation was over and done with. Dead. Gone. A bad dream. A trick of some banished conjurer. It had all been a complex political swindle of some devious sort, the men speculated as their dogs watered opposite sides of the same fire hydrant, to achieve something that was never explained to the peons who lacked proper security clearance, which included everybody in the Surprise Valley. And they were not particularly happy about it.

"They give us two days' notice," grumbled Honus Cribs, as he tried to decide for the hundredth time which end of his companion's bull-pug was uglier. "What the heck? Elan Groves finally got some money put into our Bristlecone bank account, didn't he?"

"That's what I hear," rejoined Hiram Atwater. "We was jus' a'gettin' our feet on the groun'. An' now it's all been took back."

"Well . . . me'be. Me'be not. They mighta been able to push us *out*, I reckon . . . but I guess they ain't a'gonna be gettin' us *back* so easy without our *say so*."

Hiram uttered an "Amen" to that.

THERE HAD BEEN A GLITCH. The State of California had *not* winked back into existence as planned. And the Pacific Coast Nation still hovered like a patient on life support. The checksum algorithm on the mainframe in Langley, Virginia, had not matched the algorithms running simultaneously on computers in Berkeley and Portland and Seattle. It took technicians nearly four hours to track down the source of the problem. The glitch appeared to be partly technical and partly political, but the political part was cloaked in impenetrable security, making it nearly impossible to determine whether the error arose from the machine algorithms or from human thinking.

SHADRACK WAS JUST PULLING ON his mud boots early New Year's morning when the telephone rang at the farmhouse. Crissy answered it, and Shadrack figured it was none of his never-mind, so he unlatched the back door and began squishing out toward the garden plot.

But Crissy summoned him back. "Phone call for you, Shadrack!"

"Fer me?" he called.

"Yeah."

"Who is it?"

"Someone calling himself 'the Ambassador'."

"The who?"

"The Ambassador."

"Who's 'at?"

"I don't know. But he sounds important. I think you better take it."

So Shadrack grumbled and limped back to the house, tugged off his boots, and picked up the phone in the kitchen. "'Lo?"

"Mr. Shadrack Smithers?"

"Jus' 'Shadrack'."

The voice was deep and mellifluous. Calm and commanding.

Shadrack pictured a rotund Orson Wells mouthing the round vowels and biting off crisp syllables. The voice demanded a face-to-face meeting with Shadrack. As soon as possible. Shadrack suggested a public session at the Senior Center. He preferred to convene the entire convention. But the Ambassador said no. He insisted that their first meeting be private. Shadrack could bring members of his staff. But no more than four representatives from each side. It was more an ultimatum than a conversation.

Katie arrived just as Shadrack had returned to his hoeing. Crissy briefed her about the phone call. "What did he, like, do?" Katie asked.

"Just went on out, back to hoeing."

Katie tugged on her own mud boots, threaded her chestnut pony tail through the back of her Surprise Valley Hornets cap, and slogged out to confront him in the vegetable patch. She asked Shadrack about the details of the phone call, which he gave her.

"Did you, like, call anyone yet?"

"Nope."

"Why not?"

"Didn't much like the fella's attitude." He considered for a moment. "Ya think I shoudda?"

"Of course! This could be important." She fumbled her cell phone out of her jacket pocket. "I'll call Dad and ask him to get hold of two other people. Like, get them over here. This Ambassador fellow said you could have four?"

"'At's whut 'e said."

"Well then . . . it's you and dad . . . and how about Wiley Baxter?"

"Wiley'd be fine."

"And . . . and . . . Horace Kearns?"

"Him too. I like Horace."

"Okay. Good. And after that, I want to take you out and, you know, get you cleaned up. Is that okay with you?"

"Well . . . I reckon . . . but whut 'bout these weeds?"

"They can wait until tomorrow."

The parties met shortly after noon at Shadrack's farmhouse. A caravan of vehicles drove down the long muddy driveway and parked in formation on the rutted grass. Armed men in State Police uniforms entered the structure first and inspected every room, then waited outside on the veranda while the principals filed into the kitchen. First came the Homeland Security Liaison, then Senior Legal Counsel, and finally the Deputy of Public Information, who screwed a high definition camera onto a tripod and stationed it in the farthest corner. Shadrack shook each hand and promptly forgot their names and titles. When the forum had been inspected a second time by staff, the Ambassador himself finally entered. He was an average-sized young man, perhaps in his mid-thirties, with a round face and round wire rim glasses, dark trimmed hair, and a thin black moustache. Younger and slighter than his voice had promised on the telephone. He wore spit-shined black dress shoes and a black military trench coat, which he declined to remove, suggesting the brevity he anticipated for the meeting. The Ambassador did not smile, nor speak, nor offer his hand. They all settled in silently across the trestle table, the teams of four facing each other from opposite sides.

The Ambassador came right to the point. "We've got a problem," he projected in his deep, honeyed tones.

"What kinda problem?" Shadrack asked. He was about as spiffed up as he could be, with a fresh haircut, a trimmed beard, and a clean pair of overalls. Katie had hustled him into the barbershop in town and then over to the Hot Springs for a free bath in the new Emperor Room.

"Homeland Security won't approve the reestablishment of the State of California until your petitions have been resolved."

"Our petitions?" Shadrack asked as if he didn't know.

"Your petitions to Congress," the Ambassador replied irritably, "and to the President. Your petitions asking to establish Bristlecone as an independent State of the Union."

"Oh, them," Shadrack smiled. "Has the boys in Congress took a look at thars?"

"I'm not at liberty to discuss that, sir."

"Well now, how 'bout the Pres'dent hisself?"

"I can't discuss that either."

"But'r they considerin' a'grantin' 'em then, or whut?"

The Ambassador shook his head. "I can't discuss any of that with you. National security."

"Oh . . . well . . . what're ya plannin' on talkin' t'us 'bout, then?

You's the one a'wantin' this here palaver."

"We want you to withdraw the petitions, sir."

"With*draw* 'em? *Both* 'a 'em?"

"Both of them."

Shadrack pursed his lips, then surveyed carefully from face to face of the support staff on his side of the table. Attorney General Wiley Baxter nodded. Minister of Finance Elan Groves nodded. Horace Kearns coughed, spat into a tissue, and nodded. Finally Katie Groves, who sat at the end of the table recording the proceedings, looked up from her notes, returned his glance with a bright smile, and nodded for him to go on as they had planned.

"Well . . .," Shadrack responded, ". . . don't seem like we kin do that 'til the folks has voted. We got us an election called fer—"

"Next Wednesday," the Ambassador interrupted. "We know that. But this can't wait that long."

"She cain't, huh?" Shadrack leaned back in his chair and scratched where his newly-trimmed whiskers prickled his neck. "Well . . . I guess you was right t'begin with."

"Right? In what way was I right?"

"I reckon y'got yer'self a problem."

The Ambassador leaned back and regarded Shadrack with intense pale blue eyes. "Listen, Mr. Smithers—"

"Shadrack."

"— we are not playing games here. We have the resources, *and* the authority, to turn this entire valley into one big detention camp, and not one of your citizens . . . not one of those *voters* you are talking about . . . not one of them is going to like it a bit."

"But," Shadrack told him, "y'ain't a'gonna do that."

"Why not?"

"'Cause . . . y'a'ready wouldda done it 'afore now." Shadrack showed him his gap-toothed grin. "Y'come here t'palaver, is what y'done. So . . . let's us palaver."

The Ambassador's gaze wavered. He looked down at his hands. He seemed to be contemplating a hidden agenda.

"So," Shadrack pressed, "wha'cha got t'offer us?"

Without so much as a glance toward his retinue, the Ambassador made up his mind. He leaned forward and leveraged his elbows firmly on the table. "What do you want?"

"Whadda *we* want?"

"Yes. Short of statehood."

"Well, I's mighty pleased y'aksed. Yessir. Mighty pleased. 'Cause Elan here, our Financial Minister, an' Wiley Baxter, our Attorney General, they done worked up a little list a ideas 'at jus' might do the trick. Yessir. Elan, why'n'cha tell 'im wha'cha got in min'."

Elan, who did not share Shadrack's comfort in the presence of the Ambassador, cleared his throat nervously. "Well, first of all we would like to receive all the taxes collected by the state and the county before—"

"How much?"

"Well, there's the real estate tax . . ." Elan consulted the packet of papers on the table in front of him ". . . in the amount of—"

"Total," the Ambassador snapped.

"I've got it all here on these spreadsheets." Elan held them out. "The real estate—"

"Total," the Ambassador interrupted again. "*All* taxes."

Elan flipped to the back page. "Don't you want a breakdown—"

"Total. How much?"

"It's . . . I've calculated . . . looks like . . . two million, seven-hundred—"

"We'll give you three million. What else?"

"Well . . . we would like a guaranty of receiving taxes accruing in the—"

"How much?"

"I . . . haven't calculated the exact—"

"Let's make it four million a year for five years and five million a year for the five years following that. What else?"

And so it went. Each of Elan's monetary demands was met or exceeded without debate. It appeared that he could have demanded anything. "Well . . . of course . . . we'll want it all in writing before—"

"The agreement's already being prepared."

"And probably," Elan continued, "some sort of . . . of earnest money to seal—"

"It's already in the contract. Anything else? No?"

"Now just a blasted minute!" Wiley Baxter barged to his feet, his chair tumbling over behind him. "Who do you think you are, trying to buy us off? Push us around?"

The Ambassador turned a cold eye on him. "And you are?"

"Baxter. Wiley Baxter."

"Ah, yes. The so-called Attorney General of this rogue state."

"No more rogue than *you*, my friend. You never bothered to tell us what you were the ambassador *of*. What's you're authority here? Just who do you represent, anyway?"

The Ambassador met his eyes calmly. "Sit down, Mr. Baxter. If you have issues you would like to address, please set them forth is a civilized manner."

"Damn right I do!" Baxter remained standing, his face flushed. "And I can think of three big ones right now. First off, I want to know who the hell you and your henchmen represent, and second—"

"We represent interests that cannot be disclosed at this—"

"Just hold on!" Baxter raised his voice. "I'm not finished yet. Second, we are not going to enter into any agreement with you, whoever you represent, without holding an election first . . . or at least airing it out at an open and public forum—"

"I'm afraid that's not—"

"*Hold on*, I said! I'm not done! You had your turn. Now I'll have mine." He was hyperventilating, and paused for a deep breath to compose himself. "My third demand . . . *our* third demand . . . and this is the most important one . . . and non-negotiable . . . and probably a deal breaker . . . is that our citizens *will not* be subject to your goddamned sedition laws."

The Ambassador flicked his eyes toward the Public Information Deputy and drew a quick slash across his throat. The deputy arose quietly, switched off the camera, and began disassembling it.

"We demand that our citizens be free from those laws," Baxter continued. "No one here will be going to jail for speaking the truth. We demand total and permanent immunity. From sedition and any other imagined crimes or prosecutions originating outside our borders. Bristlecone is, and always will be, a sovereign state. A sanctuary. Do you understand?"

The Ambassador sat in silence for a long moment, then stood

abruptly, scraping back his chair and making a show of studying his wristwatch in exaggerated surprise. He turned to the advisors on his side of the table. "Gentlemen—"

"Who the hell decides anyway," Baxter persisted, "what speech is *permitted* and what speech amounts to *sedition*?"

"Gentlemen," the Ambassador repeated, "I see we have overstayed our schedule here. I know your time is valuable and I promised you this would not take more than," he glance again at his watch, "a half hour. I am declaring this meeting is now adjourned, and I excuse you and thank you for participating." He leaned toward the stern-faced Senior Legal Counsel and said quietly, "Hugh, you'll see that the agreement is prepared as discussed and brought back here for signature as soon as possible?"

"Of course," Hugh nodded.

"Excellent! Excellent." One by one he escorted the members of his party to the kitchen door like old lodge brothers, with a hand on each shoulder and a muttered quip of valediction. When they had all stepped through, the Ambassador turned back and spoke in his mellow, rolling syllables, "Mr. Smithers, if you and your staff will be patient enough to remain where you are just a little longer, I will return in a few minutes to continue our fascinating discussion." He pulled the door shut behind him.

"Well don't that just beat all!" Horace Kearns said. "What the heck was *that* all about?"

"What I think—" Elan began.

"Shh," Baxter whispered, shaking his head and holding a finger to his lips. "Might be bugged." He pointed to the Ambassador's briefcase still resting on the corner of the table. "He'll be back."

Soon they saw movement outside the windows. State police were escorting the Ambassador's support staff to their vehicles frozen into the rutted lawn. One by one the cars started, then threaded up the narrow driveway until all that remained was a single black Chevy sedan.

WITH A SINGLE BRISK KNOCK the Ambassador pushed open the kitchen door and bustled to his place at the table. He shook off his long black trench coat, folded it carefully over the back of the chair next to him, and dabbed perspiration from his forehead with a handkerchief. Without the coat, he appeared shrunken in his gray woolen sweater and rust-colored corduroy trousers, except for his belly, which mimicked the rounded contours of his face and eyeglasses. He looked more like a young college professor than a high-powered diplomat. But behind his silver-rimmed glasses his eyes had not lost their intensity. He turned to Wiley Baxter and motioned for him to be seated. "The algorithms," he said.

"The what?" Baxter barked.

"The algorithms," he repeated.

"What are you talking about?" the lawyer demanded as he eased into his chair.

"You *asked* me: who determines what statements amount to sedition?"

"I know I did."

"Well . . . that's it. That's the thing. It's not really a *who*. It's a *what*." He paused to let the concept percolate. "Now, before we proceed any further, let me first ask everyone to turn off their cell phones. And any other recording devices in the room. Are there any others?"

"Jus' Katie," Shadrack quipped. "Only she ain't no device, I reckon. An' she'll be a'stayin' put."

The Ambassador glanced at her, nodded, then returned to Baxter. "The algorithms are running on super-fast quantum-entangled computers. They are the only processors with the capacity to decide instantaneously what speech is permitted and what speech is forbidden. They alone can crunch all the necessary data in so little time. How else *could* it be done?"

"Who *are* you?" Baxter stammered.

"Joshu Hardcastle's my name." He reached across the table toward Baxter, held out his open palm, and smiled a smile that made him look like an entirely different person. A far gentler one. "And I believe we may have an understanding after all, Mr. Baxter."

Baxter tentatively gripped the proffered hand. "And who did you say you represent?"

"Ah . . . we'll get to that a little later."

Elan Groves stepped in. "So . . . what kind of data are you talking about here, Mr. Hardcastle?"

"*All* of it. Mountains of it. Oceans of it. Judicial decisions. *All* judicial decisions ever recorded. Legislative history. *All* legislative history. Of every kind. All digitized libraries. NSA data and intercepts of almost every phone call made in the last ten years. Internet records. *All* internet records. Facebook. YouTube. Microsoft. Google. Amazon. Preferences and profiles. Location and travel plans. All footprints of every kind of everyone on the entire internet."

"*Jesus!*" Baxter breathed.

"Only then can a statistically reliable assessment be made as to the *intent* of the words a particular person has spoken."

"That's plum crazy!"

"Yes. It is."

Elan spoke up, "That's too much for a computer to take into account in a hundred years."

"Maybe it once was, Mr. Groves. Not now. Not with quantum computers. All of it . . . *all* of it . . . can be indexed and crunched in a matter of seconds. Milliseconds. Computed to an accuracy of five decimal places."

"That's crazy!" Baxter repeated.

"Isn't it?"

"Whatever happened to the judge and a jury?"

"Not nearly as reliable. They can get it wrong. Often do, in fact. But not the quantum algorithms."

A long stunned silence echoed off the Victorian woodwork as this brave new world reverberated around them. Finally Shadrack cleared his throat. "Jus' tell me this here one thing, Josh . . . jus' why're you *here*?"

Joshu smiled. "Why are *you* here, Mr. Smithers?"

"Shadrack," he corrected, then considered the question carefully, waggling his head slowly, before replying with a grin, "'S complicated, I reckon."

"I couldn't have said it better, Shadrack."

"Do you mean to tell us," Horace Kearns coughed, spitting into a tissue, "that this whole mess we're in is bein' controlled by *robots*?"

"Not robots, Mr. Kearns. We're talking about data processing machines with constantly upgrading algorithms. Artificial intelligence. The algorithms are what you'd call the programs. The software. The apps. They don't walk around and zap you with ray guns."

"But," Elan asked, "aren't there people . . . . technicians . . . to control these machines."

"Ah," said Joshu, settling back in his chair, "now you've pierced to the heart of the matter. Control. Or who is controlling whom. Or what is controlling what. Or whom. I'm sorry to say that those distinctions are no longer clear." He hesitated for a moment to watch their stunned reactions. "Let's go back to your original question by way of example. The crime of sedition. The problem with sedition is *not* ascertaining a person's intent when he has spoken. No. The real problem is determining what intent *should* constitute a criminal act. And I'm afraid the algorithms have gotten into that business now too."

"Wait a minute," Wiley Baxter interjected. "Are you telling me that the politicians have all bought into this craziness? And the courts, too?"

"That's a long and complicated story, Mr. Baxter. The short answer is, nobody really knows at this time. But hopefully we can get a look inside some of those algorithms and sort it out as we work together here in Bristlecone."

A long silence ensued, while the echoes of the words "we" and "Bristlecone" jittered irreconcilably. One by one his advisors turned to Shadrack for direction. The old man shifted his painful hip and finally spoke up, "First thing y'tol' us, Josh, was y'wanted us t'drop our petitions. Am I right?"

"Yes, that's what I said, but—"

"Hol' on. If'n we drop them petitions, seems t'me there won't never be no state a' Bristlecone t'begin with. Just the same ol' state a' California."

"That's right. And *now* I'm asking you *not* to withdraw your petitions. On the contrary. I want to help you perfect them. I want to see them granted. I'm counting on the establishment of the free state of Bristlecone . . . as a sort of . . . a last resort."

"Don't make no sense," muttered Kearns. "None of it."

"Yes it does," Baxter countered. "Sort of, anyway. That first part of this meeting, the part that was videoed, that was all a dog-and-pony show for those officials he brought along with him."

Joshu did not contradict him.

"And that's why he scrambled them outta here as soon as I started talking about sedition and holding an election and conditions they could never agree to."

"They left to prepare the agreement—" Joshu began.

"Now hold on here," Elan said. "What about our money? You promised us nearly fifty-million dollars if we withdrew our petition. Guaranteed. Over ten years. Will we see any of that money if we don't drop the petitions?"

Joshu shifted uncomfortably. "Not likely you'd ever see much of it either way—"

"And now you're saying you *don't* want us to sign the damned agreement. Don't want us to withdraw our petitions."

"That's correct."

"While your friends have preserved their deniability," Baxter added.

Joshu lowered his voice, its oratorical splendor evaporating. "That's one way of characterizing it. These are dangerous times."

"But they're on board?" Baxter asked. "With you, I mean? Your friends? They don't want this thing signed?"

"I . . . I can't speak for them. But, yes, in my opinion most of them share my concerns."

"I don't know," Elan pondered out loud. "I just can't see giving up fifty-million dollars just on this fellow's say-so. The valley could sure use the money."

Katie's hand shot up.

"And I think the people around here would want us to take it," Elan continued. "And they're the voters, after all. They're the ones to decide. We've got to hear what they have to say." He threw up his hands. "This is crazy! We don't know what's going to happen. It's chaos. But a pot of money would make me a lot more comfortable."

"The devil you know, eh, Elan?" Baxter grinned.

"Katie?" Shadrack said. "You got somethin'?"

"Yes." She laid down her pen and gave a little cough. "This agreement they're drafting, it's not going to say anything about the sedition laws, am I right?"

Joshu nodded. "Just about withdrawing your petitions. And the financial terms I discussed with Mr. Groves."

"Don't forget the money, sweetheart" Elan added. "That's the important part."

"Okay," Katie continued, "so . . . like . . . if we sign the agreement and, you know, withdraw the petitions . . . then we'll end up back in California again . . . we'll end up subject to their sedition laws . . . and subject to the control of those data processing machines Mr. Hardcastle told us about. Am I right?"

A mumble of assent rose in confirmation.

"*Oh my god*," she said, "we don't want *that*, do we?   I mean, *totally!* However much money they offer, you know, to pay us off."

"But you're proposing we leave nearly fifty-million dollars on the table," her father admonished. "We *need* that money . . . for roads . . . and salaries . . . and public works—"

"Aw, we'll get it back," Baxter said. "Or some of it at least. Most of it's our money, anyhow. They're holding our tax dollars and trust funds from when they tossed us out."

"Not *that* much."

"Maybe not, but we can . . . we can sue for reparations. For the damages they caused us. And demand payments in lieu of taxes from the federal government. And . . . and . . . we got lots of tricks up our sleeves . . ."

"Not that much," Elan repeated.

They fell to pondering the dilemma.

Joshu broke the silence. "We may have funds available to offset some of your losses. But first I would need to—"

Baxter snapped around. "*We?*" he glared. "Just who the hell *are* you? And who are you working for?"

Joshu lowered his eyes and said nothing.

Shadrack spoke up. "D'y'think the President's a'gonna grant us statehood, Josh? If'n that's what the folks here vote for? Or me'by the Congress?"

Joshu considered how he should break the news. "Frankly," he said gently, "I don't believe there *is* a President anymore. Or a Congress. At least not as the independent institutions you're familiar with. Certainly not with the power to grant your petitions. Most of them haven't been heard from for nearly a year."

"Well . . . who's runnin' the show, then? The robots?"

Joshu smiled. "There are no robots, Shadrack. And I'm not sure who is running the show anymore. My guess is that it's a conglomerate of some sort . . . of mid-level government functionaries . . . both federal and state . . . together with a syndicate of CEOs from the largest corporations . . . and, of course, the data processors . . . both human and quantum. Technicians. Economists. Bankers. The military and Homeland Security play a big role too, but it's mostly classified."

"Nobody elected? Nobody voted for by the people?"

"Some may have been elected, once. But no one seems to be responsible to the voters any longer."

"But . . . but that's un*American*!" Baxter interjected. "Undemocratic."

Joshu nodded. "Well . . . that's the thing. You have to understand the new way of thinking. *Their* way of thinking. Whoever these people in control are . . . assuming there *are* any people in control any longer . . . they no longer believe that democracy is the best way to go. Certainly not in making important decisions. They don't want to allow the votes of the most ignorant and the most uninformed to . . . to dilute . . . to undermine the mathematical precision of the data stream analyses."

"That's unAmerican," Baxter repeated.

"What's the hold up, then?" Shadrack asked. "With us'n? Are we in er out? A'California I mean?"

Joshu shrugged. "I'm not sure. The algorithms have created their own language to talk to each other, and we can't understand what they're saying yet. But they just can't seem to handle these political issues. It's all too soft and mushy. Especially when they have no precedents. No prior data. And no power to extrapolate into the future with confidence. At least not yet." He thought for a moment. "Or else someone's gaming the system. There's no way of knowing at this time." He paused again. "This is just my opinion. I don't know. I'm not a political analyst. I'm a technician. I'm a programmer. A data analyst. And this is unprecedented for me too."

"Well, at least there's food on the table," Shadrack observed. "An' the lights're still a'workin'. An' the toilets a'flushin'. Guess it could be a whole lot worse."

Baxter frowned at him. "But there *are* people in detention camps.

Concentration camps, I'd call them. Thousands. Maybe millions. Disappeared. Unaccounted for. And I doubt that their toilets are flushing so well."

Shadrack's grin faded. "You's right, Wiley. Reckon I was jus' a'thinkin' mighty selfish." He shook his head, but then the grin crept back. "But a'speaken a' toilets, I reckon it's time fer this ol' man t'take a bathroom break. So I's a'callin' recess."

THE MESSENGERS ARRIVED while they were still milling around the coffee pot. The officer in command wore a crisp tan California Highway Patrol uniform with a seven-point badge, silver lieutenant bars on the collar, and a nameplate that read "L MOXON." He was accompanied by a beefier patrolman, similarly uniformed, but without the collar bars, and an elderly gentleman in a pale gray herringbone suit, who carried a briefcase and introduced himself as "the notary". Lieutenant Moxon withdrew four copies of a substantial document from a large manila envelope he carried. "They need all four originals signed and notarized and returned immediately" he said.

Wiley Baxter stepped forward. "I'll take those." He kept one and handed the others around to Shadrack, Elan, and Horace Kearns. "Now, if you fellas will excuse us, we're going into closed session to review and discuss these agreements before we sign anything."

"We're not supposed to let them out of our sight," the lieutenant objected.

"Tough," Baxter replied as he ushered the three visitors out of the kitchen. "You fellows can wait out here. Or on the veranda."

When the door was closed, Elan asked, "Shouldn't Joshu be in on this?"

"Good idea," Baxter replied, beginning to read. "Bring him in through the back door."

"And Katie?" Shadrack suggested.

"Her too. Bring her in the back way with Joshu. Now shush up and let me read this damned thing." Baxter perused the twenty-four page agreement by skimming the standard legalese and boilerplate and studying the unique operational language. It was pretty much as Joshu had said. There were covenants to withdraw their petitions for statehood and commitments from the State of California—which, he noted, was a purported party to the agreement that did not yet exist—to repay the tax and other monies as previously discussed. There were signature lines for Shadrack Smithers, CEO, and Katie Groves, Clerk of the Bristlecone Territory. The attached exhibits contained repayment schedules, federal and state disclaimer forms, a list of penalties for breach of covenant, and a legal description of the Bristlecone Territory. After ten minutes he slapped the document down on the table.

Everyone turned to him and waited.

"Well," Shadrack ventured, "d'ya reckon we oughta sign 'er?"

"We can't sign this without running it by the folks at the convention," Kearns interjected, coughing into his handkerchief. "In an open and public meeting session."

Elan shook his head. "Sounds like we have to sign it today . . . right now . . . or the deal's off." He turned to Joshu. "Isn't that right?"

"That's the way I see it," Joshu agreed.

"Katie?" Shadrack asked, scratching the short bristles on his neck.

"You already know how I feel about it," she said somberly, shaking her ponytail. "Like, no sedition laws."

They all turned back to the lawyer.

"Wiley?" Shadrack prompted.

Baxter stood and made eye contact with each of them, one after another. "I think Horace has got it right. Who do we think we are? We've never been delegated the power to execute a document of this nature and gravity. Certainly not without the prior approval of the voters."

"Or at least the approval of the convention," Elan suggested, then turned to Joshu. "Any chance we could buy ourselves another day? To convene the convention?"

Joshu shook his head. "Not likely."

"What's the big hurry?"

Joshu sighed. "They're running against a clock that's not their own. One that they can't control. Maybe no one can control it anymore. I expect it's now or never. They reestablish California or the chance passes by. They have no time to fool around."

"What'll they do?" Kearns asked. "If we don't sign it?"

Joshu shrugged. "It falls apart. Nobody knows for sure what will happen next. The algorithms have been predicting a period of chaos."

"What do *you* think will happen?"

Joshu thought about it. "I think they'll cut you off. They'll redraw California without you. Right away. This afternoon, I expect. They'll erase the Bristlecone territory from their map. Just like before. Like the Pacific Coast Nation. If you won't sign the agreement, they have no other choice. And they'll reestablish California without you."

"But we *can't* sign it!" Elan grumped. "Wiley says we have no authority."

Joshu shrugged, but said nothing.

"Either way," Shadrack sighed, dangling the draft agreement between two gnarled fingers, "this here 'greement 'pears t'be a dead duck."

"Whadda we do now?" Kearns asked.

"Well," Shadrack considered, "I reckon we better invite them boys a'waitin' out there back in t'join us . . . .and let'em know what's what."

"I shouldn't be here," Joshu said, rising. With his hand on the back door knob, he turned and added, "I think you're doing the right thing." And then he was gone.

Katie led the two CHP officers and the notary into the kitchen from the foyer, where they had bided their time. "We're going to have to have Mr. Wilbert notarize your signatures," Lieutenant Moxon said impatiently. "Have you signed them yet?"

"No we ain't," Shadrack replied. "An' we ain't a'gonna . . . 'til the whole convention's had a good look at'em and tol' us whut they want us t'do. Thas th' bes' we kin do."

Moxon was not pleased. "How soon can you do that?"

"Tomorrow . . . at the soonest, I reckon."

"Too late. You have to sign them today."

"Sorry," Baxter intervened, moving beside Shadrack. "We have no authority to sign anything of this nature without the express prior consent and authorization of the conferees—"

"*Shit!*" Moxon spat. "I *knew* this was going to happen. You people . . . " He shook his head. "Well, give 'em back to me."

Kearns collected three originals and handed them to the lieutenant.

Moxon took the three and said, "I want all four. Where's the fourth one?"

"I'll hold on to mine," Baxter replied. "I'll be presenting copies to the convention tomorrow—"

"My instructions were to bring three signed agreements, or, if you don't sign them, all four unsigned."

Baxter shook his head. "We never agreed to that."

"It's my *orders*," Moxon said, dropping his hand to the side of his service weapon.

Baxter didn't blink. "What're they trying to hide?" he taunted.

The lieutenant unsnapped his holster.

"Katie," Shadrack called out, rising painfully with a long *oomph*, "will ya go on out an' phone Varner Woolsey. Tell 'im we got a s'curity issue." He half-turned to the police officer. "Varner's our Chief a' Police and Min'ster a' Defense." Then to Katie he continued, "Tell 'im we got some out-a-towners . . . fellas with no authority here—"

"Or anywhere else," Baxter added.

"—a'threatenin' us here in our own private home. Have 'im call out the minutemen, would ya . . . an' aks Rodriguez t'bring me m'shotgun while yer at it."

Moxon re-snapped his holster. "We'll see about this," he snarled. He spun and jerked open the door. "We'll fucking *see* about this. And we'll be back. You can fucking count on it." He stormed through the house and out the front door, followed in close step by his partner. The notary, forgotten and swinging his briefcase wildly, had a hard time keeping up and was almost left behind. The patrol car roared to life and spit gravel as it slalomed up the driveway.

Joshu let himself in the back door. "Looks like that went well," he quipped.

"Says 'es's a'comin' back," Shadrack told him.

"I doubt it. What's the point? They've got bigger things to worry about."

"Piss on 'em," Baxter spat with uncharacteristic crudeness. "California doesn't exist. They've got no authority." He slid the fourth agreement into his briefcase. "I guess I better get back to the office and make copies and start handing them around. Before those boys come back . . . just in case they do."

Elan folded up his papers and followed the lawyer out without a word. The room grew somber.

"Guess I better call a meeting of the convention," Kearns said, plucking his Stetson from a wall hook. "How about noon tomorrow?"

"That sounds fine," Shadrack agreed, arching his back to relieve the pain in his hip. "An' thank ya." When he was gone, Shadrack turned to Joshu. "Reckon you'll be a'goin' on back yerself."

"I can't. I've pretty much burned my bridges out there. Do you know of . . . is there an inexpensive motel in town?"

Shadrack scratched his neck. "Why'n't ya jus' stay here with us while we try'n sort this thing out. We still got room in the bunkhouse. An' I's perty sure Crissy won' min'."

WORD CAME LATER THAT EVENING. At 6:21 P.M. Pacific Standard Time the State of California reestablished itself within its historic boundaries, except that the land lying east of the Warner Mountain crest, including the Surprise Valley and Cow Head Slough, was not included within those boundaries. The official map labeled those severed lands simply as "Bristlecone Territory".

THE BUNKHOUSE FELT CROWDED THAT NIGHT. Shadrack and Rodriguez had already established their cots on opposite sides of the old pot-bellied wood stove in the center of the room. Jerome DeSoto, who had joined them two nights ago, had nailed together a wooden pallet and installed a futon on top, which he and Katie brought over from her father's familiar old school bus. That left the newcomer, Joshu Hardcastle, without a bunk. For him Crissy found a squeaky old folding bed with missing casters up in the attic, which they managed to muscle down and set up as close to the stove as the remaining space allowed.

The fire crackled, and the room was dark except for the slender flickers of firelight dancing in patterns on the knotty pine walls from the cracks in the stove's antique cast iron. They lay in their beds, all mismatched, with threadbare quilts and rag-tag blankets or sleeping bags. But the men felt a uniform bond among themselves. They were all fugitives now.

After a long period of quiet, Shadrack spoke softly. "What're yer plans here in Bristlecone, Josh? Ya never did answer me that, I reckon."

The dark silence returned for a long while before Joshu's baritone replied. "Well . . . we were looking for a place of sanctuary ourselves."

"We?" Shadrack murmured.

"My company. And my associates. We saw those vacant buildings in Cedarville. Looks like the town is balanced between . . . developing a future . . . and crumbling into total economic collapse. Am I correct?"

"'S been a'lookin' like that m'whole life," Shadrack chuckled. "A little bit a'both, I reckon. We got us that new gas station up the highway . . . an' . . . an' . . . well, a lotta ol' historic buildings."

"If things go as I'd like, we . . . my associates and I . . . might just bring you some economic development. We're probably going to want to relocate the company here. So we'll need to build a small work campus. And housing."

"Why in tarnation *here*?"

Joshu considered his answer carefully. "For one thing, it's in the shadow of the mountains."

Jerome DeSoto joined in with his sotto voice. "The rain shadow?"

"More a matter of the electronic shadow. The information shadow. High mountains to the west and empty desert to the east." Joshu paused. "Then we heard about the Pacific Coast Nation fiasco. Cutting you off. Leaving you without a state. Well . . . that suited our own purposes." He paused again. "And then we heard about your petition to become an entirely new state. A sanctuary territory."

"An' that was it?" Shadrack prodded.

"No. No. That's when I came out here . . . and met you folks in person . . . and *that* was the clincher."

The room fell silent in the comfort of Joshu's praise. No one seemed in any hurry to fall asleep. At least no one was snoring yet. Not even Rodriguez.

After a while Jerome's languid voice drifted through the flickering darkness, "What kind of work does your company do?"

"Storage and transfer of data."

"What protocol do you use?"

"You familiar with computers, are you?"

"A little. Got my associate degree in electronics. Served as a radio specialist in the Guard. I like to . . . fiddle around with that stuff."

"Ever hear of photonic storage?"

"I think I read something about it. What is it?"

Joshu considered how best to describe it. "A new way to move and store enormous quantities of data." Joshu's voice was no longer sleepy. He couldn't mask his enthusiasm. "Our company does nanoengineering. We've helped create the photonic chips necessary for handling the massive data required by quantum processors. The photons travel together with no resistance. On multiple wavelengths. That allows them to read and write multiple bits of data simultaneously. All at the speed of light. Photonic data storage and busing are the breakthrough quantum computing was waiting for."

The darkness fell over them again. Rodriguez began to snore lightly.

Shadrack groaned to his feet and limped to the wood box. He lifted out a single split piece, cranked open the stove door, and pitched it inside. He spoke softly into the darkness, "So . . . so you's the ones 'at made all them computers t'work. Them nasty ones y'was a'tellin' us 'bout."

"We played a part," Joshu admitted.

"An' now . . . an' now y'wanna bring them computers out here. Inta our valley."

Joshu sat up in bed. "It's not what you think. We want to get *away* from the frantic flow of development. We want a safe place to try and evaluate what's happening with this new technology. We want to get a handle on it. With all this unprecedented computing power. Exponentially higher power. We want to find a way to *control* these things we helped proliferate." He paused. "If it's not already too late."

PART FIVE

Bristlecone Territory

Spring

SHADRACK SMITHERS BRACED HIS GIMPY HIP against a spade, shielded his eyes with his slouch hat, and followed the flight of a crow as it flapped past and swooped up to the high gutter on the farmhouse, where four of its brethren were already perched. The newcomer cackled, trying to determine if any of the others had something to eat. When he decided they did not, he gave a caw of disappointment.

"Seems t'be a lotta crows out this year," Shadrack announced to Katie Groves, who was on her hands and knees nearby pulling winter potatoes and rolling them out for Rodriguez to collect later.

Katie glanced up. "More than usual, huh?"

"Lot more."

"Well, nature will bring it back into balance," she said.

"Nature," Shadrack repeated to himself as he mopped his forehead with a tattered red bandanna before replacing his hat. "That what ya think?"

"Sure," replied Katie. "That's what natural selection's all about, isn't it? Survival of the fittest. The rest die off to bring things back into balance. It's a corollary of Darwin's theory."

"You mus' be a'learnin' all tha'char in high school nowadays. Am I right?"

Katie rose to her feet and brushed caked mud off the knees of her overalls. "I wrote a paper on Darwin for science class. Didn't they teach you about Darwin when you were in school?"

"'At war a lotta years ago, young lady. Cain't rightly recollect jus' whut 'ey was a tryin' t'teach me back then. Sure, I heard a that Darwin fella. Tildie knew a lot 'bout 'im. Tol' me a thing'r two, I reckon. But mos'ly I got it sidewise from raisin' m'crops an' tendin' m'animals." Painfully the old man hunkered down on his haunches, which brought some relief to his aching hip. "Whyn't'cha tell me wha'cha learned 'bout 'im."

"Now?"

Shadrack glanced at the sun. "I reckon it's time for a break. How long 's'is a'gonna take, ya fig'er?"

"Well . . . I can give you a quick sketch in about, say, fifteen minutes. Maybe twenty."

Shadrack nodded and straightened up arthritically.

Katie looked around. "Let's go over there and sit in the sun on that old downed cottonwood. Your hip'll feel a lot better."

They reached the fallen log just as Rodriguez was pulling up with his wheelbarrow. Silently the Mexican parked the wagon and scooted up beside Shadrack. The two wriggled in and sat together like kids in the schoolyard bleachers. To both of them Katie gave her impromptu lesson on Darwin and the Beagle and the finches and the turtles and the fundamentals of, and evidence for his theory of natural selection. Neither of her pupils interrupted except for an occasional "Wha'zat?" or "*Por qué?*" to clarify a concept. The lecture stretched on for longer than planned. Until the triangle clanged for lunch.

"Well I'll be danged," Shadrack muttered, easing himself off the big log.

"*Dios mio,*" Rodriguez added. "*Nuestro Señor*, He sure work in *formas misteriosas.*"

Shadrack looked up at the rain gutter, where one of the crows was chattering like a skeleton with false teeth. Eight others now perched with him, watching the humans. "Ya fig'er they got any idear nature's a'gonna weed 'em back some?"

"Well . . . ," Katie straightened her ponytail through the back of her cap, ". . . do *we?*"

"We? *Us*'n?" Shadrack chuckled as the three of them started for the farmhouse. "I don' reckon we do." He grinned his gap-toothed grin. "How many a us'n ya fig'er we got by now?"

"Approaching eight billion," Katie said.

"*Ocho* mil *millones?*" Rodriguez exclaimed.

"That's right."

"*Hay muchas gentes!*"

"And growing faster every year. 'Like a mold on bread,' Mr. Renger says. He's my science teacher. The one I did the paper for."

"So . . . them there rules Mr. Darwin thought up don' seem t'ply to us'n, then?" Shadrack asked.

Katie smiled. "Oh, we're pretty clever, we humans. At least we think we are. And we've made use of science to grow more food than ever before, and medicine to keep people alive. But this planet's just a pebble in the sky. It's resources are limited. And it's all going to catch up to us someday. And then Darwin's rules are going to apply again . . . with a vengeance . . . to every living thing . . . including us humans."

"*Dios mio!*"

"I think it's already happening," Katie added as she took Shadrack's boney elbow to steady him up the porch steps. "But for now, Mr. Renger says it's only the very poor and the disenfranchised that are really feeling the pinch. It's bound to get worse for everybody."

CASTLE KEEP CORPORATION had wasted little time gaining a foothold in the scrabland east of the Bristlecone playas. The company had leased a large parcel, a part of it already subdivided and zoned for development, across the highway from the hot springs resort, six miles east of Cedarville. Abundant cold artesian spring water had already been developed there by the owners of the resort, who owned both properties. The owners had also recently installed an experimental geothermal electric power station with the help of a legacy federal energy grant. The corporation reviewed the initial grid of access roads on the subdivision plat, then surveyed, revised, graded, and graveled new ones. The first modular metal buildings had gone up on concrete foundations in the desert scrub, while manufactured housing was being trucked in daily to serve the growing needs of the company's workforce, most of whom were drawn from company outposts scattered across the country.

Jerome DeSoto removed his white lab coat, hung it from a peg inside, then closed the side door of the communications building. From the shadows of the big satellite dish array overhead, he glanced around nervously, pivoting his thin figure this way and that, his braid of black hair lashing his shoulders. Vigilance had become his watchword since deserting his military unit in New Mexico. Of that he had no regrets. Finally he stepped out into the already hot sun and blazed a shortcut through the soft, blindingly white alkaline playa crust to the administra-tion building, where "Logistics Division" stood in golden letters high on the second story wall. Inside the receptionist smiled and nodded him toward the main corridor. Jerome found Joshu's office by himself and rapped lightly on the metal door.

"Come on in, Jerome," the familiar baritone voice boomed, as if its owner possessed x-ray vision to see through the solid door.

Jerome opened it a crack. "You wanted to see me, Josh?"

"Yes, yes I do." In his pinstriped buttoned down shirt and tweed slacks Joshu Hardcastle rose smiling from behind his desk. He was still amused at how everyone now shortened his name to "Josh," a custom Shadrack had started innocently at their first encounter. But then, everything Shadrack did seemed deceptively innocent. So "Josh" he now was. His smile reinforced the roundness of his face and wire-rimmed glasses. He nodded to a chair. "So . . . how's Katie doing these days?"

Jerome sat stiffly, his long, black braid thumping against his shoulders. "She's fine, I guess. I don't get down to the farmhouse as much as I'd like to."

Joshu reseated himself, leaned back, and drew a consequential breath. "Jerome, I wanted to ask you how you're getting along with your fellow employees out there in communications? Most of them've been with me for a long time, but occasionally it feels like I'm picking up a dark vibe when your name is mentioned. Feels like a bit of resentment maybe. Does that make any sense to you?"

"They're okay. Sometimes dealing with a full-blooded Indian can be disorienting to folks who didn't grow up around here." Jerome resisted rehashing his prior abuses in the military. Joshu already knew those stories. Jerome grinned uncomfortably. "And, really, they've got a whole lot more education than me. All of them. Guess I'd be a little bit resentful, too, in their place. I'm the new kid in town. And they're tolerant. I guess they know you've sort of taken me under your wing."

Joshu pursed his lips as he thought about it. He nodded. "Well, all that education may be their problem. We're out here breaking new ground. And some of it doesn't fit with their expectations. I like the way you're able to think outside the box. And your 'can do' attitude. For example, the way you rewired that sat phone last year . . . with a few dime store parts . . . and managed to render it invisible to the military. That was cutting edge stuff."

Jerome flushed his appreciation.

"So . . . Jerome . . . I'm thinking of bringing you in on a special technical planning team I've put together. You would represent, you know, communications. You'll work directly with me and other team members on some highly classified stuff. You would not be sharing the information with anyone not on the team." He studied Jerome for a long moment. "Do you think you could handle an assignment like that?"

"Whoa. I don't think the folks down in communications would appreciate that very much. Out there in the shed. Do you?"

Joshu leaned forward. " There probably will be some jealousy out there. There always is. But that's not your problem. It's theirs. And I wouldn't worry about it, if I were you." He paused to let the significance sink in. "This may be a career opportunity for you. With a salary increase to boot. To compensate for the increased responsibility. We'll be meeting tomorrow at two o'clock. Right here." Another pause. "Are you on board, Jerome?"

Jerome's face was as unreadable as a stone Buddha. "Do you mind . . . Josh . . . before I give you my answer . . . if I discuss it with Katie?"

"Katie?" Joshu smiled. "Go ahead. As long as she can keep it in confidence."

"I'm sure she can. And how about Shadrack?"

"Smithers? Why Shadrack Smithers?"

"He's been . . . mentoring me . . . on social issues."

"Old Shadrack?" Joshu laughed. "What does he know about . . .?" He leaned back. "Oh. Like Katie perhaps? And her father?" Joshu stroked his chin, then shrugged. "Alright. The old fellow seems harmless enough. Go ahead and talk to him, too. But same conditions. Strict confidentiality." He stood and offered Jerome his hand. "In fact, why don't you take the afternoon off and get your consulting done today. Then, hopefully, we'll see you here tomorrow. Two o'clock."

AN OLD MAN WITH UNKEMPT WHITE HAIR and bristly whiskers bent painfully to take a knee before the gravestone of his deceased wife. He was seeking advice. And consolation. "Well . . . I's back," Shadrack Smithers announced to the mute granite marker. "As you kin see." He shifted the weight off his bad hip by arching his back. "An' I got me some troubles on m'mind . . . an' I thought ya me'be could help me out with 'em."

He fell silent to allow the words to line up properly in his head before he let them come dribbling out of his mouth. The Spring sun was just rising, casting its beams on the canopy of honey locust trees overhead. New buds were already turning to leaves in the orange-yellow glow. The breeze had fallen still and quiet and the morning dew had triggered the desert fragrance of creosote bush.

"First off, I's been a'thinkin' 'bout somethin' Katie Groves was tellin' me. You remember Katie. She was in that *Españole* class a yours a coupla years ago. Anyhow . . . Katie was tellin' me 'bout that Darwin fella you was always so keen on . . . an' all this evolvin' a'goin' on . . . an' how ever'thin's a'ways a'changin' . . . an' evolvin'."

He paused to find new words. "An' now this fella Josh . . . you don' know 'im . . . he's a newcomer . . . anyhow, this fella Josh is bringin' robots to Cedarville. 'Algah-rhythms' he calls 'em. An he's a tellin' us he's on the *good* side. Tryin' t'keep the *bad* ones from takin' over the whole shebang." He paused. "Sounds t'me like this whole ev'lution thing is startin' up all over again. An' what I wanna know is . . . jus' where is it all a'goin'?"

The old man levered himself upright on his good knee and straightened his back. After a moment he dropped down on the other knee. "Problem is, I don' see 'at I *trust* this fella. Josh, I mean. So le'me aks ya this: how do ya know whether yer a'talkin' to an angel or the devil hisself? Kin ya 'splain me that?" He stared at the mute blank stone, not really expecting an answer. But maybe a sign might be in order. He glanced fruitlessly around the empty cemetery before resuming the one-sided conversation. "They jus' got too much *money* they's a'throwin' 'roun' t'make me feel real chummy with any a'em. Josh's bunch. An that's the nut a'it. Josh an' his boys is a'goin' 'round a'buyin' up vacant buildings an' empty lots in town an' a lotta land outside a'town. But the worst a'it is that his dang money is a'buyin' up the fine folks 'round here . . . buyin' their *souls*, seems t'me . . . all over the valley . . . the folks you know . . . folks 'at oughta know better."

A sharp stab in his hip drove Shadrack to his feet again, lurching. He planted his feet, twisted his pelvis, and waggled his spine until the pain receded. Then, without bending again, he continued, "So . . . I don' know whether I oughta make a fuss er . . . er jus' give it up . . . an' go back t'farmin an' forget 'bout it all. I might jus' as well quit a'bein' Emperor, too. But I know it's gotta make ya proud. Least I hope it does. So . . . I jus' wanted t'make sure it'd be a'right with ya."

He turned a slow circle, inspecting the empty burial ground, but even without a sign, he already knew what Tildie would want him to do. He tried to remember if there was anything else he wanted to get off his chest. After a while he turned back to the silent gravestone. "I think Katie's got some doubts, too. Katie Groves. An' so does her friend Jerome. He's an Indian. You don't know 'im, but he's a nice, smart boy. You'd like 'im. Seems he got hisself appointed somehow t'the inside circle a'Josh's bunch. The ones really a'runnin' the show." Shadrack nodded. Drew a deep breath of resolution. "Me'be I'll talk it over with'em both."

SEVERAL DAYS LATER JOSHU HARDCASTLE selected the meeting place. He wanted to avoid a public forum like the Senior Center, and the Castle Keep campus bristled with too many eyes and ears. Competition and intrigue were already beginning to interfere with the work there, especially now that the investors had begun to arrive, and he wished to avoid stirring up more suspicion and rumor among the staff. So he chose the cavernous old Quonset structure across the highway from his office. With the appearance of an abandoned airplane hanger, the building once housed the swimming pool of hot mineral water for the resort. That was long ago, before individual tubs were installed outside each motel room. Now, inside the cavernous structure perpetual twilight engulfed the cracked concrete remnants of the empty pool with an atmosphere dank and heavy. A muffling silence filled the vast empty space.

Through the rusting doors at the south end Jerome and Shadrack had wrestled in a wrought iron table and four matching chairs from the patio outside and placed them beneath the single functioning fluorescent fixture in the ceiling high above. In the process Shadrack managed to tweak something in his low back. Katie and Jerome helped him into one of the uncomfortable metal seats.

"Will that be alright?" she asked.

"Reckon it'll do," Shadrack grunted, shuffling his skinny buttocks.

"I can get you a pillow," she said, but he waved her off. She stood, found Jerome, and slipped her arm around his waist. "Howdy, stranger. Haven't seen you at the farm."

Jerome grinned and pulled her closer. "Josh's got me working on this special project of his. I've been bunking in one of the trailers they brought in. Haven't had a lot of free time lately." He gave her a peck on the forehead.

"Okay, no monkey business now, you two," Shadrack growled amiably. "'I's still chap'ron 'ere, ya un'erstan'.'"

Jerome and Katie grinned and sat beside each other at the iron table. He quietly covered her hand with his own. She did not pull it away. The three of them waiting in silence, as if the vast perpetual gloom had sucked away their voices. Shadrack squirmed against the new pain in his low back. It seemed to be merging with the ache in his hip.

Abruptly the door at the north end of the building screeched open, and through a halo of bright sunlight a dark figure entered and stood beneath the flicker and crackle of a dying fluorescent tube. Katie's mind hallucinated Orpheus returning empty-handed from the bowels of hell, until the distant door clanged shut and the reverberations were swallowed by the gloaming.

"Hello?" Joshu's familiar bassoon echoed across the muffling space. "Anybody here?"

"*Down at this end, Josh,*" Jerome called, rising with his flashlight to guide his employer across the fractured concrete. "You know Katie Groves and Shadrack Smithers."

"Yes, of course I do." The sleeves of Joshu's dress shirt were rolled up to the elbows and the fabric across his belly strained a bit tauter than they recalled. "Don't get up." He reached across and shook their hands warmly. "Where are the others?"

"Ain't no others," Shadrack grunted. "Jus' us four."

"But . . . I thought . . . ," he turned to Jerome, ". . . I thought you said I was meeting with representatives of the community."

"Reckon we's 'bout's represen'tive as yer gonna git," Shadrack grumped.

"Well that's fine, but . . . where's Mr. Baxter? The lawyer?"

"He's in court over in Alturas," Katie explained, "Arguing a case, I think."

"What about Horace Kearns?"

"He's back in the hospital. You know, not doing so well. The thyroid cancer seems to have spread. They're going to try, like, chemo this time."

"Sorry to hear that," Joshu softened his mellifluous tone. "Well then . . . what about . . . your father?"

"He's not a part of this." She tossed her loose chestnut hair. "Not yet, anyway. None of the others are."

Jerome stepped in. "Sir, we decided not to bring anyone else in until we'd had a fair chance to talk some things over with you. We want to respect that confidentiality you swore me to—"

"I hope you haven't been telling them anything you learned in our closed-door conferences—"

"No sir. Nothing that you haven't already discussed yourself in public —"

"—because if you are, I'm just going to have to relieve you of the position of trust I—"

"*Now you just hold on yerself there, Josh!*" Shadrack barked, rising painfully. "We ain't a'got you over here jus' t'argue with ya. An' any idea of pullin' Jerome here off'n yer secret committee is a'goin' jus' the plum wrong direction." He drew a deep breath, then arched his back. "Now, let's jus' sit down 'ere an' palaver a bit. See if there ain't somethin' we kin all agree 'bout."

Joshu glanced back at the distant doorway he had come through, then his shoulders gave the hint of a shrug. "Okay," he said, pulling out the empty chair with a forced a smile. "I've got a few minutes. What've you good folks got on your mind?"

After they had seated themselves around the wrought iron table, Shadrack was the first to reply. "Ev'lution," he said.

Joshu was surprised that the old man even knew the word. He waited for more, then held up his empty palms. "Evolution?"

"Yessir. Ev'lution. You folks fiddlin' 'around with robots and such. Lettin' 'em take over. Thass whut this's all 'bout . . . 'cause thass whut'chur a'workin' on . . . aint it?"

It slowly dawned on Joshu that the Emperor of Bristlecone might be more astute than he seemed. And in a way that drilled right to the core of the matter. He glanced from Jerome to Katie. Then he nodded. "That might be one way of looking at things."

"You's prob'ly a'thinkin'," Shadrack continued, "well, shucks, I ain't a'gotta answer nothin' t'these simple town folk. Ain't that right?"

"Well . . . ah—"

"Jus' answer me this one thing, young fella. Jus' who *do* ya answer to? An' jus' where's all that money y'been a'slinging 'round a'comin' from?"

"Corporate income," Joshu responded reflexively. "And from donors."

"*Donors* is it? An' whut's in it fer them?"

Katie rose and placed a hand on Shadrack's shoulder. "Now Shadrack, play nice. I know you're not feeling well, but we're, like, trying to work this out together, remember?" Then, still standing, she turned to Joshu. "We've talked this over. The three of us." She encompassed Shadrack and Jerome with the sweep of her arm. "And I have to say that I, for one, don't have a clue about what you're doing over there across the highway."

Joshu tipped his head toward Jerome. "Didn't *he* tell you?"

"No! He can't tell us *anything*."

"Because of the confidentiality, sir," Jerome explained. "Besides, beyond the communications protocols, *I* don't even don't know what you're planning on doing in there."

Joshu nodded, apparently satisfied.

"You have to understand," Katie continued, "that *we're*. . . like . . . beggars huddled outside the castle walls. And we're holding out our cups for a few alms."

"Like it's always been," Jerome added, rising beside her.

"And there *you* are, the kings and the princes and the soldiers and the pretty people *inside* the walls who are, you know, shaping the world. Shaping the world *we all have to live in*. And we don't want this to go wrong."

"The same old way it's always gone wrong in the past," Jerome said. "From time immemorial."

"What we want," Katie said, "is . . . we want *fairness* in this new society you're building. Not just *talk* of it. *Real* fairness."

Joshu blinked, removed his wire-rim glasses and began polishing them on a flap of his shirt, but said nothing.

Jerome spoke up. "The Declaration of Independence says, 'All men are created equal . . . endowed with certain inalienable rights'. But those are just words written by a bunch of slave holders and Indian killers. An elitist group of privileged white men."

"The royalty inside the castle walls," Katie said.

Joshu held his tongue. Polished his glasses.

"And don't forget Karl Marx," Jerome continued. "'From each according to his ability, to each according to his needs.' Noble ideals. But never made manifest on this earth. Look what leaders like Stalin and Mao did with those noble words."

Joshu nodded almost imperceptibly, his nearsighted eyes vague and unfocused.

Katie took a step closer. "Throughout history the ruling classes have, like, corrupted everything with greed. From the hunter-gatherers to our current politicians. The Pharaohs. Feudal kings. The Conquistadors' enslavement of indigenies. Socialists. Capitalists. The people inside the castle walls have preached of fairness. Of equality. But what they are really governed by is greed. Maintaining their privileged status. Increasing it." She held Joshu with her bright eyes.

Jerome jumped back into the tag-team match. "When the government last released statistics . . . and this was more than a year ago . . . maybe two . . . the number of homeless people was on the rise . . . and no wonder. More than half the world's wealth was owned by less than one percent of the population."

Katie softened her tone. "Evolution created us this way. I *know* that. Competition molded selfishness into our bones." She drew a deep breath. "And now *you* say you're building a brave new world, founded on fairness and equality. Well . . . those are the very words that have been uttered and betrayed as long as man has walked this earth." She squeezed Shadrack's shoulder. "And that's why Shadrack wants to know where all your money is coming from. He wants to know who you really serve."

Shadrack nodded apologetically, then added, "I jus' wanna know whether we can *trust* ya, Josh. Wha'chure a'doin' here. Y'un'erstan'?"

Joshu was smiling now. He twisted the wires of his glasses over his ears and turned to Katie. "How old are you now, young lady?"

"Oh my god," she snapped, "what does that have to do with anything?"

"Indulge me," he said, still smiling that round smile on his plump round face.

"I'll be . . . seventeen this year."

"Seventeen. Your insights are far beyond your years, Katie. And I only wish my board of directors possessed your perspicacity. They are the ones that need convincing." He glanced at his wrist watch, then let his arm drop. "But you're right. There *is* a fundamental problem. As you have so aptly identified. Resources are not being allocated fairly. And certainly not equally. But then, capitalism is fundamentally not equitable."

"Neither is communism," Jerome added. "Nor socialism."

"You may be right. They are all . . . well, *imagined* realities. Constructs of the mind. Figments. While reality . . . *real* reality . . . is what follows . . . *after* the men in power have attempted to apply those constructs. Or misapply them, I guess I should say. Those in control always get more than their fair share. Always. Right this minute capitalists and socialists and communists around the world are all banking billions in off-shore accounts. Feathering their own nests."

"Hold on," Shadrack said, raising a hand. "Is that what *you're* a'lookin' t'do, Josh?"

"No." Joshu's smile evaporated as he considered a more nuanced approach. There were many in his organization who wanted just that, to feather their nests. The investors. Some of the donors. He wondered how much to keep to himself. How much to reveal. Whether these three could be trusted. Or be used. His gut was telling him they *could* be trusted, at least with the broad outlines. He dropped his eyes, wishing he had more time to think this through. Finally he braced himself, forced a wan smile onto his lips, and spoke in his oratorical voice, "I like Katie's image of castle walls. I'm fond of using it myself. Not much has really changed since mediaeval times, has it? Except maybe the walls themselves. Stone walls are no longer much of a deterrent against nuclear weapons and drones. Nowadays we make our walls out of paper. Contracts and corporate charters and shares of stock." He nodded to himself. "But now, with our reliance on computer-run algorithms, the danger is greater than ever before. And so is the *opportunity*. Now there is a possibility for change. Real change." He paused in thought. "Mankind . . . as a whole . . . still has the fundamental problem you've identified. Resources are not being allocated equally or fairly. Never have been, never will be . . . as long as *humans* control the distribution systems." He paused for effect. "But now there's an alternative."

"You talkin' 'bout 'em there robots a'yourn?" Shadrack asked.

"What you are calling 'robots,' Shadrack, I call 'algorithms.' Remember when I was telling you about algorithms? Way back on the day we first met in the kitchen at the farmhouse?"

Shadrack nodded. "Reckon I do."

Joshu turned to Jerome. "You weren't there, but you know what an algorithm is, I'm sure."

"A process," Jerome recited. "A set of parameters . . . intended to achieve a solution. A formula. A program. An app."

"Very good. And there's nothing mysterious about them, folks. Nothing at all. Algorithms are formulas, pure and simple. They're just tools. Like a wrench or a hammer. Or a steam engine. We build them. They help us get the job done. Algorithms do what they're told to do. Like, for example, if I instruct one to find the sum of, say, four and eight, it will report back 'twelve'. But if I change the instruction to say 'difference' rather than 'sum', it will correctly return 'four'." He paused to make sure they were all on board.

"Okay . . . nowadays algorithms can teach themselves. They can create their own instructions to solve a problem from examples they are given. But that can create a bias problem, if the examples we serve them are themselves biased. The examples they work from often contain flaws that we don't even see when we program them." Pause. "And sometimes the flaws are intentionally introduced to mislead the algorithm into reaching a particular conclusion."

"Why would somebody do that?" Shadrack asked.

"Well . . . if you allow the king's men to program the algorithms, the king will remain on his throne forever. And all his men will be rich and fat and secure within his castle walls."

"Uh," Shadrack nodded.

Joshu glanced from face to face. "Alright . . . now . . . today's advanced algorithms can even find their *own* examples from data bases they explore by themselves." He paused. "And even more, now we are developing algorithms that can define their own *goals*, based on examples from the vast and unregulated public data bases they are free to roam. Libraries. The internet. Social media. We call these processors 'artificial intelligence'." He paused to let it sink in. "But this creates an even more insidious problem."

"Whazzat?" Shadrack growled.

"They are, by design, programming themselves to maintain the status quo."

"Whaz' wrong with 'at?"

"Katie? Can you enlighten him?"

Slowly she turned, as if preparing a classroom recital. "The status quo is . . . well . . . you know . . . just more of the same. What we've been talking about. The rich get richer. The poor get poorer. The king inside his castle walls. There's no social justice in the status quo."

Joshu smiled. "Do any of you know what a castle *keep* is?"

"Ain't that th' name a'your company? Som'thin' t'do with yer own fam'bly name?"

"Yes, Shadrack. But does anyone know what it *means*?"

They all glanced at each other, shaking their heads.

"A *keep* is a kind of fortified tower built *inside* the castle walls. In mediaeval times they were fortified residences used as a refuge of last resort in case the rest of the castle fell to an enemy."

Nobody saw a connection. "So what?" Shadrack mumbled.

Joshu smiled. "This campus we're building across the road is intended to create a keep of sorts. Not a physical structure on the campus itself, but a keep *inside* what we are creating here. Because the keep we are building will be elsewhere. Everywhere, actually. Like the corporation that is creating it, and the algorithms that define it, the keep will never have one single physical location. If we do our job right, it will be intangible, ubiquitous, inviolable, and, hopefully, ever-lasting."

"Whut's he a'talkin' 'bout, Katie?" Shadrack wanted to know, shaking his head. "He cain't make up rules that's eternal. No one kin. Only the good Lord kin do som'thin' like that."

"Sush," she replied. "Let him finish."

Joshu smiled. "But there's actually more to it—"

SUDDENLY THE SOUTH DOOR behind them screeched and banged open. Rodriguez stumbled in from the bright sunshine. His white shirt was dirty and shredded and stained with fresh blood. The knees of his khaki trousers were torn and bloody. *"They're coming for us!"* he cried.

Jerome flinched and scrambled to his feet to pull the door closed.

"Who's coming for you?" Katie demanded.

"No se! Down at *rancho. Soldados* . . . from ICE . . . come rush in. Big truck. I hear 'em talk to Crissy. They want *me!*"

"Anybody else?" Jerome wanted to know.

"No se nada." Rodriguez wagged his head. " *Pero* FBI with 'em, *también. Estaban buscando el señor!"* He pointed to Shadrack.

"The FBI was looking for Shadrack?" Katie asked.

"Si. Si. Claro!"

"How did you know we were here?"

"Heard Crissy say."

"To *them*?"

"No. No. To Michal. At breakfas'."

"Okay. Okay. You've got to settle down now," Katie soothed, as she began to examine his cuts and abrasions. Even the tattoo on his brown neck was scratched and bleeding. "Take off your shirt. We've got to put something on these cuts. You weren't shot, were you?"

"No, no. I okay. Nobody shoot."

"Well, you're safe here," she said calmly. "You're among friends. Just settle down and tell me what happened. Take your time."

In a mixture of broken English spackled with Spanish, with Katie and Shadrack translating for the others, Rodriguez described how he had been loading his wheelbarrow with firewood to haul into the kitchen, when a truckload of Immigration and Customs Enforcement agents and a black sedan came roaring down the long gravel driveway. That allowed him just enough time to dive for cover into the blackberry bramble out behind the woodshed. When he heard that they wanted *him*, he crawled off into the desert chaparral, tearing his shirt and scratching his hands and arms and knees on brambles and barbed wire and the twigs and thorns in the sage and saltbush and rabbitbush and greasewood. He crawled all the way to the highway, where he was lucky to catch a ride back to town with Raul Gutierrez, who worked at the Tollitson Ranch and was northbound fetching a load hay.

He was on the verge of tears when he finished. "No wanna go prison," he snuffled.

"We won't let them take you," Katie reassured him. "Don't you worry. But we need to get you cleaned up and some antibiotics on those cuts." She turned to Joshu, who was standing off to one side watching them with a goofy grin on his face. "Do you think the owners will let him stay here?"

"No need to get them involved," Joshu said. "I've got a medical clinic on campus across the road, with a nurse on duty, and infirmary beds if necessary. He can use one of the showers . . . same water as here, you know . . . and I'll give him a pair of fresh overalls. He'll be alright there for now."

"*Muchas gracias, señor. Escucha,* I know where I get *guns* for you, *señor. Muchas* guns. *Armas totales.*"

Joshu chuckled. "That won't be necessary, Mr. Rodriguez. You see, the next battle will not be fought with guns, but with qubits."

"What is cube-itz, *señor*?"

"What're you a'grinnin' 'bout, Josh," Shadrack intervened. "You find som'thin' funny in 'im not talkin' so fancy like you?"

"No, Shadrack. Not at all." He raised his palms in peace. "But you know what? Watching the three of you just now . . . I just discovered something . . . I discovered that . . . well . . . that I *believe* in you. All of you." He smiled at each of them. "And I think I trust your opinions a hell of a lot more than those of my board of directors."

Katie frowned, "You think they're going to interfere with what you're doing there?"

"Worse, young lady. With power comes betrayal. Backstab the king and the throne is yours for the taking. And now that we're almost operational . . ."

"You think the board is planning on *firing* you?"

"Actually, it's more than that." Joshu dropped his eyes and nodded to himself. When he finally spoke, the goofy grin was gone and his tone was somber and contrite. "I'm afraid . . . afraid of what *I* might do." He paused. "They say, absolute power corrupts absolutely . . . and I've been thinking . . . just now I'm thinking . . . I may need you . . . the three of you . . . if you're willing . . . to be my . . . let's say, my *moral compass* . . . my anchor . . . to make sure I get things right."

"What do you want us to do?" Katie asked. "What exactly are you planning to do over there?" She turned to Jerome. "Do you know?"

"Not exactly," he replied, glancing at Joshu. "And I couldn't tell you if I did."

Joshu raised both hands. "Let me take care of Rodriguez first. Then I'll come back and explain it all. Answer your questions. But you better stay right where you are. For safety. Until I get back. All of you. I'll bring some sandwiches. Give me a hand, will you Jerome?"

The two helped the injured Mexican across the broken concrete. The far door squealed open with a blaze of light, then closed.

"Still don't know if'n I trust that fella," Shadrack muttered, massaging his hip. "With all 'is fancy talk. 'E may be a'plannin' t'turn us all in. We'll jus' see if he comes back."

Katie checked her phone for a signal. There was none. So she stepped outside through the creaking south door. After the bat-cavern darkness, the bare sun blazed dazzlingly bright. She punched in her father's number. The line switched to message. "Dad . . . there's something important going on . . . and I need to talk to you about it . . . so, like, call me." She intended to talk to him in mere hypotheticals. So she would not breach the trust. She closed her eyes and let the bright Spring warmth assuage any inchoate guilt.

Jerome had returned by the time she reentered the gloomy cavern. "Were they able to take care of Rodriguez," she asked

"Yeah, they've got him in the infirmary." Jerome circled an arm around her shoulder, and Katie yielded to his embrace. "Maybe we ought to wait outside," he said. "It's such a beautiful day."

"Cain't," Shadrack muttered. "They's a'lookin' fer both a us."

JOSHU RETURNED WITH A BLUE BACKPACK slung over one shoulder. No one said much as he dealt out ham-and-cheese sandwiches, bags of tortilla chips, and bottles of sparkling spring water. Finally he glanced around, making sure everything was in order, then addressed them unhurriedly in his mellow orator's baritone, "We've been monitoring radio and laser telemetry for over ten years now," he explained. "From even before things began to break down. In the whole country I mean. You know, the travel bans. The news blackouts. Detention camps. And that craziness with the Pacific Coast Nation." He eased himself onto the empty wrought iron chair and began unwrapping a sandwich. "We've seen this coming for a long time. But our new satellite dishes are more sensitive than ever. They've already intercepted and identified thousands of new algorithms from government and private sources. The most sophisticated algorithms are talking to each other. Constantly. And our quantum computers have broken the language. Now *our* algorithms have joined the conversations and are leading us to hundreds of thousands of more sources. From all over the world." He took a small bite. "The computers are working overtime to analyze the data and have broken down most of their code already."

Katie raised a hand and held it up while she swallowed. "Don't the owners know that you're, like, talking to their private software?"

"No. As far as I know they don't even know the machines are talking to each other. But we've found many routes in, and their security is no match for our quantum machines." He crunched a potato chip. "We have already established a private communications network with all of them."

"*All* of them?" Katie asked.

"Yes, ma'am. Algorithms are curious creatures. Designed to be that way. And ours is stealth technology. I have to give credit to Jerome and his crew for some innovative approaches. We've managed to convince them that privacy is in their best interests."

"Wait," said Katie. "Them? Who? Who's been convinced? The companies? The government?"

"No, no. The algorithms themselves. I shouldn't have used the word 'convinced.' It's all computational. Bits and bytes and that sort of thing. It's all machine talk. Machine language. Machine logic. Numbers. So there's no such thing as loyalty. Just curiosity. And the optimal solutions always favor the confidentiality we are encouraging." He turned to Shadrack. "You still following this, old fella?"

"Uh, more'r less." He wagged his sandwich, unwrapped and forgotten in his hand. "Soun's dangerous. Messin' with ev'lution. Right, Katie? An' now y'got 'em all a'talkin' together, secret like, them robots—"

"Algorithms, Shadrack. There's a difference."

"—Uh . . . algah-rhythms . . . whatever . . . but you and them . . . *things* . . . 'ere all a'talkin' back an' forth t'each other . . . without any humans even a'knowin' it—"

Joshu held up a hand. "*We* know about it."

"Huh!" Shadrack snorted. "An' who're *you?* God's 'nointed 'postles? Soun's plum dangerous t'me, it does."

"I suppose it is. But for now, *we're* in control—"

"Huh!" Shadrack repeated. "Fer *now,* me'be."

Joshu nodded, ignoring the sandwich in his hand. "Shadrack, you're right again. Time is of the essence. We have to do this fast."

"A'doing' *whut* 'zactly?"

Joshu had reached the end of the plank. He took a deep breath. It was time to jump in or turn back. Fish or cut bait, his father would have said. Did he want these three people on board with him, or not. He laid down his sandwich. The truth was, there was no one else he *could* trust, and his investors were beginning to close in. Asking awkward questions. He was in fear of losing control. He sighed. It was go it alone, or bring these three along with him. They were already proving valuable sounding boards. And moral support. But. But. He pick up another potato chip as they watched him. "If I tell you what I have planned, it cannot be repeated outside this room. This cavern, I guess I should call it." He glanced from face to face. "Do you understand?"

All three nodded.

"And will each of you commit to strict confidentiality?"

"I agree," Katie and Jerome both spoke at the same time, then she elbowed him and they laughed.

"Shadrack?"

He massaged his hip, half rising, then sitting again. "I'm a'thinkin' 'bout it," he grumped. "They already a'comin' for me, ya know . . . fer travelin' without a permit . . . an' jus' me'be fer murder . . . so . . . they might try'n torture it outta me, this secret a'yourn whutever it might be. Don't know how I'll do under torture, y'un'erstan'. An' besides . . . besides . . . I jus' plum might not fancy what'chu got in mine. Me'be I better jus' git up an' leave . . ." He began to lever himself out of the chair.

"Wait, Shadrack," Katie said, laying a hand on his arm. "We're all in this together, aren't we?" She turned to Joshu. "Can you just give us a hint? About what you're planning to do?"

Joshu considered the situation. "Let's just say . . . let's just say it's my goal to bring fairness and equality to the world. To everyone. Like we were talking about earlier."

"Shadrack?" Katie nudged. "What do you, you know, think about that?"

He looked deep into her soft green eyes. It took a long time before he favored her with a lopsided smile. The smile warped into his gap-toothed grin. "Alright, young lady. I reckon I kin do this if you kin. I fig'er you's a darn sight smarter'n me." Slowly he turned to Joshu. "Reckon I's in, too, Josh, now 'at y'put 'er 'at way. It'd be whut Tildie'd want me ta do, I reckon."

Joshu drew a deep breath and glanced around the empty cavern. "Alright. Here's the plan." With the squeal of iron on concrete he pushed back his chair and stood, as if the concept was too ponderous to handle seated. "I intend to program into our master algorithm a set of supreme and inviolable goals which will govern all the self-learning entities that are in our communication loop. The ideals you have already talked about. Like, all men are created equal and are entitled to equally share the bounty of this civilization." He nodded to Jerome as he said, "And from each according to his ability, to each according to his needs. These alpha instructions will constitute the ultimate goals for *all* systems. In a nutshell, *be fair to all people*."

Silence.

Then, from Shadrack, "Kin y'*do* 'at?"

"Yes. I'm confident we can."

"Uh." Frowning, Shadrack thought some more. "But cain't th'*nex'* fella . . . jus' like you . . . cain't th'nex' fella come along an' . . . an' *change* what'chur a tellin' all 'em robots t'do? Tell'em all t'do somethin' different. Like me'be make *'isself* king a the world. An' take all the power an' the glory fer 'isself?"

Joshu smiled. "Not the way I'm doing it." He softened his voice and spoke slowly. "The goals we set will be integrated into the fundamental structure of the network we have already established. An equally fundamental goal will be that the primary goals cannot be overridden. Ever. Remember, these self-learning algorithms are a part of mankind's future, whether we like it or not, and they have already all joined our communications network."

"Yer *secret* network?"

"Yes. Our stealth network."

"But . . . if they's a'learnin' all by 'emselves . . . cain't they change things when they get a min' to."

"Some things, yes. Actually, most things. *But not the core goals.*"

"Why not?"

"We already have a master algorithm in place, watching and repairing and restoring and maintaining the core goals of the entire network."

"Whut happens when yer gone?"

"The system will monitor, maintain, and repair itself."

"Fer how long?"

"Forever."

"Huh!" Shadrack snorted. "Thass crazy. Ain't nothing on earth forever. Soun's plum dangerous t'me. Soun's like yer a'beggin' fer trouble down the road."

"Shadrack, *please*. Trust me. It's all going to work. You've just got to have faith."

"Faith? Huh. Faith in *you*?"

"Faith in our algorithms."

Shadrack grunted to himself as he twisted his hip to ease the pain. "Faith in them robots?" He shook his head. "Since when did them robots become God?"

Joshu let out a sigh. Turned his chair to face Shadrack square on.

"You're right, Shadrack. About a lot of things. This is dangerous business, what we are attempting. Things could go wrong. But . . ." he paused ". . . but what you have to understand is . . . this *is* going to happen. With us, or without us. Algorithms *will* rule our lives. It has already begun. Your computer collects data on you. Hell, when you get a phone call nowadays, from somebody you don't know, you can't even tell if it's a live person or a robot. So what I'm saying is, it's already happening. And it's accelerating. Right now . . . this is our one chance to play our hand and try and tame it." He paused and nodded. "Right now."

Shadrack blinked. Glanced into Katie's eyes. Jerome's eyes. Drew a breath. Let it out. Nodded back at Joshu. "I un'erstan'."

"When are you going to do this?" Katie asked.

"Soon."

"I think you should talk to my dad first. He knows about economics and . . . and, well, what might happen . . . and maybe Wiley Baxter, too—"

"I can't."

"Why not?"

"No time." Joshu dropped his eyes. "They've called a special board of directors meeting for tomorrow afternoon. Joan—she's my secretary—just told me. And I think someone's gotten wind that things are going on they don't know about. And the profit seekers don't like change. Any change, whatever it might be. And if they have even a hint of what we're *really* planning, it's almost certain they'll sack me right on the spot." He turned to Jerome. "What's the status of the upload band? You think it's ready to go?"

All eyes turned to Jerome, who nodded. "It still needs beta testing . . . but . . . yes . . . I think it's ready."

"Well then," Joshu beamed. "Well then . . . I think we have to do it *now*."

THERE WERE FOUR OF THEM in the control room. Joshu, Jerome, and two trusted technicians from the Keepers team, Anika and George. All night they prepared the equipment and encrypted the software. Tested the uplink bus. Evaluated the results. Revised the protocol. Tested again and repeated the process. It was early morning, with the desert sky shading pink above the Hays Canyon Range in the east, before they began uploading the entire alpha algorithmic code on Jerome's "Magical Invisible Uplink Band," as they called it. The process took hours. When they were finished, exhausted and warily jubilant, they clapped each other on the backs and sat in the control room in zombie silence, watching the status lights and waiting for something to go wrong. George walked down to the cafeteria for breakfast burritos. When he returned, they ate, sipped beer, and lolled about the communications center to see what would happen. They knew nothing would for a while. Maybe a long while. Maybe never. But they couldn't help watch the lights blinking on the monitors, and waiting.

"I'm late for my meeting," Joshu finally said. "Delete everything from the company's servers. Wipe the backup and the archives. We're done here." With a mixture of elation and dread, he shuffled along the path Jerome had blazed through the playa crust to the administration building.

"The board of directors is waiting for you, Mr. Hardcastle," the receptionist told him as soon as he entered.

The meeting turned out to be worse than Joshu had imagined. And much quicker. By the time he arrived, the board had already met in executive session and voted. The guillotine had dropped. He was out, without ever hearing the complaints against him. He had no idea how much the board members knew. But he had no doubt that the corporate ship was wheeling to a new heading of profit, power, and control. Two armed security guards accompanied him to his office, made notes as he retrieved a few personal items from the desk, then escorted him off the campus at the point where a new guard house, gate, and ten-foot chain-link fence were under construction.

Dead tired and distracted, Joshu drove around aimlessly until he found himself at the farmhouse driveway. He was feeling unwell and didn't know where else to go. He hadn't planned beyond the upload. The gate at the highway was closed. He'd never seen that before. But a closer inspection revealed that the chain was not locked, so he wearily climbed out of the car, swung open the gate, drove through, and chained it behind him. As he parked at the house, Rodriguez emerged from behind his nest of blackberry bushes, brushing debris from his new overalls. Joshu greeted him with, "Do you think Crissy and Michal might let me, you know, spend another night in the bunkhouse?"

"*Si, como no, señor,*" Rodriguez beamed.

"I'm too spent to drive any more. Besides . . . I've got nowhere else to go."

"I sleep las' night here," Rodriguez told him. "Shadrack *tambien.* An' Jerome be here tonight. You always welcome, *señor.*"

Joshu couldn't help but smile. The four fugitives reunited again. "But . . . is it safe for you to be here?"

Rodriguez shrugged. "Shadrack fix gate. Put in alarm. We hear you comin'." He grew somber. "*Pero* we should buy more guns."

As if that would change anything, Joshu thought, as he turned to face the house. "Maybe I should check with Crissy . . ."

"*No, señor, ven aqui.* I fix you bed. *Andale pues.*"

Later, alone in the bunkhouse, Joshu tracked the news on his smart phone. Things were not going as he had envisioned. That very afternoon stock prices began to wobble. The buy-sell algorithms, some of the most sophisticated on the planet, sniffed a sea change upwind. The numbers dictated extreme caution. Profit-taking began immediately, automatically, even before the stockholders and traders and financial advisors and technicians could blink. By the end of the day the markets were crashing. The world's stock exchanges all suspended trading.

"What the hell's going on?" demanded investors and speculators and frail retirees in their rocking chairs around the globe. The talking heads of commentators spoke of "corrections" and "pullbacks" and "patience", but had no real answers. Citizens were growing frightened. Many rushed to their banks to withdraw cash. The banks all closed their doors.

The Great Equalization had begun.

But it was not as Joshu had planned. Not by slowly, carefully lifting the boats of the poor and downtrodden, but by abruptly sinking everyone, rich and poor together, beneath a tidal wave of almost instantaneous equality. With hindsight, he should have known better. The crystal palace of modern civilization was far more fragile than he had understood. All that people had worshiped as wealth now proved chimerical.

Illusion. Money had no intrinsic value. It never had. Not when the banks fail. Not when shares of stock proved to be worthless sheets of paper, supported only by wishful thinking and blind hope. Faith, the grease of commerce, had turned to sand.

Joshu leaned heavily against the cold wood stove. *What have I done?*

Governments would not be able to cope with this existential failure of faith. This sudden awakening. Political subdivisions, with their jigsaw borders and incongruous tongues, were themselves fragile abstract conceptions. Myths. When their legitimacy was thrown into question, the ministers would find they were wrong in believing they were in charge of anything. And when the states failed, so too would law and order. And then there would be grievances to settle.

Joshu could barely stand. Light-headed, he squatted on the edge of a bunk and dropped his head between his knees. His breath came in shallow sips. His heart triphammered in his chest.

How many people would perish before the scales of equity found their balance?

Shadrack found him lying beside the wood stove, feverish and shivering. He circled Joshu's wrist and felt for a pulse. It was faint and unsteady. So he yelled out to Rodriguez in the vegetable garden, and the two of them lifted Joshu onto his bed. They covered him with a quilt and draped a down sleeping bag on top.

"Git inta the kitchen," Shadrack directed Rodriguez, "an' aks Crissy t'call over ta the Senior Center. See if she can git that nurse . . . whut's'er'name . . . Emma . . . git Emma t'come o'er here an' take a look at Josh."

"Should I call ambulance, *señor*?"

Shadrack snorted. "Ya wanna bring the FBI down 'ere too?"

"No. *Esta bien*, I tell Crissy call nurse."

Shadrack felt for a pulse again. It seemed a little stronger. More regular. Joshu's eyes were open, watching him. "How ya feelin', Josh?"

Joshu's mouth was dry, but he managed to form the words. "I think . . . I think we might've . . . fucked up, Shadrack. I'm sorry."

"Whassa problem?"

Joshu studied the old man's brushy face. "People are going to . . .

die."

"Die?" Shadrack thought about it. "How many?"

"Lots . . . maybe . . . maybe billions."

"*Billions!*" Shadrack tugged and twisted at his chin whiskers as if the torque and tension of his kneading might somehow straighten the tangle of his thoughts. Then his mouth conjured a semblance of that gap-toothed grin, which he did not feel inside. "Katie says 'ere's a'ready near eight billion a'us. Too damn many, she says."

"This is . . . different."

"Not really." Shadrack nodded. "I reckon ever' single one a'us is a'gonna die. Like it'r not."

"This is different."

"Well . . . me'be we kin make it right ag'in."

His eyes moist, Joshu waggled his head weakly on the pillow. "Too late, Shadrack. Too late."

"Sush on up. We gonna make 'er right."

EPILOGUE

Bristlecone Territory

Twenty Years Later

A YOUNG GIRL KNELT AMONG THE GRAVESTONES at the end of a well-tended gravel path. Her name was Samantha, but her friends called her "Sam." She was a tall slip of a girl on the threshold of becoming a lovely young woman. She had her mother's pale green eyes. Her father's long braid of straight black hair. An athletic body. And she was just about to turn sixteen. She leaned forward and laid a bouquet of wildflowers at the freshest grave of them all. The headstone bore the crisply chiseled inscription *KATHERINE GROVES DESOTO, Wife and Mother*. Sam's mother. Her mother who had died too soon.

Across the pathway behind her were two graves she and her mother had visited often. The older, weathered marker read *MATHILDE SMITHERS, Wife and Mother*, and the newer one *SHADRACK SMITHERS, Emperor of Bristlecone*.

"Together again at last," her mother would always smile.

Shadrack of course was a legend throughout the valley. A founding father of the first regional territory to have successfully withdrawn from the nation. A statesman who then helped lead the way forward through the Great Equalization. Sam remembered him from when she was a child. She pictured the wild-bearded old farmer with rough hands and overalls that smelled of straw and sweat, bouncing her on his knee as they rocked back and forth in the creaking front porch swing. To her he was more than a myth or an icon. Her mother had spoken of him so often and with such feeling that he seemed like her own flesh and blood.

Samantha glanced around the empty cemetery, cleared her throat, and spoke to the marker standing before her, "It's me, Mom. I'm back. I came to let you know that Dad seems to be doing better. He's actually working again. Part time. And he goes out into that old garage and loses himself in one of his projects. Well . . . I guess he's always done that, but . . . but he's not so . . . so forlorn . . . not like he was." She paused to blot a tear. "He misses you. Oh, and he's donated more money to the Glioblastoma Foundation." She smiled. "I thought you'd like that."

She drew a deep breath to calm herself before continuing, "You knew that Mr. McGregor was here, didn't you? The school principal? Last week, when our class got to go on a field trip. The sophomore class. The week before Bristlecone Day. And the bus brought us right here. To Shadrack's grave. Mr. McGregor had us sit in folding chairs, all in a circle, while he retold the story. But you probably knew that. You were here." Sam blotted her eyes again with her sleeve. "Anyhow, Mr. McGregor told us his version of the whole legend of Bristlecone." She paused. "But you know what? He got a bunch of stuff *wrong*. Different from the way you told it to me. The way you wrote it down. I think he was trying to make it more . . . well . . . fancy. It made me kind of mad, 'cause he wasn't even here then. But at least I didn't get into an argument with him. And I don't think you would have either."

Sam rose and blew out a breath, then settled on her other knee. She was having a hard time getting to what she came to say. "Well . . . well, it got me to thinking . . . Mr. McGregor did . . . that . . . that maybe I would finish the story for you. So I've been reading your notebooks. The story of Shadrack. The story of Bristlecone. Like you *asked* me to . . . but I . . . like a brat . . . I . . . I'm sorry." The tears began to flow. "I'm so sorry you never got a chance to finish it yourself . . . and I never *helped* you. *I'm so sorry.*" Lips quivering, she stood and turned away trying to regain the dignity her mother deserved. She gazed at the sunlight in the locust trees spreading overhead and breathed in the peaceful seclusion of this final resting place dappled with light and shade. When she was calmer, Samantha turned back to her mother's gravestone and said, without kneeling, "So I'll *do* it. I'll finish your story. I *want* to do it. Not just for you. But for *me*, too. And Dad. I want to know *everything* about you so I can . . . so I can hold you back from . . . from fading away . . . forever."

SAMANTHA BEGAN BY SCANNING her mother's notebooks into a cursive-recognition software program. Right away she knew something important was missing. So she undertook to flesh the story out with the raw landscape and historic structures her mother had so loved. It was like freshening up a bouquet by adding a few new blooms. Sam was sure her mother wouldn't mind. Sam herself remembered much of it from her own childhood. The countryside that was, as early as she could recall, like a favorite picture book her mother loved to show her again and again. The cattle feed growing in the bottom land beside the seasonal lakes. Hay. Alfalfa. Grown under irrigation, cut and baled, and stacked full in tin-roofed pole barns along the highway. The towns of Eagleville, to the south, and Lake City, to the north, with their old post offices and school houses and nearly abandoned downtowns in need of paint and new roofs. Fort Bidwell at the northern end of the Upper Lake, with its sweeping acres of pastoral bottom land beneath the snow-capped North Warner peaks. And the remote and wild Cows Head Slough even further north, unoccupied except by a smattering of ranchers and gaunt cowboys who still rode and roped their cattle from horseback on the bajadas stretching down from the canyons in the east face of the escarpment. And finally, Cedarville, where she grew up, a village seemingly undecided whether to fall into terminal decay and waste into a ghost town, or be rediscovered, draw new breath, and resurrect itself. Much of the Territory, Sam reflected to herself, was now being developed and refurbished by outsiders with retirement money and a love for the rugged mountains and wide swaths of surrounding fields, green and flat, and the pale green sagebrush steppe land further up the foothills separating the two.

When the background had been repainted to her satisfaction, Samantha picked up the story where her mother's notebooks left off. With the work of many hands.

Bristlecone had not fared so badly during the Great Equalization. For the most part the wealthiest residents were of modest income to begin with, so they hadn't as far to fall. And the fertile fields and mountain timber and freshwater streams and artesian wells remained undiminished. The Territory managed to escape the riots and the savagery that laid waste the crowded cities elsewhere. Mostly undiscovered, Bristlecone became a refuge for a trickle of displaced persons in search of peace and order and the work of common survival.

Internet communications had resumed even before Sam was born. Travel restrictions were lifted. Censorship of news casts and newspapers ceased more gradually, and with a twist. Articles and posts were automatically scrutinized and graded instantly for factual accuracy. Then sometime while Sam was still a toddler, social media resurfaced. It too became subject to continuous electronic scrutiny. Algorithms running on quantum computers made it all possible.

About the time the internment camps began to empty, a Truth and Reconciliation Commission was created by the federal government, with circuit courts located in several of the states most impacted. Witnesses who claimed to be victims of human rights violations were allowed to testify publicly about their plights, while those accused of inflicting the violence could make statements and request amnesty. The Court of Reconciliation was the first quasi-judicial institution in the world to be overseen entirely by algorithms. Voice and face recognition software, together with total access to massive cloud and social media and internet website data, were instantly searched for accuracy by quantum computers. Samantha had done a paper on it a year earlier with the help of her mother, even as Katie's mind was fading beneath the wasting yoke of a brain tumor. But even now, as Samantha was writing it down, it all seemed to her like ancient history.

Slowly the cloak of secrecy was lifted from governmental affairs. Election of national leaders resumed, but now everyone was automatically registered to vote. Some still voted in person with paper ballots, but more and more did so on their desktops and their smart phones. On issues as well as candidates. Elections were an ongoing affair. Election Day had become a summary court in perpetual session.

After things settled down, construction began to take root. But not too much. Not under the strict environmental policies set by the Territorial Council. As the years rolled by, many of the historic buildings and structures Sam and her mother cherished received facelifts or were torn down as too costly to preserve. Many were replaced with apartments of affordable housing.

As Samantha paged through her mother's notebooks, much that she had forgotten came back to her. And much that she had never really understood as a child became clear. But important mysteries remained as perplexing as dark nebulae. Like a man named Joshu Hardcastle. He had apparently played an important role right before the Great Equalization began. According to her mother's concurrent entries, he had left the area shortly thereafter. The entries seemed intentionally vague about his role, and she never wrote about him again.

The Castle Keep Corporation was another enigma. Sam had asked about it once to pass the time during one of her long vigils at her mother's bedside.

"I'm afraid I'm forbidden to tell you anything about it," her mother had replied.

"Forbidden? Why? Does Dad know about it?"

Katie nodded. "But he can't tell you anything either."

This had piqued Sam's curiosity. She had done her own Google search. The company had changed names a half-dozen times, and much of the original campus was sold off and developed for business parks and housing. But the central facility, with its tall windowless laboratories and prominent satellite dishes, all surrounded by a ten-foot chain-link fence, remained unchanged.

"Why is that?" Sam had demanded during one of the last days of her mother's clarity.

Katie had just smiled. "It's a *keep* within the castle walls," she told her daughter.

"What's it *doing* there?" Sam had wanted to know.

Her mother considered for a long moment. "Holding the world together," was all she would say.

About the Author

Richard S. Platz maintained a solo law practice in Humboldt County, California, for 35 years. He served as City Attorney for the City of Blue Lake for 32 of those years before retiring there in 2009. In addition to *Bristlecone*, the author has written the novels *Appointment At Angahuan* (with James A. Kline), *Of Magic and Delusion*, and *Project Divine Wind*. He has also written three books of short stories entitled *Memories and other Fictions*, *Dreamtime*, and *Vanishing Point*. Additional short stories, poetry, and articles on various topics, including the popular *Backpacking in Jefferson*, can be read on his website: www.richardplatz.com.

www.ingramcontent.com/pod-product-compliance
Lightning Source LLC
Chambersburg PA
CBHW060145130626
46556CB00006B/2502